His Jilted Bride

ROSE GORDON

HIS JILTED BRIDE

© 2013 C. Rose Gordon
Front cover image © 2013 Lily Smith
Back cover design © Liberty Digital Graphics Designs
All rights reserved.

Published by Parchment & Plume, LLC
www.parchmentandplume.com

Other Titles Available

SCANDALOUS SISTERS SERIES
Intentions of the Earl (Book 1)
Liberty for Paul (Book 2)
 To Win His Wayward Wife (Book 3)

GROOM SERIES
Her Sudden Groom (Book 1)
Her Reluctant Groom (Book 2)
Her Secondhand Groom (Book 3)
Her Imperfect Groom (Book 4)

BANKS BROTHERS BRIDES SERIES
His Contract Bride
His Yankee Bride
His Jilted Bride
His Brother's Bride

OFFICER SERIES (AMERICAN SET)
The Officer and the Bostoner
The Officer and the Southerner
The Officer and the Traveler

Coming Soon!
GENTLEMEN OF HONOR
Secrets of the Viscount
Desires of the Baron
Passions of the Gentleman

~Prologue~

1800
Watson Estate

"You're it!" five-year-old Lady Amelia Brice squealed as she pressed her dirty hands against Elijah's back.

Elijah remained seated in his shady spot on the grass and swatted at the neighbor girl who had an odd tendency to think of him as her playmate. "I'm not playing."

"And why not?" She put her hands on her hips and pursed her lips.

He shrugged. "I don't want to."

A sound of annoyance erupted from her throat and she stomped her foot. "Elijah Banks, you are no fun!"

"He isn't, is he?" Henry, his twin, chimed in, grinning.

Lady Amelia twisted her lips and enthusiastically nodded her agreement. "He sure isn't. But I know how to get him to play."

"Oh?"

"Sure do. He just needs a little kiss!" She puckered her lips and leaned forward.

Eight-year-old Elijah was off his bottom and to his feet before she could come within a foot of him, let alone touch her puckered lips to his skin.

His standing position didn't deter her. Lips still puckered and ready, she stepped closer to him.

He took a step back.

She came closer to him again.

This time, he fled.

"You'd better run, Elijah, because when I catch you, you'll be

1

getting this kiss whether you want it or not," she called as she chased him around the field. Her unpinned, mud brown hair whipped wildly in the wind as she chased him around the maple tree and down the stone walkway leading to the shed, trampling over his mother's wildflowers before running up the large hill that led to the house.

"I'll get you," she called to him with a wild giggle, making kissing noises as loudly as she could while she chased after him.

"No, you won't," Elijah shouted back. He crested a hill and came to a halt when he saw his brother Alex, who was home on academic leave from Eton, sitting under a tree and reading some boring tome about plants.

Elijah pressed his finger against his lips then ran behind a large oak.

From behind the tree, he positioned one eye so he could watch Lady Amelia.

She reached the top of the hill, her dark hair plastered against her sweaty face.

"Alex," she said, gasping for breath.

Alex nodded to her and Elijah moved his head back behind the tree, debating about just when he should start running again.

A twig snapped from somewhere in Alex's vicinity and he peeked around the tree just in time to meet Lady Amelia's grey eyes, then he was running again. Only this time he didn't have the same lead as before.

In front of God, Alex and everybody within hearing distance, Lady Amelia called for him to stop so she could grant him his kiss. But he didn't. He ran as fast as his bare feet could take him.

Just then, the door to his family's estate swung open, revealing Mother and Father.

Elijah came to a halt and Lady Amelia ran straight into his left side, knocking them both to the ground.

She must not have noticed his parents standing there, for right then, without a second's hesitation, she pressed her lips against his in a slobbery kiss.

Immediately, he pushed her away and ran the back of his hand over his now moist lips—that's what a boy was supposed to do when kissed, wasn't it?—then shoved to his feet.

"Mother, Father."

Lady Amelia stood, her eyes as wide as tea saucers. If she'd been anybody else, it'd be terror that would make her look so scared. But Elijah knew better. Amelia Brice was the most stubborn, shameless girl he'd ever met. She wasn't terrified; she was merely surprised.

"Elijah, Lady Amelia," Mother greeted, favoring them both with a warm smile.

"And what has the two of you running as if the Angel of Death is nearby?" Father surprised him by asking. Father had no real shame, either, and often asked blunt questions just to see the expression they elicited on someone's face. So the fact that he hadn't made mention of what Elijah would forever have to remember as his first kiss caught him unawares.

"She was trying to kiss me," Elijah blurted.

"It didn't look like she was trying to me, my boy," Father said. "I just hope you've used your tooth powder recently or that might also be your last kiss."

Elijah's cheeks burned. "Well, if not using tooth powder will keep *her* away from me; I'd better go throw all of mine into the fire right now."

Mother's face fell and Father sent him a sharp look at his unkind words.

"Elijah, you know what you must do," Mother said softly.

Elijah swallowed and turned to face Lady Amelia. He twisted his lips. "I'm sorry if I hurt your feelings," he muttered.

Mother shook her head and extended her hand down toward Lady Amelia. "Come. I was just about to take tea in the drawing room and I'd love for you to be my guest."

A grin split Lady Amelia's red face. "Truly?"

"Truly. Come along now before it gets cold."

Elijah watched in silence as Lady Amelia accompanied his mother into the red brick house.

Shaking his head, he turned to go find Henry.

"Elijah," Father called.

"Yes, sir," he said, turning back to face his father.

"Come sit, I want to talk to you about how you treated your friend."

Elijah scrunched up his nose at the way his father had referred to her as his friend. "She's not my friend."

"Is that so?" Father drawled, leaning against a tall white pillar in front of the house. "You seem to play with her quite a lot."

"Only because she comes over here all the time."

"She does that because she likes you, son."

"Why can't she find anyone else to like?" Elijah asked through gritted teeth.

Father shrugged. "I have no idea. She might find a friend who'd treat her better if she did though."

Shame washed over Elijah. "I apologized to her," he said in a tone that matched the one he'd used when he'd issued said apology.

"Yes, you sure did mumble one, didn't you? And you even made sure to allow yourself a measure of pride by letting her know that your apology was only being made *if* you'd hurt her feelings."

Elijah shrugged. "She's the one who chased me around the estate trying to kiss me. I doubt I hurt her feelings."

"Perhaps not," Father conceded. "But that doesn't matter. When an apology is made, it needs to be sincere or not made at all." He pushed off the column and ran a hand through his dark blond hair. "Son, you might not like her now, but one day you might. Then what will you do when she wants nothing to do with you because of the way you treated her?"

Elijah burst out with laughter. "Do not worry, Father. The chances of Alex having a love match are far greater than my being attracted to Lady Amelia."

~Chapter One~

Late April 1819
Dover

Blast it all to botheration and back!

Lady Amelia Brice would have bellowed every word of that sentence if she had not been trying to prowl around Lord Nigel's study undetected.

She eased the large drawer to his desk closed as calmly as she could, considering the frustration and irritation currently flowing through her. Had her brother, Philip, been even slightly more specific about what she was looking for, she might not be so frustrated.

All she knew was she was looking for a bundle of papers that may or may not be kept in a leather portfolio. Very helpful, indeed.

Scowling she gripped the handle of another drawer and pulled. Then again. She frowned. Drat, this drawer was locked.

Perhaps a locked drawer was a good thing, she thought as she slid a pin from her hair. She straightened it as best she could then stuck it between her teeth while she ran her fingertips along the smooth drawer in search of the keyhole.

Finding it, she jammed the end of her hairpin in and jiggled it around until the distinctive *click* that signaled a successfully picked lock echoed in the room. She stilled and held her breath, which was absolutely silly. There was so much noise coming from the rest of the house that nobody could have been able to have heard that lock turn unless they'd been in the room with her. And even that was doubtful.

She took a deep calming breath and slid open the drawer.

Reaching her hand inside, she felt around. She scowled. Loose cigars and whisky flasks seemed to be what Lord Nigel considered so important that he had to lock them up? Ridiculous. For as long as she lived, she'd never understand the opposite sex and what they found to be of greatest importance.

Her fingers brushed something that felt unmistakably like paper and her heart pounded. This had to be it. Slowly she brought the bundle of papers out from the back of the drawer and unfolded it. She walked to the window and held the stack of papers up in the moonlight and blushed. This couldn't be what Philip was talking about. These were...were...sketches. Sketches of an unclothed lady, to be precise.

She shook her head and walked the papers back to his desk. She'd always thought Lord Nigel to be a lecher. Now she didn't just have to think it, she had confirmation.

Amelia shoved the naughty pictures back into the drawer then shut it with a soft thud. There was only one unexplored drawer left and after that... She didn't even want to think of what would come if she didn't find what she was looking for in the last drawer.

She pulled out the leather chair that was in front of the large oak desk to give her enough room to open the skinny drawer that was below the desk's writing surface.

Amelia ran her hand along the front of the drawer and frowned. There wasn't a handle. She curled her fingers under the edge of the wood and pulled. Nothing. Falling into the chair, she put her other hand under the edge of the drawer and pulled again. It didn't budge.

She moved her hand under the drawer and frowned when her fingers collided with the support beam that ran down the center of the desk. There was certainly a drawer here. She just didn't know how to get it open.

Biting her lip so not to groan in frustration, she blindly groped for some sort of release latch on the bottom of the drawer.

Nothing.

Sighing in frustration, Amelia finished off the glass of punch she'd brought with her then pulled the five-candle candelabra that sat at the far edge of the desk toward her. She'd been reluctant to light any candles, lest the hint of light was seen under the door and she was discovered. But she could no longer avoid it. The moon was falling behind a neighboring house, stealing her light, and this blasted drawer had to have some sort of trick release and she was helpless to find it in the dark.

She quickly lit a single candle, snuffed the match, and froze.

In the low glow the candle had given off, she could see the outline of a decidedly male form sitting on the settee not fifteen feet away.

Panic pounded in her chest, but she was too terrified to move, much less speak or think.

A moment stretched into two, the silence of the room growing louder than the din just outside the room.

Wordlessly, the man stood and began to walk in her direction while she sat still frozen behind the desk. Her eyes stayed focused on his face, which was ridiculous since, like her, he wore a mask that concealed everything except his eyes.

Unlike most men she knew, his boots made no noise as he made his way over to her, then just as quietly, he reached a single hand in front of her and pushed the section of wood directly in front of her that marked the front of the drawer that she knew had to be there. As soon as he moved his fingers, the drawer popped open.

"As you were," he said in a deep voice that sent a shiver down her spine and woke her from her fog.

Amelia licked her lips, feeling somewhat naked and vulnerable in this stranger's presence. "How long?" she heard herself ask.

"How long have I been here?" the man asked. His voice so low and soft it was a miracle she'd heard him over the blood roaring in her ears.

She nodded. It was all she could do.

"Long enough." He walked back over to the spot he'd vacated on the settee and took a seat. "Don't let me stop you."

Amelia's blood turned to ice. When Philip brought her to their cousin's costume party tonight, he told her that everyone would be too interested in the activities going on in the drawing room to notice her exit and she'd have as much time as she needed to locate the papers as long as she did nothing to attract attention to her whereabouts.

But somehow she'd attracted attention. But whose and how, she didn't know.

"You do plan to continue, do you not?"

Amelia stiffened. "Just who are you to inquire about my intentions?" she asked, inwardly congratulating herself on her frosty tone that didn't falter once.

"And who are you to go through a man's desk?"

"How is that your concern?" she countered. "Did you attend tonight's party with the same intent?"

"I don't know," he said slowly. "Why don't you tell me exactly what you're doing and I'll tell you if my intentions are the same?"

Amelia's mind raced. Whoever this man was, he was a master in turning the conversation around on her.

"Don't let my presence interrupt you," he said again a few minutes later.

Who was this man? He wasn't her cousin, she was certain of that. She'd recognize his loud voice and even louder footsteps anywhere. Besides, he wouldn't be half this calm if he'd found someone digging around in his desk. And then there was the way her skin tingled and her stomach became uneasy each time he spoke...

Or perhaps those responses could be because she was nervous. That was actually a very logical explanation, and likely the right one.

"And what of my presence? Why are you letting it keep *you*

from *your* task?" she asked with a sudden urge to giggle.

The man didn't respond, or if he did, Amelia couldn't hear his soft voice because just at that moment, she opened her mouth to ask him yet another giggled question, but instead of words coming past her lips, she belched. Then she giggled. "Oh dear," she said, covering her mouth. What was wrong with her? A minute ago she was able to form a coherent thought and now... Now she was giggling and making the most unladylike noises.

She'd have been embarrassed by her sudden outbursts, to be sure, if only she could stop giggling.

Just then, something appeared in front of her. It was like a circle made up of dozens of shades of every color she'd ever seen and it was swirling.

She grabbed for it, giggling. But she couldn't reach it.

She reached again, this time standing—or trying to, at least. But just as she half-stood to grab it, it moved out of her reach, and for some reason, this made her laugh all the more.

"Madam?"

Amelia turned to where the voice had come from right beside her. When had he gotten so close? And when had that wheel of vivid and vibrant colors joined him? She reached forward again in an attempt to grab it and her hand collided with something hard, his chest, perhaps. Or possibly even his shoulder. She really couldn't tell because her big ball of spinning colors was blocking her view of him.

Her subsequent endeavor was halted by two strong hands that clasped onto her wrists and didn't let her go. He pulled her to a standing position and before she knew what she was doing, she wrapped her arms around his neck.

"Hullo," she trilled, tipping her face up to his.

"Did you have something to drink?" His voice reminded her of when she was younger and she and the Banks twins would go underwater in their creek and one of them would say something then when they came up, everyone would guess what it was.

"Perhaps," she said, giggling as if it were the most humorous thing she'd ever heard. "You're tall."

"What did you drink?"

"Some punch," she said on another peal of uncontrollable giggles. She let go of her hold around his neck and bent backwards at the waist, spreading her arms as if she were falling backwards into an endless pit behind her.

His hands kept their firm grasp on her hips and didn't let her fall despite the way she swayed and arched against him. "You need to go lie down." He pulled her back into a standing position and her breasts pressed against his chest.

Her skin prickled and tingled as he slid his hands up toward her arms, exciting her in ways she'd never known existed until now. Her blood pumped and her body sang with a need she couldn't comprehend.

"Come," he said; his lips so close to hers she could almost feel them against her heated skin as he said the word.

She couldn't come. Or go. In fact, she couldn't move at all. Her legs felt as if they'd suddenly turned to lava. Two hot, tingling, burning columns of immovable lava.

As if sensing her inability to leave the room on her own accord, the stranger scooped her into his arms and carried her across the room.

She opened her mouth to ask where he was taking her; but doubted the correct words came out because he didn't respond.

The steady rhythm of his footsteps was reminiscent of a lullaby; a very upbeat and strangely lively lullaby with his heartbeat now joining in the harmony. She closed her eyes and her circle of color returned, bursting with each "beat" she heard.

The sounds of boot heels on rock soon added to the music. She had the strangest sensation she was being carried up stairs, but couldn't pry her eyes open to confirm her suspicion.

Suddenly she felt cold and realized the stranger was moving her away from his body and down...down...down she went to fall against a soft feather mattress.

Exhaustion—or perhaps a strange hallucination—took over and suddenly she was transported back to a game of chase she'd played with Elijah Banks where she'd threatened to kiss him if he didn't play. "Wait," she called—whether in her dream or in real life, she'd never really know.

There was a response, but what it was, or who said it—eight year old Elijah or the stranger who'd found her in Nigel's study—she may never know.

She reached forward, trying to grab Elijah by the suspenders, or the twin shirttails flying behind him, or any part of him she could get her hands on really. Fabric. So many times she'd reached for him and never gained purchase. But this time she held fabric.

Amelia clenched her fingers into a fist so not to let him get away and gave a hearty tug to pull him to a stop. "I got you, Elijah Banks," she declared proudly before yanking him closer to her and planting her lips squarely on his.

This was the moment in which Elijah's hands usually found her shoulders and threw her off, no matter who was watching or how undignified it made them both look. But this time it was different. His hands came to her shoulders, but instead of pushing her way, he held her in place and the strangest thing happened: he kissed her back.

Soft yet firm, demanding yet gentle, his lips moved with hers in a kiss far more intoxicating than she'd ever dreamed possible.

~ *Chapter Two* ~

The Next Morning

Amelia's head was about to explode.

Or would that be implode?

No matter, she could worry about the difference between explode and implode later. Right now she just needed something to relieve the intense pressure she felt behind her eyes.

She lifted her hand to block the sun streaming in through the nearby window that only served to make her head throb more. Where was she? None of the furniture in the room was hers. It was all vaguely familiar, mind you, but she couldn't place where she'd seen it before.

She moved to sit up in the bed and frowned in discomfort. She was still wearing her blasted corset. Part of it anyway, she amended when she glanced down and glimpsed almost her entire bosom. She gasped and placed her hand on her chest to cover herself. How had her dress gotten that way? And why had she gone to bed wearing her gown in the first place? And at a strange place, no less. Something wasn't right, but what?

Amelia pushed to her unsteady feet and immediately wished she hadn't when a wave of nausea unlike anything she'd ever experienced before engulfed her as the room spun in fast circles around her. The need to retch was overwhelming. She grabbed the nightstand next to her to regain her balance.

She took a deep breath in through her mouth—something a proper young lady should never do—then exhaled. Then again. She'd do it as many times necessary if it'd settle her stomach without the need to shoot the cat. Whatever it was she'd ingested last night was not agreeing with her. But for the life of her she couldn't remember anything she'd eaten for dinner. Or where she'd eaten it.

Closing her eyes to block out the movements around her, she racked her brain, but nothing was coming back to her. Her legs began to tremble, and she moved her hand to get better purchase on the nightstand, her fingers brushing something hard and cold.

Slowly, she turned her head toward the nightstand and opened one eye. A glass. And a note of only two words: DRINK THIS.

She frowned. She didn't recognize the giant, stiff writing, but a snatch of memory of accepting a glass of punch from Philip flashed in her mind. Then she'd... What had she done with it? She hadn't drunk it right away; instead, she'd walked around and then gone into a dark room. Yes, a dark room where she'd set it down on a desk. But why was she in a dark room alone?

Unable to stand any longer, she sank down to the mattress and picked up the liquid. She sniffed it then jerked it away from her face with so much force she nearly spilled it. That was the foulest smelling thing she'd ever been unfortunate enough to inhale. There wasn't a chance in the world she was going to drink it. Not like that sweet, fruity punch she'd tasted last night.

More snatches of last night came to mind. She'd been taking sips of her punch while digging through drawers. Her frown deepened. That couldn't be right, could it? Why would she be digging in drawers in a darkened room?

She looked around the room, hoping to find some sort of clue about what had happened last night other than her drinking some very delicious punch. But there was nothing in the room that looked out of place. Oak armoire. Vanity with a large oval mirror hung above and a plush pink-topped stool underneath. The nightstand next to her with a three-candle candelabra and the note. The demi mask at her feet. The pine che— The demi mask at her feet? Despite the revulsion in her stomach, she dropped her gaze to the floor where a white and gold demi mask lay at her feet.

As if suddenly the pressure of rising water broke through a

dam, incomplete memories came flooding back to her.

The first was of Philip asking her to find a bundle of papers. That's what she'd been looking for in the drawers.

Then she'd been frustrated she'd drank the entire glass of punch at once and lit the candle. That's when the mysterious stranger appeared...

They'd talked, about what she couldn't say. Then she'd... Then he'd... Then they'd...

Fractured memories of him holding her and carrying her to this room formed in her mind. But then, suddenly things were very clear. She'd been chasing Elijah around his father's estate, threatening to kiss him, and when she did, he'd kissed her back.

Her blood turned cold. That kiss was real. It had to be. It was far too vivid not to be, which would mean...

Her hand flew to the gaping bodice of her gown What had he done after they'd kissed? She searched her brain but nothing was coming to mind. Clearly the masked scoundrel from last night had seen fit to undo the top of her gown, but had he touched her anywhere else? She might never know.

Tears stung her eyes, blinding her, and she pushed to her feet. She needed to leave this awful place and go home.

She exited the room and padded down the hall. Not a soul was in sight. She'd been to her cousin's house often enough to know her way around and found the stairs easily enough.

Several loud snores filled the air and Amelia gripped the handrail tighter as she descended the stairs as quietly as she could and found a relatively new footman, rather than the aging butler who'd known her for her entire life, to send a carriage for her.

Shame and uncertainty and even fear settled in her stomach as she rode back to Mumford Hill, her family's country estate. Mother and Father were in London and likely by wearing the disguise Philip had selected for her, she hadn't been recognized last night. But that did nothing to replace her lost innocence and eliminate the other consequences she might face now. No not *might*, even if she didn't conceive, she was now impure and that meant she was unmarriageable.

A sob built in her throat and a lone tear slipped from her eye and by the time she arrived at her house, she was a sobbing mess.

"Where the blazes have you been?" Philip slurred without preamble before she'd crossed the threshold.

Amelia blinked at her brother. He looked nearly as bad as she felt. His face had several nasty cuts, both of his eyes had large purple circles around them and the entire left side of his face was swollen. "What happened to you?"

"Never you mind that." He likely attempted to scowl at her as he said it, but his face was too swollen and bruised to tell. "Where the hell did you go last night?"

"To Nigel's study to look for the papers as you instructed."

Philip crossed his arms. "And did you find them?"

"N-no." She wet her lips. "I looked for them, but I couldn't find them. I—I'm sorry, Philip."

"It's of no account," he said as crisply as his swollen mouth would allow. "We can try again. Now, you go upstairs and get presentable. Lord Friar is expected to come for a visit this afternoon and I do believe it is time you accept his suit."

"W-what?" Amelia stammered. Lord Friar was one of the most vile, ungentlemanly creatures she'd ever met. He'd pursued her relentlessly since her come out five years ago, and to her good fortune, Father had rejected his suit, no matter how strong his argument of having plenty of funds and of Amelia swiftly becoming a spinster.

"You're ruined," Philip burst out, gesturing to her dress.

She'd nearly forgotten her own state of undress at seeing him. "We don't know that yet," she said, hopefully. Frankly, being condemned to spinsterhood was better than being trapped into a marriage with Lord Friar and his leering eyes and wandering hands.

"You might have escaped that house unseen," Philip allowed.

"But you are still ruined."

"How do you know?"

"I just do," he said, lifting his chin a notch. "And you will marry him within the fortnight, so if there's a child, he will assume it's his."

Amelia blanched and her hands went straight to her abdomen. "I cannot marry that man." She refused to say the word "gentle" in regards to Lord Friar.

"Then do you plan to be branded a whore and bring shame on your entire family?" Philip countered, a hardness in his eyes Amelia had never glimpsed before. He sighed. "Don't you understand this is what you must do now? Your chances of making a match are diminishing by the day as it is and now that you've— you've—" He gestured toward her abdomen. "You cannot afford not to marry."

"I could go off to live in the country," she said in a broken whisper.

He snorted. "Is that what you think to do? Go off and live in the country?"

"It's a possibility." Not one that most young ladies dreamed about, but when one found herself in a delicate way without the bonds of marriage, it was certainly a possibility.

"Not for you it's not. You know as well as I do that Father doesn't have the funds to keep his townhouse in London. Keeping you hidden in the country is the equivalent of building a castle in the clouds."

"I don't have to have my own cottage," she pointed out.

Philip's jaw dropped. "Are you suggesting you and your bastard live *here?*"

"It is my home, too."

"No," he snapped. "It's Father's home and one day it will be mine and I will not let you and some bastard bring shame to it."

She blanched. "We don't even know that I've conceived."

"Nor do we know that you haven't, and won't for a while yet, I expect. Which is why we need to accept Lord Friar's suit today. Tell him you'd like to have the wedding before the end of the month, so you get to enjoy the majority of the Season with your husband. He'll understand that. Then in nine months when there's a grand event, he'll just assume it's his."

"You seem to have everything worked out," she remarked. "But I wonder why he'd be so inclined to want to marry me once he finds out about my ruin."

"Do you plan to tell him?"

Her face heated. "No. I thought you would."

"Amelia, listen to the nonsense you speak. If I tell him then he won't marry you."

"But if you don't and he finds out after we marry he might petition for a parliamentary divorce,"

Philip twisted his lips. "All right. I'll inform him, but you must promise that if he doesn't mind that you're no longer chaste that, you'll marry him."

That was a promise no young lady wanted to make. But it was also one that Amelia couldn't afford *not* to make. At least this way her mother and father wouldn't have to suffer the scandal of a bastard grandchild, she whispered to herself as the last rays of hope that one day Elijah Banks would come back from one of his many travels and fall in love with her.

She took a deep breath. "I promise."

~Chapter Three~

Two weeks later
Brighton

Elijah Banks clenched his hands into twin fists and willed himself to stay seated.

He shifted on the hard bench and took a deep, calming breath. It had only been forty minutes. Lord Friar could still arrive.

The silence that filled the room seemed louder than the crowds who gathered each night at Vauxhall.

Or mayhap that was just the steady tattoo of his blood pounding in his ears.

"Would you relax?" his twin Henry whispered. "It's not your wedding."

And what a pity that was. For as much as he'd denied the possibility to his father when he was younger, he'd gone and fallen in love with Lady Amelia Brice. And desperately wished it *was* his wedding today. "It might not be my wedding, but she *is* my friend."

"Do you think he woke up this morning and realized he was about to marry a spinster?" one of the ladies sitting in the pew behind him asked with a slight giggle.

Elijah bridled at her remark. Amelia might be four-and-twenty, but she wasn't what he'd consider a spinster. Besides, if anyone was getting the bad end of this bargain, it was Amelia. At least she was young and attractive. Hiram, Lord Friar was older than her father; and though Elijah had never actually seen the man, as he mixed in circles that even Elijah wasn't welcome in, the man's reputation of being one of the worst sort of no-good, lecherous scoundrel preceded him.

Henry lifted his eyebrows at him and Elijah jerked his gaze away. In a moment such as this, he wished he wasn't a twin. For as odd as it might seem to others, he and Henry had the ability to finish each other's thoughts and sentences with no difficulty, and with something as simple as an exchanged look, they could communicate every thought and feeling they had to the other. And right now, he didn't want his twin to know a single thing that was racing through his mind.

"Only five more minutes, then I can claim my winnings," another lady said behind him.

The hair on the back of Elijah's neck stood on end. What was she talking about?

He was saved from asking when one of the lady's companions inquired.

"Nothing you'd be interested in, Griselda," the woman said archly. "Just a little wagering."

"You placed a wager on the wedding today?" the lady who must have been Griselda said in shock.

"Perhaps."

A little sputter of laughter passed one's lips and Elijah's temper flared. Amelia had been his friend as long as he could remember and he'd be damned if he'd continue to sit idle while she was mocked behind her back.

He shoved to his feet. "Excuse me," he murmured, pushing his way down the pew and to the aisle, where he dodged a multitude of curious looks on his way to the back of the sanctuary.

Closing the large oak door behind him, he exhaled and swallowed. He could do this. He *needed* to do this. He owed it to Amelia.

Chancing a look down both sides of the hall to make sure her father or brother weren't stirring about, he knocked softly at the door to her bridal chamber. "Amelia?"

No answer.

He twisted his lips and considered knocking again, then dismissed the idea. She was in there, he was certain of it. Quiet so not to startle or upset her, he turned the knob and opened the door.

"Amelia," he said, uncertain if his word was a question or a statement as his eyes fell over her quiet form.

She half sat, half lay on a floral settee that blended into the equally flowery wallpaper, wearing one of the fluffiest dresses he'd ever seen. Her shawl lay in a little pile of white silk next to her, which was exactly where it should be, not draped around her, covering up her delicate shoulders or the tops of her luscious breasts. He swallowed. She'd always been a beautiful young lady, but just now she was absolutely breathtaking as she sat there and idly twirled a fallen lock of her silky, dark brown hair.

He found an empty chair from across the room and pulled it over to her so he could sit beside her. At least when they were both sitting, the height difference between her petite five foot frame and his towering five foot-eleven didn't seem so noticeable; and that was much the way he preferred it: equal.

"I should have known he'd do something like this," she whispered.

"I'm sorry," Elijah whispered just as softly as she'd spoken.

"Don't be. It's not your fault he jilted me at the altar."

No, but it is my good fortune, because now I won't even have to halt a wedding and pray your answer will be yes. He shoved the thought from his mind. If she truly wanted to marry Lord Friar, he'd have stepped aside and blamed himself for taking too long to tell her how he felt. But since he knew as well as she did that a match between Amelia and Lord Friar would be the equivalent of a death sentence, he'd come today to make one last appeal. Not to her father, to *her*. Fortunately, Lord Friar's absence had afforded him an opportunity to offer her marriage without the same risk of scandal or rejection.

He hated the bitter taste that word put in his mouth, but it didn't change the truth of it. Amelia was no longer the simpering miss she'd once been around him, talking of love and marriage to him. Instead, she seemed guarded around him and spoke as if those sorts of feelings no longer existed.

"Nobody has to know he jilted you," he said, reaching forward to push the hair sweeping across her forehead behind her ear.

She shook her head; her grey eyes shining with unshed tears. "They already do."

"No," he corrected. "All they know for sure is a wedding is not currently taking place. What they don't know is if it was the groom who jilted the bride or the bride who jilted the groom."

Amelia eyed him curiously. "No, I'm fairly certain they all know it was the groom who jilted the bride. My mother and father are both out there."

"Yes, and they are doing a wonderful job acting as if they're waiting for their daughter's wedding to take place."

"Acting?" she said, her eyes narrowing in on him.

"Acting," he confirmed. "See, your mother is sitting in her pew, dabbing her eyes with a handkerchief while your father is pacing a hole in the wooden platform just outside the front door of the church. Both are playing their roles perfectly, giving off the illusion to the rest of the guests that they are just waiting for the wedding to begin any moment."

"Which seems to be less likely to happen as the minutes pass."

"Exactly," Elijah agreed. "Which is why you need to act now before someone discovers your game."

"My game?"

He nodded once. "Yes, madam, your game." He picked up her petite hand and wrapped his fingers around it. "I'm not as dimwitted as the rest of them. I see what's really going on here."

"At least you do, because I have no idea what you're talking about."

He ignored her. "I almost fell for it, too."

"Fell for what?" she burst out in hysteria, presumably due to her current situation, lacing her voice.

"You're jilting your groom," he said evenly, meeting her eyes.

A shadow crossed her face and she cleared her throat. Twice. "What are you suggesting?"

"I'm not suggesting anything. I'm just merely making mention of the fact that the wedding has yet to begin, and both the bride and the groom have yet to be seen. How does a guest such as myself truly know whether it was the bride or the groom who didn't come today? How do I—a random guest—know that the bride and groom were not so in love with the other they could hardly wait another day and decided to elope?"

She snorted.

"All right, well, perhaps *that* scenario isn't very believable, but the other very well could be possible." He took a deep breath. "Amelia, listen to me, I know you're a very strong young lady and you come from a very important family; but none of that will matter come tomorrow when this is all over the scandal sheets."

"I know," she said with a swallow.

"Then see the sense in what I'm saying and marry me."

***

Amelia's jaw would have hit the end table next to the settee had she had the mouth of an ostrich. Elijah Banks was offering her marriage as a way to escape a scandal?

"Elijah, you don't have to do this."

He laughed at her weak protest. "I know I don't have to. I want to."

"Why? To make amends for dumping a bucket of cold water on me after I told your father that you wouldn't let me ride your mare?"

"No, nor is it because I feel bad about volunteering you to sing during the reception at Edwina's wedding."

"I knew it was you, you scoundrel!" She clapped a hand over her mouth.

He grinned at her outburst. "What do you say, Amelia? Will you be my wife?"

Had his question been asked because he loved her, she'd have dissolved into a watering pot on the spot. But it wasn't. Well, perhaps it was, but not love born of a romantic feeling; but rather that of a friend. A pang of sadness pierced her heart. Elijah was the only gentleman she'd ever wanted to marry. Since she was a young girl running around his parents' estate when spending summers with her aunt and uncle, she'd fancied herself in love with Elijah. He was the reason she'd turned away any gentlemen who wished to court her, hoping one day he'd see her as more than a friend. How unfortunate he never saw fit to feel the same for her.

She bit her lip. Hard. She needed to put that thought out of her mind immediately. If she let emotions get in the way and didn't take him up on his offer, she'd forever face a life of shame. But what of her other problem? The one that made *this* hasty marriage necessary. It had only been two weeks and she still didn't know whether she carried a life inside of her yet. A lump formed in her throat. "I can't."

"Can't what?"

Amelia blinked back her tears. "Elijah, I cannot marry you and condemn you to—"

"Nonsense," he cut in. "Amelia, if I didn't want to be here right now, I wouldn't be. You know that. No amount of goading and threatening can make me do something I don't want to do. I want to help you. You're my friend."

She inwardly flinched at his confirmation: she was just a friend. She knew that of course, he'd told her for years he was only her friend and had even gone so far as to help her find another gentleman to give her attentions to. Gently, of course. He'd never been cruel about her feelings or dismissive of her as a person, just the sincerity of a young girl's feelings. But try as she might, she couldn't fall out of love as easily as she'd fallen in. Only now, she didn't dare let him or anyone know the truth. He wanted to be her friend and that'd have to be good enough. "But what if I have a secret?" she challenged.

He pulled a face that reminded her of his late father. "It's not that you're genuinely in love with Lord Friar, is it?"

"Most certainly not! It has nothing to do with him." At least it had better not. She'd still yet to determine the identity of the masked stranger, and for all she knew it *could* have been Lord Friar. Her stomach lurched at the wretched thought. "It's something else."

Elijah's gloved fingers tilted her face up toward his. "As long as it's not that, I don't care what it is. Now, what do you say?"

A lead weight lowered on her chest. He might say he didn't care about her secret, but how would he feel in nine months when she presented him with a child that wasn't his? Or even sooner when he went to take her innocence only to discover it was already gone?

His deep sigh pulled her from her thoughts. "You'd be doing me a favor, wouldn't you know?"

How could *she* be doing *him* a favor? "How so?"

"Now that Weenie and Alex have both married, Mother has nobody to play matchmaker for except me and Henry, and if I'm married...that only leaves Henry."

Amelia nearly laughed. "Your mother doesn't play matchmaker, Elijah." She played the role of confidant and voice of sanity to perfection, but never once had Amelia caught Regina Banks, the dowager baroness, playing matchmaker.

"Just because she hasn't yet, doesn't mean she doesn't intend to," Elijah pointed out. "She and my Aunt Carolina have been spending *a lot* of time together recently. And there is nothing that can stop *that woman* when she takes a notion into her mind. So what do you say? Will you spare me the unpleasant fate that would befall me otherwise?"

"All right, but only if you promise me something."

"Anything."

"No matter what happens, you won't regret this?"

Elijah grinned and shook his head. "I accept your condition.

Now we just have to sneak you out of here." He walked over to a window and opened it just far enough to poke his head out. "Perfect." He pushed open the window as far as it would go and motioned for her to come over. "All right, I'll climb out first and then help pull you through."

She cast him a tentative glance. "Is that really necessary?"

He stared at her as if she'd just asked the stupidest question ever. "Do you know another way to get out of here without being seen?"

"No." But that still didn't mean she wanted to climb out a window.

"Don't worry, Amelia. I'll be right there to help you."

"Wonderful," she muttered as he threw his left leg over the window sill, then his right.

He jumped down and took a step back. "All right, Amelia, let's see those superb leaping skills you used to boast about having."

Had she a heavy object at her disposal—and not been in the middle of escaping what was sure to be the scandal of the season— she'd have brained him right then and there. With as much grace as her heavy satin gown would allow, she made her way to the window, pulled her skirt up as far as she could, and then threw one stocking-clad leg over the windowsill.

And that's as far as she got.

Between the heavy skirts and the voluminous petticoats underneath them, she couldn't move.

"Elijah, help me. I think my skirt is stuck."

He grinned at her.

"Elijah, why are you just standing there?"

"Just admiring the view," he said with a wink.

"Elijah!" She gave her dress a hearty yank, but it would seem her iron hoop stays were too wide to go through the window. "You can gawk all you want later. Just help me out."

"Promises, promises," he muttered, coming up to her.

If she honestly thought he was genuinely interested in seeing her naked body, she'd be flattered by his staring and excited by his statement. But she knew better. He was just enjoying the fact she was stuck in the window!

He walked over toward her and reached his hands up inside her skirt to find the ties that would release her stays. The bare skin of her thighs burned at the feeling of his gloved hands brushing them.

"Just cut them," she blurted.

"Are you sure?"

She'd never been more sure of anything in her life. "Yes. I have no idea why my mother insisted I wear these hoops anyway, they're nearly twenty years past fashion."

"All right, I'll cut them. Step back into the room and lift your skirt."

"How charming," she said under her breath.

"I try," he said with a smile. He reached into his pocket and pulled out his penknife. "Ready?"

She nodded as nervous excitement coursed through her. It was bad enough she'd been jilted today. It'd be even more awkward if someone were to enter the room at this very moment and see her holding her heavy skirts up so Elijah Banks could reach in through the window and cut her stays away. If her bridegroom not showing up wasn't enough to make her a laughingstock already, this particular situation would get her name whispered behind fans for generations.

The sharp sound of cloth—not just any cloth, but the cloth under her gown—being torn sent chills up her spine. Chills of excitement or danger or uncertainty, she might never really know.

"Turn," Elijah commanded.

She turned and he continued cutting the fabric until suddenly the sound of fabric-covered metal hitting the wooden floor floated to her ears.

Elijah put his knife away and then reached up toward her. "Let's go."

Without hesitation, she leaned out the window, wrapped her arms around Elijah's neck and let him pull her out of the church and away from the public shame and embarrassment she'd be condemned to as a jilted bride.

~ *Chapter Four* ~

Blood thundered in Elijah's ears. How far would they get before Elijah's absence was remarked on and the bride was found missing? They'd never make it to Gretna Green without being discovered. It was too far, and with only Elijah's horse, they didn't have a chance of arriving there anyway.

He'd be sure to send up a prayer of thanksgiving tonight that she'd been so easy to convince. But then again, she hadn't really had much of a choice because if she'd been her stubborn self and refused his offer, she'd have ended up a pariah for the rest of her life.

He twisted his lips. Thinking of it that way, her acceptance wasn't nearly as flattering as he'd like to pretend.

But that didn't matter. His offer had already been made, she'd accepted it and now they'd just have to ride three hours east to the Archbishop of Canterbury's residence, the only man close enough to issue a special license and marry them tonight.

"He's not home. He's visiting his nephew in Dover," the archbishop's purse-lipped butler intoned when Elijah and Amelia arrived on his doorstep.

Elijah graciously thanked the man and tried his best to reassure Amelia everything would be all right as he helped her back onto his horse.

Blessedly, Elijah had attended school with the bishop's nephew, Lord Templemore, and was counting on that very old and thin connection to help him gain an audience with the archbishop while he was visiting his relations. It might also secure the man's approval for a special license, he thought as he directed his horse down the lane. And if that didn't work, he'd tell the bishop there was a possibility she was increasing.

Chancing the occasional glance over his shoulder, he rode on. It would likely be nightfall before they reached where the bishop was staying. No matter. Just as long as they reached him before anyone found them, everything would be fine.

Three and a half hours and one horrible case of muscle cramps later, they arrived at Templemore's residence, where the archbishop was staying.

"Banks," Templemore greeted, coming into his study.

Elijah nodded. Templemore had attended Eton with Elijah and Henry. Templemore stood at least six feet tall with black hair and green eyes and was of exceptional intelligence. The young ladies swarmed to him in his first Season, but he hated the attention and chose to keep to himself, doing God only knows what in his townhouse. So it was to Elijah's surprise that when he returned home a few months ago he learned that Templemore had actually married last year, but it was not so surprising to find he was now spending the first part of the Season still in the country. "This might seem an odd request, but is your uncle in residence?"

"Of course," he said automatically, craning his neck around to get a good look at Amelia. "He's in the library right now—praying."

Elijah and Amelia exchanged looks. "Do you think he'll be finished shortly?" Elijah inquired.

"I suppose," Templemore said with a shrug.

If Elijah wasn't so tired from riding a horse all day, he just might strangle the man. Templemore had always been insolent, rivaling only Henry with his trite answers and infuriating quips. "Do you suppose you could go fetch him?"

"I suppose," Templemore said. "But do *you* suppose you might introduce me to your companion first?"

Elijah flushed. "Of course. Amelia, this is my friend Caleb Law, Earl of Templemore. And, this is Lady Amelia Brice, soon-to-be Mrs. Elijah Banks, I hope."

"I see," Templemore said, drawing out the words.

Just then, a dark-haired, lady joined them in the drawing room. "Oh, excuse me; I didn't realize you had company," she murmured to Templemore.

"Anne, I'd like you to meet a friend of mine, Elijah Banks and his...er...intended, Lady Amelia Brice." Templemore pulled the woman closer to him. "Elijah, Lady Amelia, this is my wife, Anne, Lady Templemore."

"It's nice to make your acquaintance," Elijah said automatically. Surely, Amelia said something to her, too, but Elijah didn't hear her. He was still in shock that Templemore had found someone who could actually tolerate him well enough to marry him.

"Thank you." Amelia's voice floated to his ears and he shot her a questioning look. "He's sending the butler to find the archbishop."

"Very good. You two don't mind being witnesses do you?"

"Do we have a choice?" Templemore asked.

"No. Not really."

"Well then, we'd be honored," Templemore said dryly.

A few minutes later the Archbishop of Canterbury lumbered into the room. "I understand my presence has been requested."

"Yes, sir," Elijah rushed to say before Templemore could say anything that might dissuade the old codger from performing the ceremony. "Lady Amelia and I would like for you to marry us. Now."

The older man pursed his lips and cocked his head to the side. "I'd be honored to perform the ceremony, but this is hardly the time or place, son."

"Is it not?" Elijah challenged. He heaved an exaggerated sigh. "I suppose you're right. Come along, sweet. We'd better start for Gretna Green now if we'd like to arrive in the next fortnight. Lady Templemore, do you happen to like Lady Amelia's gown? I think it's far too extravagant for her to ride across the country in while sharing a horse with her groom-to-be." He dropped his voice to a stage whisper. "Not to mention it might be too heavy for her to wear at night and she—"

"That is enough, young man," the archbishop snapped. He ran a hand over his wrinkled face. "Your point has been received. The wedding shall take place tonight."

"Excellent," Elijah said, beaming at his bride, who looked too travel weary to counter the not-so-flattering insinuation he'd made to the archbishop.

A few minutes later, the ceremony had begun.

Despite her ripped and dusty gown and wind whipped hair, Amelia made a beautiful bride. He squeezed her hands. She looked just as ragged as he felt. They'd both sleep very well tonight. Which was a good thing considering all the gossip they'd have to start fending off in the next few days.

"Elijah," Templemore all but shouted.

Elijah started. "Yes?"

"You may now kiss your bride," the archbishop said for what Elijah was certain wasn't the first time.

"Right," he said, meeting Amelia's grey eyes. A long ago memory of her chasing after him and threatening to kiss him suddenly came into his mind. She'd gotten him once or twice, too, if he remembered right. And always in front of someone, too. Of course that made it worse as he had an image to protect; and he'd always been sure to make a show of wiping off his mouth, or cheek, or forehead, or wherever it was her lips had landed. He shook his head to rid himself of the juvenile thought and pressed a quick, chaste kiss to her lips.

At least that's how he'd intended the kiss to be. But even for how fast and devoid of any tender emotion he'd intended to make it, he found himself craving more. Which would not do. While he desired her with his entire being, now wasn't the time to let her know.

"Do the two of you have any plans for the evening?"

Templemore asked, crossing his arms and leaning against the doorjamb.

"Just to go to bed," Elijah said without thought. His eyes flared wide and his face burned when he realized what he'd said, and how the unintended meaning his friend—and the bishop—likely took from his words. "That is— I mean—" He cleared his throat. "We've been traveling most of the day, I should think we'd like to have baths then go to bed."

Templemore's green eyes danced with laughter. "You're welcome to stay here tonight, if you'd like," Lady Templemore offered.

Elijah looked over to Amelia. She had dark circles under her eyes from their travels. It'd be at least another hour ride to the nearest inn, and that was if there was any vacancy. For as awkward as it might be for her to spend their wedding night in his friend's home, the bed would be far more superior and so would their fare. "Thank you. We'd love to stay."

Templemore nodded, then rang for Bennett, his butler. When he arrived, Templemore whispered some commands to him and only a short time later, Bennett was leading them up the stairs.

"You'll sleep much better this way," he whispered to her as they followed Bennett to the guest rooms.

She nodded but didn't say anything else.

Bennett moved the large brass eight-candle candelabra he carried to his left hand and opened the door to a large room with an oversized bed.

Elijah swallowed.

"This will be your room, Mrs. Banks," Bennett intoned. "And now if you'll come with me, Mr. Banks, I'll show you to yours."

For the best, he supposed. It might be their wedding night, but they'd been traveling all day and were in the residence of one of his friends, for pity's sake. No lady would wish to be deflowered under such circumstances.

He stepped into the room the butler indicated as his and

looked around. It was arranged much like his wife's with a large poster bed made out of mahogany that matched the wardrobe and vanity perfectly. The coverlet was the same shade of crimson as hers had been; and just as the basin and pitcher in her room were royal blue with six white lines creating a decorative border at the top, his were identical. Everything in this room was much like the other, only it lacked one thing: Amelia.

He sighed and fell onto the bed, exhausted. She'd acted just as tired as he. She'd probably appreciate—and perhaps expect—a slight reprieve for the evening. Besides he wasn't exactly in a hurry to share intimacies with her as clearly his feelings for her weren't returned. They'd need to, of course, if she was to— He closed his eyes to extinguish the thought. Tomorrow. He'd initiate intimacies with her tomorrow night and then all would be well.

***

Amelia willed the knot in her stomach to go away and stared blankly at the tapestry above her bed. It was too dark in the room to actually make out the designs embroidered into the fabric, but still there was enough of an outline to study to rid her mind of thoughts of her husband.

Oh, who was she trying to fool? She could no more forget his presence in the room next to hers as much as she could deny that she was the one who put that scar above his left eyebrow when he snuck up behind her, startling her so much she threw a rock at him.

Would he visit her tonight? She'd peeked in the hall to confirm that Bennett had put him in the room next to hers...with the adjoining door. So where was her groom? Mary, Lady Templemore's lady's maid had helped her undress and left her to wait more than an hour ago.

She'd spent that time thinking of what she'd say to him once he entered, and still couldn't decide. Should she try to put him off tonight or tell him all of her shame and live with whatever consequence came from it?

She flipped over and shoved a pillow under her stomach, but it did nothing to alleviate the nausea that swirled in her gut. All day Elijah had been nothing but kind to her; and how was she going to repay him? With a cuckoo. Now, *that* would endear her to him for life, to be sure.

~ *Chapter Five* ~

Death would be a welcome part of life just now. Yes, *death*.

Similar to that awful morning two weeks ago, she had a horrible headache and was nauseous, presumably due to the bundle of nerves she'd been last night; unfortunately, she couldn't blame this particular feeling on a fruity drink.

She *had* to tell him. He deserved to know.

Wearily, she rolled out of bed and rubbed her tired eyes.

"Good morning, Mrs. Banks," a familiar voice said from the adjoining door.

"Elijah?"

"Or am I Henry?" he teased.

She offered him a weak smile. "That never worked with me."

"I know," he said, frowning. He walked further inside and kicked the door closed behind him. In his hands, he carried a tray filled with several pastries and fruits. "Templemore had these sent up, and I thought I'd see if you'd like to have breakfast with me?"

Her face burned. "Can't we just leave?"

Elijah set the tray down on the vanity. "Is something not to your liking?"

"It's not that. It's just—" She tucked a tendril of her dark hair behind her ear and swallowed her unease. "They think we're up here becoming better acquainted as husband and wife."

"And we're not?" Elijah asked, gesturing to the tray of food.

"You know what I meant."

"Indeed." He lifted the tray again and walked toward her bed. "But I feel compelled to ask when you started caring what other people think about you?"

Since I woke up to find I'd been unknowingly stripped of my virtue, might be carrying a child and foolishly agreed to marry Lord Friar. She forced a shrug. "I don't want to seem impolite or inhospitable."

A sharp bark of laughter filled the air. "You're a new bride the morning after her wedding, nobody expects you to be holding court in the breakfast room." He snorted. "Clearly, Templemore didn't even think *you'd* be awake yet."

Amelia's cheeks burned. "You are your father's son, aren't you?" she mused, remembering all the times his father had made some sort of dry remark that hedged on the side of being considered scandalous.

With a hint of a smile, he did a mock bow. "Guilty, I'm afraid."

"Do you miss him?" she asked, taking a strawberry tart from the tray.

Elijah set the tray down on the bed next to her and then made himself comfortable on the other side. "Sometimes; but not the same as Alex and Weenie," he added, snatching a biscuit.

"Because you have a twin and they don't?"

"No. I think Alex was closer to Father because he was the oldest and they shared more common interests, what with their love for all things science and Alex being his heir and all. Then Weenie was the youngest, and his only daughter." He shrugged. "I would never say that I didn't feel any attachment at all for him or him for me. I certainly did, but I just wasn't as close to him as the other two. Neither was Henry."

"Because you had each other," she murmured again between bites.

"I suppose so. I never really thought about it that way, but now that I've said it, I suppose you're right."

"I usually am," Amelia retorted, smiling. Something about the way Elijah looked at her in return made her smile falter. There was a certain intensity in his eyes she hadn't expected to see just then. She cleared her throat and shifted. "Where do you plan for us to go now?"

Elijah lifted a single brow.

"Certainly you didn't expect us to live out the rest of our lives here with your friend Lord Templemore, did you?"

"Well, no," Elijah conceded, twisting his lips into an overdone frown and nodding once. "But if you'd like to, I'm sure arrangements could be made..."

Amelia shook her head and grinned. "No. And I wouldn't think you'd like that, either."

"No, I wouldn't like to live out the rest of our lives here, but —" his voice dropped to little more than a soft whisper— "I see no reason to leave immediately."

Amelia's breath caught and she nearly lost hold of her tart. "Y-you don't?"

***

Elijah wanted to laugh at her naivety. "No, I don't," he whispered, leaning toward her.

"Wh-what are you doing?"

This time Elijah did laugh—inwardly, anyway. He'd never be so ill-mannered as to humiliate her by actually laughing at her innocence. "Just relax," he murmured, leaning in toward her again.

Her nervous giggle was the equivalent of her throwing her hands up to stop him. He frowned at her. "Is something humorous?"

"N-no," she said. There wasn't laughter lacing her voice any longer, but neither was her tone as soft as usual.

He ignored the uncertainty stamped on her face and pressed forward, closing the gap between them. His lips found hers and she pulled away. Not to be deterred, he brought his hand up to cup her face and held her still while he leaned in for another kiss.

Unfortunately, this one was far less satisfactory than the one yesterday. He pushed the thought from his mind and kissed her again, but missed her lips and kissed her cheek when she moved her head to evade him.

"I don't think this is a good time," she said with a slight hitch in her voice.

"No, it's the perfect time." He tucked a tendril of her fallen hair behind her ear, then swallowed his unease and brought his lips to hers again.

Hard and unyielding, kissing Amelia was what he imagined kissing a stone would be like. He fought the urge to frown and continued to kiss his marble statue.

"Amelia," he said, pulling back. "Kiss me back."

Her cheeks flushed. "I can't."

"Yes, you can. First you need to relax your lips, then you need to mirror my actions," he said, leaning toward her for what he hoped would be the final time.

"I-I don't think so." She pulled away from him and put her fingers to his lips to stop him from kissing her again.

Elijah's hand slowly encircled her wrist and pulled her hand away from his face. "Is something wrong?" he murmured half-heartedly.

"No, not wrong." She bit her lower lip and let her eyes wander the room. "This just really isn't the time."

Elijah wanted to groan. For a young lady who'd once made it a habit to chase him around the lawn, trying to kiss him, she sure didn't seem too interested in kissing him when the time was finally appropriate. He raked a hand through his hair. Considering the circumstances, it was probably for the best. Likely she was still tired, and for as much as he might be ready to initiate lovemaking, his friend's house was probably not the best place.

From beneath his lashes, Elijah noticed Amelia was fingering the top of her chemise, presumably trying to keep it pressed firmly to her skin, depriving him of any glimpse of skin he might have been afforded otherwise. He touched the back of her hand with the tips of his fingers. "Stop fussing. You're decent—enough."

Her blush made him grin. "Perhaps I should don my gown from yesterday." She cast her eyes to the crumpled blue and white mess just to the left of where her dainty, stockinged foot dangled from the side of the bed.

He twisted his lips. "You enjoy your breakfast, and leave your wardrobe to me."

A burble of laughter passed her lips and she cast him a quizzical look. "I wait with bated breath to see what you deem appropriate."

He frowned. "What is that to mean?"

"If a lady's wardrobe was left to her husband to decide, she'd spend her days wearing—" She abruptly broke off, then cleared her throat.

Elijah casually reached forward and took another tart from the tray, hoping she'd continue where she'd left off. He couldn't say why, but he was truly interested in what she might suggest. Of course he had an idea of what she was about to say, but wanted to hear it from her—and more curious than that, why had she stopped? She should know him well enough by now to know nothing she could say, and he truly meant *nothing*, could possibly scandalize him or make him think less of her.

When it had become clear she had no intention of resuming her former thought, he said, "Don't worry, one of Templemore's maids can help you dress before we leave."

"And exactly where will we be going?"

He hesitated but a moment. "Watson Estate."

"But isn't your brother and his wife hosting a house party there?"

"Yes; but we won't have to attend, if you don't wish to." He picked up a blackberry tart and brought it to his lips. "I don't have a country home, so it's either there or London."

Amelia idly twirled her hair around her fingers and looked decidedly unconvinced.

"Don't worry," Elijah said, brushing off the excess sugar from his fingers. "It'll just be my family. A more scandalous lot I have yet to meet."

She cast him a dubious look. "You must be talking about your cousins, because I've never heard your name, or that of any of your brothers attached to a single scandal."

"Indeed," Elijah said slowly. "But you forget. I do have a sister."

"No, I haven't forgotten her; nor how to properly pronounce her name." she said, not quite meeting his eyes.

Elijah chuckled as for a mere moment it seemed the new constraints of their relationship evaporated and they were both transported back in time to when they could share private jests with a few simple words and secret expressions.

~ Chapter Six ~

From beneath her lowered lashes, Amelia watched as Elijah sighed and leaned his back against the red velvet squabs of the carriage Lord Templemore had insisted on loaning him for their trip to Watson Estate.

Amelia wondered what he was thinking, but didn't dare ask and continued to pretend she was sleeping. It appeared at first as if he were in deep contemplation, but now he was squeezing his eyes shut so tightly lines that looked like he'd just been scratched by the claw of a crow fanned out from the corners of his eyelids.

She had no idea what would make him act in such a way. It wasn't he who had a damning secret. Nor was it he who'd been married the day before only out of pity. Amelia immediately tried to swallow the large, uncomfortable lump that had suddenly taken up residence in her throat.

Yesterday, she'd foolishly convinced herself everything would turn out all right. Elijah was her friend. But that was just it. Elijah was her *friend*. He had no other interest in her and his horrible charade earlier this morning proved it. The stiff, impersonal way he'd tried to kiss her turned Amelia into a walking contradiction of herself. She'd always dreamed of kissing Elijah, and fancied herself in love with him for as long as she could comprehend, but she'd had no desire to kiss him back. And it wasn't because of the secret she possessed or because they were at his friend's, but quite simply, his actions were cold and devoid of any emotion, done solely out of obligation—a fact that hurt worse than a simple, honest rejection.

A raw, strangled sound broke the silence in the carriage.

"Elijah, are you feeling all right?" she asked before she could stop herself.

Elijah snapped his eyes open. "Yes. Are you?"

Amelia ignored his question. She'd already given herself away that she was not sleeping; she might as well make the best of it. "Are you sure you're all right? Your hands are clenched into fists and your face was just contorted the same way it did the time Henry hit you with the end of his pall mall mallet."

He winced and like it always did when this topic was mentioned, his right hand drifted down to idly rub his shin. "That is undoubtedly one of the most painful memories of my boyhood."

"Yes, I know." She changed positions and tucked her stocking-clad feet up under her. Lady Templemore had graciously offered her one of her traveling gowns and though reluctant, Amelia had accepted. She'd have been a fool not to. "You actually cried."

"I did not."

"Yes—" she pinned him with her gaze— "you did."

He scoffed. "I most certainly did not."

Amelia arched her brow. "Hmmm, I seem to recall things a little differently. First there was the shriek—"

"I know for certain that I did not shriek," he cut in, scowling. "I might have yelped, but I did not shriek."

She grinned at him. "All right, and how do you explain the moisture that surrounded your eyes following your yelp?"

"Perhaps a bug flew into my eye and I was trying to flush it out."

"Into both eyes at that precise moment?" She shook her head. "No, you were crying. Just admit it."

"All right," he said, throwing his hands into the air. "I admit I had tears in my eyes. Who wouldn't after having a two pound chunk of wood collide with the front of their leg in such a manner?"

She shrugged. "I don't know. You were the one who denied you cried about it."

"That's because it's unmanly," he informed her, crossing his arms.

"It's unmanly to cry?" she asked for clarification that he had in fact just said the stupidest thing she'd ever heard.

"Of course it is." He twisted his lips. *"Unless you're a molly,"* he grumbled almost inaudibly.

"And what, pray tell, is a molly?" She nearly laughed at the look of shock that had come over his face at her question. "You ought to know by now that my hearing is good enough to hear when you mumble under your breath."

Elijah flicked his wrist. "Don't worry about what a molly is. In the unlikely chance you ever make the acquaintance of one, he probably wouldn't cry in front of you."

She frowned. "I've seen Philip cry and I'm fairly certain he's not a molly, whatever that is."

"Was he ten years old and standing too close when his sibling swung their pall mall mallet, too?"

"No. He lost his prized thoroughbred in a card game and when Mr. Maxwell came to collect his winnings, Philip—"

"Please, stop, I pray you," Elijah interjected, lifting his hand to halt her words. "I'm sure there was just a bit of stable dust in his eye."

"Ah, is that what you gentlemen call it?"

"When we're genuinely tearing up, yes," he said with a grimace. "But I have difficulty believing Philip cried about losing his horse. In that situation, I think he really did have something in his eyes."

"No, I'm fairly certain he was crying. It was his *prized thoroughbred.*"

"Prized thoroughbred or not, no man cries about losing something. He might frown or scowl, but he doesn't cry."

"So when does a man cry?"

"He doesn't," Elijah burst out.

"Ever?"

"Ever."

"But what if he's hurt? Do his eyes not water?"

"They might water, but he does not cry."

She twisted her lips and crossed her arms. "Is there a difference?"

"Yes."

"I fail to see it," she said, giving her head a slight shake. "Tears are tears."

"Then I suppose every time a man's eyes water when he yawns or sneezes you think he's crying?"

"Well no," she allowed. "But I'm certain Philip was crying when he lost his horse."

"If you say so," he grumbled.

"It's still pain, Elijah. It might not be the same kind of pain you felt when Henry hit you with the mallet, but I'm sure it hurt him all the same."

Elijah lifted his hands in defeat. "All right, you win."

"Ha! I knew it, men do cry."

"No, I was just acknowledging that Philip cried about his horse," he teased.

She laughed. "All right; but since you said I won, I demand you still allow me my boon."

"I wouldn't dream of denying it from you."

***

Not that he'd ever dreamed her boon would be so...so...infuriating, he amended as his jaw clenched in agitation.

"I beg your pardon?"

"I said, I'd like a separate room," Amelia repeated as if she was announcing what she'd like for luncheon.

Despite the heat crawling up his face, Elijah turned to the innkeeper of the little inn just outside of London they'd stopped at for the evening. "We'll be back in just a moment. Amelia, can we talk a moment?"

Amelia followed him over to the little corner. "Yes?"

"What are you about?"

She shrugged. "I won a boon, didn't I?"

"Yes," he said slowly. "But I thought you'd want a book or a shawl or some sort of other bauble."

"No. I think my own room tonight should do."

Well, it wouldn't do for Elijah. He'd missed his opportunity to bed her last night and this morning. He didn't want to waste another chance. "You do realize when we reach Watson Estate we'll have to share the same bedchamber?"

She frowned. "I thought there were more than sixty guest bedchambers. Surely Alex's wife isn't planning to invite that many people, is she?"

"No," he allowed. "But neither do I intend to take my new bride to live in the main house. Alex has a hunting cabin just a half a mile or so away from the main house. We'll be staying there."

Her frown deepened. "You want us to walk half a mile back and forth each day to get to their house?"

With any luck, they wouldn't be going to Caroline's house party every day. "No, we can ride a horse, if you'd rather. Or I can even order the carriage to transport us." Whatever it took to please her, he'd do. Almost. He did have his limits, and right now, she was testing them.

"We can talk about this later. For now, I just want my own room for the night."

He scowled. "Why?"

"Because I won a boon," she said, lifting her chin a notch.

To her left two burly looking fellows had stopped their conversation and were now watching Amelia and Elijah with unmasked curiosity. Elijah twisted his lips. It was becoming clear that if he didn't wish to have such a private matter discussed publicly, he'd better just agree to let her have her own room. "Fine. You can have your own room tonight. But don't think for one minute you'll get your way tomorrow night."

"I will if I win another boon," she said; that old, familiar spark in her grey eyes.

"I wouldn't spend too much time counting on such an occurrence." He took a step closer to her and dropped his voice. "I have no desire to allow you another win."

She took a step in his direction, and matching his tone, said, "You won't have to let me win. I'll win all on my own."

Elijah had the strangest urge to wipe that smug smile straight from her lips, preferably with a kiss—the kind from yesterday at their wedding, not one similar to the travesty this morning; but instead, he just nodded and walked off. Now wasn't the time to push her. If she reacted so horribly to him while they were alone, God could only know how she might act if he tried to kiss her with an audience present.

Elijah stalked back to the counter where the innkeeper stood. "We'll take two rooms," he said, unable to look the older man in the eye.

The innkeeper chuckled, but sobered instantly when Elijah shot him an icy stare. "Here is yer keys." He handed Elijah two keys. "But there's a connecting door," he added with a wink.

Elijah closed his eyes, waiting for Amelia's pert reply about the connecting door being unnecessary that he was expecting; but no such reply came. He turned to look at her and if he didn't know any better, he'd say she either hadn't heard the man or was pretending she hadn't. He shook his head. For as long as he might walk the face of this earth, he may never understand the creature he'd married.

***

Amelia desperately needed a new gown. While it was nice that Lady Templemore had loaned Amelia one of her best traveling gowns, it didn't fit quite right. They were close to the same height, both just a touch above five feet tall, but it would seem Amelia had a tad more curve to her bosom than Lady Templemore did.

One of the maids had been able to let the seam out enough to allow Amelia to wear it somewhat comfortably and at least she could get this one on and off herself, she thought as she scowled at her image in the mirror. She turned to the side and ran her hands down her smooth stomach. Was that a bulge? Nonsense. It was too early to be showing signs of increasing. Sadly, she hadn't yet experienced the one symptom that guaranteed she was *not* increasing, either.

She frowned and moved away from the mirror. Likely Elijah was waiting for her downstairs.

Or right outside her door, she amended as soon as she opened the door to be greeted by his pale blue eyes.

"Is the carriage ready?"

He nodded. "Everything's ready, but you." He cocked his head to the side. "Are you feeling all right?"

"Just fine," she lied. Was it that obvious she was hiding something?

He nodded slowly then flickered a glance inside her room, to her bed, if she had to venture a guess. She fought not to scowl and quickly, she closed the door. What was his obsession with her bed? If he truly wanted to take her there, all he'd have to do is kiss her properly, with true and genuine emotion and she'd undoubtedly be at war with herself about what to do. Of course, she'd then have to tell him of her shame—which would kill the romance and magic of the moment faster than a stampede of elephants could trample a rose garden—then they'd be right back in the situation they currently found themselves.

She sighed and pursed her lips. It was for the best that he wasn't truly interested in her. Once she knew whether or not she was increasing she could tell him everything, and they could start that particular aspect of their marriage with honesty. Unfortunately, her own uncertainty of the situation might kill her first.

"Are you feeling all right?" Elijah repeated, pulling Amelia from her fog.

She forced a smile. "I already told you that I was."

He cast her a dubious look, but didn't argue. "Shall we?" He offered her his arm and led her to the carriage.

Amelia was beyond relief when the familiar trees and rolling landscape of Watson Estate came into view, followed by the well traveled lanes to the dowager house and hunting cabin. Elijah, however, didn't look quite as relieved, perhaps that was because the curtains were drawn in the heat of the day, flooding that little building with more heat than might be comfortable.

"Is something the matter?"

She expected him to make a jest about his asking her that this morning, but surprised her when he didn't. "No." He turned to face her, a stoic expression coming over him. Without consulting his pocket watch, he said, "We'll go into the main house first and greet our gracious host."

Amelia stared at him in confusion. He looked no more fit for company than she did, and he was insisting they go inside? Why?

"What has you grinning like a cat who's spotted the cream?" Elijah asked with no hint of emotion in his voice.

She put her fingers to her lips. Indeed, he was right and she was grinning wildly. "Nothing. I was merely thinking that perhaps *you* do have a scandalous side, after all."

"And you came to this conclusion because I think we should greet our hosts?" he asked, confusion marring his handsome face.

"Dressed like we've just spent the last two days—and nights— wearing the same crumpled costumes, yes."

His blue eyes lit with laughter. "Have no fear, my sweet," he said in a voice that sent shivers down her spine. "Our dreadful state of dress won't scandalize them nearly as much as the thoughts that will be cycling through each one of their heads about *how* we came to be in such a disheveled state. Don't forget, each and every one of them had a love match."

Amelia's cheeks heated as Elijah's soft chuckle filled the carriage. That scoundrel!

~ Chapter Seven ~

Amelia had never felt as nervous as she did right then walking into the drawing room filled with Elijah's closest female relatives.

"Amelia," Regina, Elijah's mother, called. She got off her blue settee and walked over to wrap Amelia in a tight hug. "I am so glad to see you. I didn't think my son would be kind enough to share you so soon."

Amelia almost snorted. Elijah seemed more than happy to "share" her with his family as soon as they approached Watson Estate. And the fact that the host and hostess had already gone off to entertain their guests didn't deter him one bit. Instead, he ushered her down the hall and to the drawing room so quickly it was simply miraculous she hadn't fallen on her face. Then without preamble, he slung open the door and declared that Lady Amelia Banks had arrived—as if the entire room of ladies had been waiting for that very moment. Before she could say anything—or cast him the icy stare he deserved—he was gone. Off to be away from her and with his brothers, if she had to guess. "Surely he just wanted me to meet his family while you were all so close."

"Yes, I'm sure that's it," Regina said quietly; then she cleared her throat. "Well, since my son seems to lack any sort of manners, please allow me to introduce you to the room."

Amelia scanned all the faces and swallowed hard. She'd had no sisters or female friends growing up. How was she supposed to survive being in a room with seven other ladies?

"Wait, Aunt Regina," a dark-eyed woman with long, curly brown hair called. She stood up and picked something up from the top of the secretary in the corner, then came over to Amelia and handed her a sheet of paper and a short pencil. "To take notes."

Grinning, Regina shook her head. "It's true, we have a large family, but once you meet everyone, you'll find it's easy to identify who is who. For instance, the forward young lady who so helpfully handed you this paper is my niece Brooke, Lady Townson. Next to her with the light blonde hair and blue eyes is her sister Madison. She's married to a duke who has similar features." She turned to face another settee full of ladies. "Over there is my final niece, Liberty Grimes and next to her is the brave woman who raised all of these girls, Carolina." She brushed out her skirt. "And of course you already know Alex's wife Caroline and Edwina."

Amelia nodded quietly. She'd heard Alex had married a lady as scientific as he a few years ago, but had only seen her in passing at Edwina's wedding. And of course, she'd played with Edwina when she was younger. Being exactly three years younger than Elijah and Henry and three years older than Edwina, had put her in the position of being all of their playmates at different times. Once Elijah and Henry were old enough to go off to Eton, Amelia and Edwina had become friends until it was decided Edwina was to attend a girls' school.

Regina affectionately squeezed her arm. "It'll be all right," she whispered. "Just stay close to me and together we can fade into the wallpaper."

Amelia offered her a slim smile. "If only such a thing were truly possible."

Regina's eyes crinkled around the corners. "Nonsense. My son would be quite disappointed to come back and find his new bride had made such a tragic transformation."

"Tragic?" Amelia echoed, knitting her brows.

Regina nodded once and dropped her voice. "My husband may have passed a few years ago, but I recall well enough that no gentleman wants only a lady whom he can look upon and occasionally touch in passing."

Amelia was even more confused. Regina was talking cryptically, she realized. Something that Amelia had never known her to do before. Not that she knew Elijah's mother *that* well. Sure, they'd had numerous amounts of afternoon teas together after Regina had caught Elijah being beastly to her. But they'd always spoken about Amelia's clothes, flowers, or other pleasantries— they'd even discussed Amelia's feelings for Elijah, or rather Amelia had confided in Regina her feelings for Elijah a time or two; but never had Regina spoken in any sort of code like she seemed to be doing now. Unfortunately, for as intelligent as Regina must think Amelia to be to understand her hidden message, Amelia was undeniably befuddled. But instead of asking for clarification and risking embarrassing herself right along with everyone else in the room, she just nodded and said, "Yes, he'd find *that* to be a great travesty, indeed."

Regina's eyes flared wide but for a moment and a hint of color rose in her cheeks. She coughed to clear her throat. "Shall we sit?"

Numbly, Amelia nodded and took her seat. What had she just said that would cause Regina to act so...so...oddly?

"What exactly do you have planned for this party, Caroline?" Madison, the duchess, asked.

"Nothing too extravagant—"

A wave of relief washed over Amelia at her sister-in-law's words, causing her not to hear anything else she said until the words, "And then of course on the final night we'll invite a few neighbors and invite others from London for the annual costume ball."

"A costume ball?" Amelia choked before she could stop herself.

"Not to worry," Caroline said, smiling warmly at Amelia. "I have a few spare dominos. You're welcome to borrow anything you might like."

"Thank you, that's most gracious," Amelia murmured, inwardly cringing. The last thing she wanted to do was attend a ball with members of the *ton*. At the house party they were only in the company of Elijah's closest family and friends—nobody here was likely to mock her or be so cruel as to ask questions about her disastrous wedding, if they'd even heard of it yet. The same couldn't be said for the throngs of people who might come from London. She sighed. At least she'd be in disguise.

"Of course if you don't wish to come, being newly married and all, we'll all understand," Regina said softly.

Amelia shot her a grateful look, but knew it'd be considered rude to accept her mother-in-law's invitation to escape. "It's more than a week away, surely by then we'll be settled enough to attend."

Elijah's Aunt Carolina gave her a doubtful look, then said the last thing Amelia ever expected a woman of her years to say, "Regina's right, dear. With the way you two stole away to Gretna Green to marry, we're all rather surprised you're even here."

Amelia flushed. "Gretna Green," she choked.

"Gretna Green," Edwina confirmed before anyone else could say anything. "I do wish Elijah had thought enough of his family to have held just a small ceremony, but alas he didn't."

"That's because when a Banks man takes it in his mind it's time to marry, then it's time to marry," Carolina said, her voice full of conviction, a wistful smile on her face. "And if that means a girl must sneak out of her window under the cloak of darkness and travel to a seedy part of town to do it—then she must go."

The room grew quiet as everyone exchanged looks—most notably expressions with raised eyebrows, but nobody said anything directly to Carolina's strange pronouncement.

"Just so," Regina agreed at last. "It's just unfortunate that we all missed out on the wedding."

No, they were quite fortunate they *had* missed the wedding, but Amelia wasn't about to say that. "May I ask how you knew of Gretna Green?" She hoped that sounded better to their ears than it had to her own. But the truth was, she'd never been to Gretna Green, and if there was a rumor going around that she'd been there to marry Elijah, she would do well to know what was being said about her before attempting to set things straight.

"It was in Elijah's note," Edwina said easily.

"His note?" Amelia repeated, her words more a statement than a question.

Edwina opened her reticule and pulled out a note and handed it to Amelia.

I have just learned of Amelia's engagement to Lord Friar. A more mismatched pair, I couldn't imagine. I'm off to Brighton to steal the bride and take her to Gretna Green before the wedding. Wish me luck. I shall see you soon.

EJB

Amelia stared at the note in disbelief. It had to have been written by Henry. Did he write that to spare her reputation or his family's honor? Or did it matter now that they were one and the same? Either way, she certainly owed him a debt of gratitude. And possibly a thump on the head for taking such a risk. Had Elijah's aunt not said anything about Gretna Green she could have very easily ruined the illusion he'd tried to make.

Regina exhaled. "Such a pity Henry didn't see fit to show, the two-week old note, to any of us until this morning. I knew they were staying in London and I just saw your wedding announcement last week, but I had no idea he'd hauled you off to elope!" She shook her head. "I have no idea what I'm going to do with those two. Actually—" a hint of a smile took her face— "Elijah is now *yours,* Amelia. As I once told Caroline after she married Alex, I did the best I could and now it's your turn to make something respectable of him. But I'm sure that'll be an act of love, for you," she added, grinning.

Was it so obvious she held the same torch for Elijah as she had when she was a young girl or was this inferred due to the Gretna Green story? She contemplated asking, but dismissed the notion instantly.

"It seems like a difficult task, but I'll do my best."

Carolina grinned. "And where the Banks gentlemen—and young ladies," she added casting her daughters a sharp look, "are concerned, that's all you can do."

~Chapter Eight~

"Alex, have you ever lied to Caroline?"

Alex, his oldest brother, blinked his brown eyes at him from behind his wire-rimmed spectacles. "No. Why?"

Elijah leaned back against the cushions on the settee, refusing to meet either of his brothers' curious gazes. "I just wondered."

"A man doesn't just wonder that," Alex commented.

"At least not if he knows what's best for him," Henry finished, an unspoken message meant for only Elijah in those words.

Elijah ran his hand through his thick hair. "Forget I said anything."

"We can't. You've already done said it," John Banks, Elijah's uncle, said plainly as he led a small group of gentlemen who included Elijah's cousins' husbands and his brother-in-law, Sir Wallace Benedict into the room. "Now we're all curious."

"Just so," Andrew Black, Earl of Townson, one of Alex's closest friends and the husband of Elijah's outspoken cousin Brooke, agreed as he found a seat on a nearby settee.

Alex didn't seem to mind the intrusion and Elijah didn't even want to venture a look at Henry. He already knew Henry's reaction to being joined.

"Don't be shy to talk about your marital problems, now," Paul, another cousin's husband, intoned, his lips twitching. "Besides having two vicars present, we're all family. And if that doesn't convince you, you can take comfort knowing a similar conversation has happened with all of us."

Elijah doubted that.

"You look like you don't believe me," Paul continued. "Say, Alex, do you recall—"

"Yes," Alex bit off. "I was trying to explain a very fascinating discovery I'd made about hedgehogs and you three—" he nodded toward Andrew, Paul and Uncle John— "kept asking questions about how Paul and Liberty were rubbing along."

"If I recall correctly, I gave you leave to continue discussing your findings on hedgehog mating," Paul grumbled.

Benjamin Collins, Duke of Gateway, the husband to his other cousin, Madison, snapped his head around to face Alex. "You wouldn't still happen to have those notes you took, would you?" he asked hopefully.

Uncle John groaned and turned toward Alex. "If you do, please keep them to yourself. Nobody here, especially him—" he pointed an accusing finger over to the duke— "wants to hear about hedgehog procreation or any other scientific discovery you might have made, of that, I'm quite certain."

Alex sighed. "Why is it every time we've crossed paths these last five years you ask a battery of questions about my science experiments?"

"No reason," Benjamin said with a shrug, his blue eyes holding not a clue to what he was thinking.

"Enough of that," Andrew said, twisting his lips.

"No, I'm truly interested," Alex argued. "If he wants any more of my science bits, he'd better—"

"Alex, setting aside the fact that other than Caroline, Benjamin is the only person of your acquaintance who seems to find any interest in your 'science bits', I wouldn't complain. At least it gives you someone to discuss your experiments with without risk of sending them into a state of unconsciousness," Andrew said. "Besides, we're not here to discuss either of you two or any of your science discoveries, but to prod Elijah until he reveals the lie he's keeping from Lady Amelia."

Elijah almost snorted. They could "prod" him all day long, if they'd like, he had no intention of telling them anything. He shrugged. "There's nothing to tell."

"Sure there is," Uncle John said. "You're lying to your wife. Now, just tell us why and we'll help you decide what you should do."

Elijah cleared his throat, his eyes momentarily locking with Henry's. They exchanged a look: a simple message and understanding, if you will. "My marriage is not up for discussion," Elijah said coolly.

"No matter," Benjamin said, repositioning a gold pillow behind his back. "You've already said enough. You've lied to your wife. As a man who...er...might have done something similar for reasons I'd rather not say, I might be able to offer some advice."

All eyes went to the duke. A more scheming, cryptic individual Elijah had never met—outside of those he'd been paid to see, that is.

"Why would you lie to your wife?" Alex asked Benjamin without a hint of emotion.

Benjamin shrugged. "It was for the best."

Sir Wallace, Elijah's brother-in-law snorted. "I haven't been married nearly as long as you, but even I know it's not in anybody's best interest to lie to one's wife."

Elijah shifted his gaze to Sir Wallace. Though a little unusual with his habit of counting when uncomfortable and his somewhat irritating need for perfection, he seemed a decent sort. Elijah hadn't always thought so, of course, but he'd had plenty of time to observe and speculate and now understood just what it was about the man that made Sir Wallace an excellent match for his sister, Edwina: he was genuine. He didn't lie or cheat to get his way. He wasn't the type to grow angry over trivial matters, or even the majority of important matters, either. But neither did he have a menacing bone in his body. Gossip could fly about the man faster than a swallow escaping a tabby, and he wouldn't so much as mutter an impolite statement in response. Yes, Sir Wallace Benedict was odd, indeed; but his oddness was exactly what made him a good match for Edwina.

"Normally, it's not a brilliant idea to lie to one's wife," Benjamin conceded a moment later. "But sometimes it must be done. Perhaps that's the situation in which Elijah currently finds himself."

"No," Elijah said, giving a lopsided shrug. "It was just a question. Nothing more."

Five snorts rang out, leaving Elijah and Henry the only two who didn't find humor in his statement.

"It's never just a question," Uncle John said. "Especially not that one."

"I don't think it's wise to lie to her about anything," Alex said, garnering nods of agreement from Andrew, Paul, Uncle John and Sir Wallace.

"You wouldn't," Benjamin muttered, crossing his arms. "The fact is, sometimes it's just the way it has to be and if someone sees a problem with it, then it's because they're too simpleminded to understand."

A series of snorts, guffaws, scoffs, and head shaking by all the other married men in the room followed the duke's words, but he didn't seem to care. Benjamin Collins was the kind who didn't care what others thought of him or said about him. He was who he was, he said what he felt like saying, and did whatever he wanted; and if you didn't like that, he didn't care. Except when it came to his wife. Madison's opinion seemed to be the only one he cared a whit about. Apparently she didn't mind his fibbing or he wouldn't be advocating it so much.

"Tell me, Benjamin, how exactly did your wife feel when she learned the truth? And don't think for one minute that I'll believe that she never learned of it, I know my daughter better than that. All three of my daughters can sniff out the truth even if it's buried under a thousand pounds of manure," John mumbled.

Benjamin shrugged. "She didn't care so much and I expect that Lady Amelia won't, either."

"Didn't care so much," Andrew muttered, shaking his head.

"From what I heard from her sister—who just so happens to be my wife—I'd say she might have cared more than you'd like to believe."

"Well, that might be what she told Brooke," Benjamin said with an overdone frown. "But I don't think so. Madison has no qualm telling me when I do something she doesn't like. If my omission had displeased her that greatly, she'd have said so. Besides, she's the one who insisted I lie to her."

Elijah's interest was piqued, but he kept quiet. In all of his travels he'd learned that in situations such as this that one gains far more information by being silent than by asking questions.

"How the blazes did you reach such an illogical conclusion?" Alex burst out, taking the words straight from Elijah's mind.

"She said she didn't wish to discuss a certain matter, so I didn't. Therefore, she had no one but herself to blame for my omission."

Elijah nodded slowly as conversation went on around him. His situation had many similarities, but was still different. He chanced another glance over to Henry. Everyone said they were identical, and perhaps they were with their father's blond hair, blue eyes, and tilted grin, but their personalities were not so identical. Never mind the fact that Henry would not have made the decisions that had led Elijah to this situation, but if he had, he'd just do whatever he felt was his duty without worrying about hurt feelings or damaging a friendship. Henry was more like their father and Alex in that respect. Henry relied on logic and duty to make his decisions while Elijah had a tendency to let his heart interfere—a trait that seemed to be leading him into more trouble with each passing day.

He resisted the urge to scowl at the realization and pushed to his feet. Amelia had not looked overly pleased about being forced to join the ladies for a bout of drawing room chitchat. Surely by now she would certainly be in need of rescuing.

~Chapter Nine~

"Cake?"

"Cake," Amelia repeated with a nod as she removed her bonnet and tossed it over the back of the leather chair that was positioned in the middle of the common room in the hunting cabin. "I think you should treat me to a slice of the best cake Bath has to offer tomorrow."

"You are a very strange young lady; did you know that?" he asked, chuckling. Who knew Amelia had a hankering for cake? No matter. If cake is all she demanded of him for having to endure his female relatives for the better half of an evening, cake is what she'd get.

"Well, now that I'm an old married matron, it won't matter what I eat," she said as cool as could be as she set her unneeded red scarf on the edge of the pale blue settee.

He removed his grey coat and set it next to her discarded scarf. "And it did before?"

"Of course," she murmured, running her hands down the front of the pink gown she'd borrowed from Lady Templemore.

Without meaning to, Elijah's eyes followed the path her hands made over her ample bosom, down to her slim waist, then flared out with her hips.

He cleared his throat to tell her something reassuring, but it would seem nothing worked to relieve himself of that strangled feeling. "Amelia, it wouldn't matter if you weren't married. You're...er..." The invisible hands that were strangling him finally choked him tight enough to end his words.

Her lips formed a half-smile. "It's all right. I don't expect you to compliment me."

He loosened his cravat, whether because he needed to in order to take it off for the night or because it seemed to suddenly be choking the life out of him, he might never truly know. She was his oldest friend. He'd complimented her many times when she'd found some clever way to best Henry at a game and even a few weeks ago he'd complimented her dancing at his sister's wedding. He cocked his head to the side. How strange. He had always complimented things she did, never actually *her*.

"Amelia?"

She smoothed her skirt and kept her eyes trained on whatever it was on the floor that had managed to capture her attention. "Hmm?"

"You are a very beautiful young lady."

"Thank you." Her cheeks turned the palest shade of pink and she kicked off her cream slippers. "Don't worry. I shan't overindulge too often."

Elijah sighed. "I'm not worried about you gaining a few pounds, Amelia. I just wanted to tell you—" He shrugged. "Well, I already said it, so now you know."

Amelia twirled a tendril of her fallen hair around her finger. "Thank you."

"You're welcome."

Amelia gave her head a little shake, almost as if she were shaking off his words, then she bit her lip. She'd been acting most strange since they'd entered the cabin. Surely she wasn't afraid to be alone with him.

"Amelia?"

"Hmmm?"

Elijah ignored her half-hearted response and took a step closer to her. She'd been able to put him off for two nights. But tonight she wouldn't have an excuse. "Amelia," he murmured, leaning in to kiss her.

She swallowed audibly and stood stock-still.

Slowly, Elijah brushed his lips across hers, hoping to fan some internal flame she had.

"I—I'm not ready," she blurted. She cleared her throat and took a step away from him. "This is all so sudden."

He stared at her. Sudden? How could she even think to claim his actions were sudden? They'd been married, or on their way to marry, for the better part of three days, surely she understood that most ladies were expected to share their husbands' beds within hours of being married. It didn't seem sudden at all as far as he was concerned. "You were prepared to do this with Lord Friar two days ago, were you not?"

Amelia's eyes widened at his frank words, then she clasped her hands in front of her. "Of course."

"Then I see no reason for you to have any reservation when it comes to me."

"Of course you wouldn't," she murmured.

He lifted his eyebrows.

"As you know," she said, taking another step backwards. "I was promised to Lord Friar for a fortnight. It gave me plenty of time to prepare for..."

"Coitus," he supplied for her.

Her cheeks turned crimson. "Yes, that."

"Well then, you had two weeks to get accustomed to the idea of sharing your body with him and an additional two days to rejoice that you don't have to. That doesn't sound sudden at all, if you ask me."

Her silver eyes bore into him. "Perhaps it doesn't to you. It seems to me you're rather willing to jump between the sheets with anyone in a skirt."

"That's not true."

She crossed her arms and held his gaze, a glint of fire in her eyes. "Isn't it?"

He studied her. Why did she appear so angry? Had she heard some undesirable rumor about him? He nearly scoffed. There wasn't such a rumor to be heard. As much as he'd hate to admit this publicly, he'd followed right in his father's and brother's steps and had managed to avoid any type of scandal whatsoever.

"I still don't see the problem." He crossed his arms. "You've had plenty of time to 'prepare yourself', as you so delicately termed it." By the shade of red her face had now grown, she was about to combust with fire if he didn't stop, but an observer of their conversation would have never known she was uncomfortable about their conversation by her next words.

"Yes, well, as charming as you might think you are, I require more time to accept that you'll be my lifelong bed partner."

He ignored the sharpness in her tone and the way the meaning of her words hit him like a punch in the gut. Turning his head to the side a fraction, he lifted his chin a notch and looked at her through his lowered lashes. "I am charming, aren't I?"

"Not as much as you seem to think," she said, lacking any sense of emotion.

Elijah straightened. What the devil was wrong with her? He'd expected her to giggle or at least crack a smile at his nonsense, not be so dismissive of him. He stared at her for a moment. If she were anyone else treating him this way, he'd let loose the scathing retort that was on the tip of his tongue.

"Very well." Elijah nodded, then taking care not to brush her crushed skirt, he exited the common room and entered the bedroom.

***

Amelia inhaled a deep breath, then blew it out. She'd never been one to keep a secret from Elijah. Perhaps she ought to tell him? She bit her lip and resumed twisting a lock of her hair around her finger. She could, she supposed. Actually, no not could, she *should*. He deserved to know. Her teeth bit harder into her lip. What would he think of her? Even if she weren't carrying another man's child, would he lose all regard for her for giving away her virtue so easily?

Tears welled up in her eyes. How could she have been so

careless? One minute she was digging around in a desk looking for an elusive piece of parchment the next she was seeing colors and being talked to by a stranger with a deep voice, then...then she was kissing him, only to wake up and not know what happened between them.

What would Elijah think of her when she told him? He might not care so much about her loss of innocence in an intimate or possessive way since he didn't see her *that* way. But would he think less of her as a friend or as a person? Would he see her only as a fallen woman? One who had no hope of a future except to marry the biggest reprobate who'd ever walked the soil of England?

She swallowed the lump of raw emotion in her throat and blinked away the tears. She couldn't tell him. Not yet anyway. She'd stick to her earlier decision and tell him everything when she knew for certain if she was or wasn't carrying a child.

For now, however, she'd just have to keep putting him off, which seemed to be getting easier with each time she did it. Perhaps if he didn't seem so impassive and disinterested, she'd find it harder to resist him. But his expressionless face and cold, chaste kisses made the task simple.

Amelia released her hair and sank down onto the settee. Was she that undesirable that every time the subject of intimacy was broached, Elijah transformed from a trusted friend and confidant to a stranger who acted like his business with her was to collect what she owed, then be on his way? Or perhaps this was his way of being nervous and unsure? Though she'd never read his name in the scandal sheets as being seen with a mistress, didn't mean that he hadn't had one or hadn't frequented bawdy houses during his many travels, giving him plenty of experience in the matter and no need to be nervous.

A shaky laugh passed her lips. Even if he was the greatest lover in all of England and no one knew, he wouldn't be nervous around her. She wasn't a diamond of the first water, nor so high on the instep that she'd be considered unapproachable. Besides, she'd seen him nervous before: he'd rake his hand through his hair like his father was fond of doing, then he'd twist his lips into all sorts of strange shapes, all while shifting on his feet and clearing his throat every fifteen seconds. Granted she hadn't seen him behave that way in several years, but she doubted much had changed.

No he wasn't nervous. He was disinterested. All the more reason to stay true to her convictions.

She sighed. She'd had all these same thoughts cycle through her mind before. Nothing had changed.

"Amelia?"

She jumped. "Y-yes?" She cleared her throat and turned her head to flash Elijah her best attempt at a smile. But her smile faltered.

Standing in the lowly lit room was Elijah like she'd never seen him—or anyone for that matter—before. He wore nothing more than a white lawn shirt with tails settling just four inches above where his white drawers tied at his knees.

"Are you coming to bed?" he asked, not seeming to notice how she was affected by him.

Unease settled over her. *Coming to bed?*

Elijah padded over to her in his bare feet and sank down to the haunches in front of her. "Amelia," he started softly, taking her hand in his much larger one. "Come to bed. You're in no harm of being ravished by me tonight. I promise. Just come." He stood up and pulled her up with him.

Instinctively, she stood up to go with him and a surge of comfort like that of a warm blanket on a cold snowy day overtook her when he squeezed her hand. It was all the reassurance she needed and followed him to the bedchamber.

~ Chapter Ten ~

Elijah couldn't sleep. In fact, he was so restless he doubted he was even feigning it very well. This was the third night in a row they'd both gone to bed, and would wake up just as virginal as they'd both been before they married.

While that wouldn't have posed a problem under different circumstances, the fact that he *needed* to bed Amelia had not escaped him.

He curled his toes and squeezed—a habit he'd begun in recent years to take the place of a sigh or any other annoyed or nervous gesture that might give himself away. Why was she so resistant toward his advances? What was he doing wrong? He'd been chased by bulls and escaped an Irish prison with little help from his brother, and yet, he couldn't get a lady who'd once gone around and proclaimed to anyone who would listen that one day she would be Mrs. Elijah J. Banks to so much as kiss him, much less share her body with him just once.

He squeezed his toes again. Considering the frequency he'd been doing this since he'd married Amelia, he might not be able to walk without a limp in a few days. He needed to bed her—and soon if he didn't want her to think something was wrong with her —that was just the facts. The details of how he'd convince her were to remain a mystery, he supposed. But the fact remained: it was his duty to bed her and he would.

Unfortunately for him, fate—or in this case, Henry—had once again stepped in before Elijah could make his next attempt.

"Can this wait?" Elijah asked without ceremony when he answered the soft knock at the door.

Henry lifted his eyebrows, his lips twitching. "Seeing as how you're dressed in nothing but your small clothes at the advanced hour of noon, I shall take that to mean you don't plan to attend Caroline's luncheon today."

Elijah scowled at him.

Henry laughed. "What was that name you coined for Alex shortly after he married Caroline? Amorous Alex, was it? Who's the one with seduction on his mind now, Enamored Elijah?"

Despite the heat that flooded his face at his brother's insinuation, Elijah ignored him. "What do you want?" he all but barked.

"Did you get it?" Henry's voice was so low it was almost inaudible.

Elijah ran his hand through his unkempt hair and scratched his head, then leaned against the doorframe, purposely taking his time in answering his brother—just to return the feeling of irritation Henry had stirred in him. "Yes." He'd found Henry's message of the escape.

A look of relief crossed Henry's face. "Very good. You can go back and enjoy your wife now."

"I thank you for your permission," Elijah said in a tone that dripped with sarcasm.

Henry twisted his lips into an overdone frown. "No thanks are necessary."

Elijah was *this* close to closing the door in his brother's face, but his next words and louder tone kept him from doing just that.

"Of course it was very difficult to tear myself away from Caroline's festivities to make sure you both knew you were invited to join, but it was a task done out of love."

"All right, we'll be there soon," Elijah said with a grunt borne of irritation. His skin prickled. Amelia must be standing close behind him.

"And when shall I expect to see you?"

"Whenever I walk through the door." When had his twin become so dratted annoying? Couldn't he just go away already?

Henry waggled his eyebrows suggestively and said, "I hope it is soon. Caroline was most adamant I come over and extend a formal invitation to the lovesick duo. She said she wanted to make sure Amelia was able to get better acquainted with everyone—" he dropped his voice to a near inaudible whisper— "and not just you."

Elijah narrowed his eyes on Henry in a warning. "Our attendance today depends on Amelia and if she'd prefer to attend Caroline's house party or lie in bed with me a while longer," Elijah said with all the confidence of Prinny himself.

The gasp from directly behind him, robbed him of his confidence in less time than it took for his heart to beat.

Elijah spun around to face Amelia's whose face was just as pink as the traveling gown she'd borrowed from Lady Templemore that she'd insisted on wearing to bed last night. "That didn't come out how I'd meant it," he blurted for lack of anything else to say at the moment.

She stared at Elijah, then cut her eyes toward his brother.

"Not to worry, Lady Amelia," Henry said quietly, almost as if he were uncertain of just what to say. "I shall inform Caroline that you two are undecided for the day."

"No, no," Amelia rushed to say, fruitlessly trying to smooth the wrinkles in her crushed skirt. "If she's invited us and has sent you to invite us personally, then we should go. Tell her we'll be there following—"

SLAM!

Amelia wheeled around to face Elijah. "What was that for?"

Elijah shrugged. "He deserved it."

"He came here to invite us to Caroline's house party and because house parties are so awful to attend he deserved to have the door slammed in his face?" Amelia reasoned in a mocking tone.

Elijah nodded enthusiastically. "That was my logic, too."

Amelia heaved an overdone sigh. "You're incorrigible."

He grinned. "Really?"

"No."

Elijah followed Amelia back into the little bedroom they'd shared last night, running almost right into her back when she stopped just inside the doorway. "Ooof."

"Sorry," she murmured, her eyes trained on the bed.

"Is something wrong?" he asked quietly by her ear.

She shook her head. "What do you think he's telling them?"

Elijah put his hands on her shoulders and gently rubbed up and down the tops of her arms which were knotted with tension. "Don't worry," he whispered softly. "He won't say anything that will embarrass you."

She nodded once, but her body didn't relax like he'd hoped.

Elijah took a deep breath and spun her around to face him. "I know to a lady it's considered vulgar, bad taste, not done, and a string of other similar adjectives for people to know you've ever participated in marital intimacies, but while everyone pretends such things don't exist—we all know they do." Her eyes widened and he inwardly cursed himself. That hadn't been the right thing to say. "Amelia," he tried again. "He won't shame you. I won't let him."

Amelia parted her lips to voice something, a protest if he had to guess, but was cut off when pure unadulterated instinct came over Elijah and he pressed his lips against hers, capturing them in a kiss as sweet and delicious as the one they'd shared at their wedding. Releasing his hold on her shoulders, Elijah slid his hands down the back of the rumpled fabric of the gown she wore. His fingers brushed against the top button and quickly unfastened it. Then the one beneath it and the one after that.

He parted his lips, drawing her lower lip between both of his. She sighed his name, and his blood rushed through his veins. He slipped the last button free and brought his hands beneath her chin, gripping the loose fabric that capped her shoulders. Without breaking their kiss, he tightened his grip on the edge of her gown and gave it a swift tug.

"Ouch," she squealed, taking a step away from him. Her hands flew to her still covered chest and attempted to fix her terribly askew bodice.

His eyes drifted to the exposed skin at the top of her chest. Despite the way he'd imagined his movements working out in his mind, she was still wearing that dratted gown. "I'm sorry," he rasped, reaching for her again. "I didn't mean to hurt you."

She shook her head. "It's all right. I know you didn't mean to. The sleeves and bodice have ties— "

Elijah clamped his jaw and nodded once. "Please accept my sincerest apologies. I was unaware.."

"Elijah," she interrupted, her voice as uneven as his had been a moment before. "It's not about that. Well, perhaps it was a little, but what I wanted to say was—"

He pulled her back toward him and kissed her again, not giving her the chance to offer up some sort of excuse about this not being the right time. This was the perfect time. Her earlier response to his kisses had only confirmed it. If he gave her the chance to protest— No, he wouldn't even think about it. "Kiss me back," he said against her lips. He abandoned the ties at the top of her bodice and fisted his hands into the mass of skirts she wore, pulling them up at a frantic pace, intent to touch the skin he'd been treated to glimpsing Saturday when she'd lifted her skirts for him to remove her stays.

Anticipation was almost too much as his imagination had been able to think of little since that afternoon.

***

Everything was happening so quickly. Elijah's hands were lifting her skirt—and then...then his warm hand was blazing a fast trail along her thigh, going higher. He cupped her derriere, eliciting an involuntary jerk from her. His left hand joined his right, caressing her where she'd never thought anyone would ever touch. As wicked as it might sound, she actually *liked* him touching her thus.

His hands slid up and captured the top of her drawers with his thumbs just as his lips captured hers in another kiss. He moved his lips on top of hers, exerting just a hint of pressure while his fingers worked to loosen the knot in the front of her drawers.

A second later, he pulled the final string and her drawers fell to her ankles, making her suddenly aware of what his intentions were. She couldn't let him do this. Not now. His fingers brushed the curls that hid her most intimate areas, and her heart nearly beat out of her chest. No. This wasn't right, she reminded herself, opening her mouth to protest.

Her protest died on her lips when his lips left hers and he lowered his face to the crook of her neck, his wandering fingers moving closer to her— Rational thought fled as her face began to heat and an ache she couldn't find the words to describe formed not far from where he was touching her. He slid his fingertips along her sensitive flesh, and she gasped. Never before had she felt such an intense pleasure as she was right now.

He touched her again and sparks of pleasure took flight inside of her body. Her breath hitched. What was he doing to her? Why was it that the more he touched her, the harder it was for her to breathe, let alone think?

Elijah shifted his hand to where his fingers had greater access to her most intimate area. Her heart slammed in her chest. And not in a good way. If he touched her much more, he might discover her secret.

She sobered instantly. She had to tell him. He deserved to know. "Stop! Stop!"

Elijah froze. "Stop?" he repeated tonelessly.

"Stop," she confirmed. How could his speech and breathing be so normal when she was practically gasping for her next breath? Bringing both of her hands up to his chest, she gave him a hard shove.

Elijah stumbled backwards a few steps, never taking his eyes from hers. Despite the pain that was rapidly forming in her chest, she held his gaze. Just as they'd been all the other times he'd come to her room, his eyes had an intensity that she'd never seen before. But it wasn't the warm intensity she'd noticed in Lord Templemore's eyes when Lady Templemore had joined them. This was a different sort. Almost like he was distracted, perhaps?

"Are intimacies all you think about?" she demanded, trying to distract herself from the harsh realization that she'd practically fallen into his snare. A snare he'd laid for what reason? His expression and actions wouldn't suggest his interest in her had been sincere.

"No," he said easily. "I think about plenty of things other than intimacies."

"Are you sure? It seems you keep suggesting it and won't even let me speak more than a sentence before you're ready to make another attempt."

Something foreign and fierce flashed in his eyes. "That's not true." He took a step toward her. "Perhaps I wouldn't have to keep *attempting* if you'd stop putting me off." He took another step closer to her, bringing his large, imposing body within mere inches of hers. "Someone around here has to be concerned about our marital duties and since it doesn't seem to be you..." He shrugged.

"That's not fair," she choked out. *Marital duties, is that how he thought of bedding her?* Bile rose in her throat. "I—I—I—I—"

"You what? You need more time to prepare yourself?" he snapped. "Is that it? Well, Lady Amelia, how is this for preparation, before the sun rises tomorrow morning you won't be in the same state of chastity you are in currently."

Angry heat surfaced in her face as a storm raged in her heart. This cocksure man thought he knew everything, didn't he? "Would you care to place a wager on that?"

A smug smile took his lips. "As a matter of fact, I would."

Amelia met his unblinking gaze with her own. "All right, and if you're wrong and I wake up tomorrow in the same state I'm in now—" she coughed— "I want you to leave me alone about marital intimacies for the rest of our lives."

"You don't mean that."

She lifted her chin a notch. "Yes, I do mean that. You might think you're irresistible, but believe me, you are not. Irresistible, that is."

"Is that so?" He rocked back on his heels. "And what is it that I'm to get when I prove *you* wrong. Besides, your innocence, that is," he added with a wicked grin.

She stared at the insufferable man. What had come over him to make him speak to her this way? No matter. He wouldn't get his way and bed her, and in the unlikely event that he did, she'd still win the wager. So truly, it didn't matter, she had nothing to lose—except perhaps her heart, but it would seem that had been lost long ago. "You may have whatever you want."

"A biddable wife who does exactly what I say without questioning me?"

She nearly laughed at his request. "If that's what you want, then yes, those can be our terms."

"Excellent." He frowned at her. "Just so we're in agreement, you're not going to do something foolish to become dreadfully ill between now and nightfall, are you?"

"No." She shook her head for emphasis. Did he think she was a complete imbecile? "I have every intention of being in perfect health."

"Very well, madam," Elijah said with a wide grin. "Challenge accepted."

~ Chapter Eleven ~

Amelia didn't know if she should be relieved, worried, or remorseful about the challenge she'd issued and its potential consequences.

She supposed she'd have regretted it if she thought her marriage would ever have any semblance to a love match. But it didn't now, nor would it ever; and for as much as she'd like to have children, Elijah didn't need an heir to pass a title or fortune to, rendering the *need* for children unnecessary.

As it was, not only were children not a necessity where Elijah was concerned, neither was her love—only her body it would seem. Why he'd suddenly taken such a keen and determined interest in bedding her, she'd never know. At least he'd shown he *could* be gentle. Until he suddenly became savage, followed immediately by cold disinterest, she thought grimly.

Wordlessly, she stood at the end of the four poster bed and watched as Elijah dragged on a pair of dove breeches and a clean shirt, then hastily tied on snowy white cravat. He sat down on the edge of the bed and pulled on his leather boots, then shrugged into a yellow waistcoat followed by a blue coat. Then without so much as a backward glance at her, he was out the door of their bedroom.

The door handle to the front door turned, followed by the door creaking open. Elijah's heavy boot falls quieted and the door shut again.

Closing her eyes to hold back the tears welling in her eyes, Amelia sank to the bed.

Marrying Elijah was once all she'd ever dreamed about. It was the reason she'd refused her mother's encouragement to allow other gentlemen to court her or call on her. But now that it'd happened...

The hot tears she'd tried to keep in her eyes spilled out onto her cheeks.

She lifted her hand and used the back to dash away her hot tears. It was ridiculous to cry over their quarrel. Elijah had told her many times when they were younger that his interest in her was only that of a friend. She'd have done well to have heeded his advice and conducted herself accordingly.

She took a deep sniff and used the tips of her fingers to dry the bottom rims of her eyes. As composed as she could be with tearstained cheeks and a crushed gown, Amelia lifted her eyes and stood.

"Elijah," she gasped, startled.

He stood right in front of her like a stone wall with that same infuriating expressionless face he'd taken to wearing more often than not recently.

"If you're done now, I'll see if Caroline can find you something to wear until your wardrobe can be fetched."

For the second time since he'd suggested they marry, she had the strangest urge to grab the heaviest object nearest her and brain him with it. She settled for clenching her fists and letting a string of unladylike remarks fly through her head. "Don't bother," she said, taking to her feet. "I should hate to have my absence remarked upon. I'll go ask Lady Watson myself."

"You don't need to do that. I'll speak to Alex in the library and have him speak to Caroline." He raked his gaze down the front of her in a way that made her feel naked. "Wouldn't you rather have your absence remarked upon rather than the crumpled state of the very dress they saw you in yesterday?"

***

If beautiful young ladies were considered diamonds of the first water, then Elijah was most definitely a cad of the first water. Never had he seen Amelia cry before and to know he'd been the one that caused her tears made it even worse. He was a cad, indeed.

Tamping down the sudden urge he had to turn around and go comfort and apologize to her, he focused his eyes on the little window just above the front door of his brother's estate and kept walking forward.

Henry's impromptu visit this morning had ignited his fury, not Amelia. She hadn't deserved for him to treat her that way. Their sudden marriage and his persistence couldn't possibly be any easier for her than it was for him. But dash it all, it was for her own good, and if she'd stop being so stubborn she'd realize he was trying to help her.

"What has put such a serious expression on your face, son?"

Elijah snapped his head to the side to look at his mother. "I don't have a serious expression."

A smile spread his mother's lips. "If you say so."

Were she anyone else, he'd try to deny her charge. Unfortunately, he'd never been very good at convincing his mother she was mistaken.

"Does this have anything to do with your new bride?" The concern in her voice was unmistakeable.

Elijah studied his mother carefully. She and his father had had an arranged marriage and had somehow managed to find a semblance of love, even if his siblings failed to see it, Elijah had noticed their exchanged glances and hidden remarks. That's what he was trained to do. But their circumstances were different. They had to be.

Even though his parents had never been overly affectionate in public nor felt the need to discuss details of their marriage with their children, he knew enough to know the two had only met once before they married, which meant love for them had to have come later. He and Amelia, however, had known each other for most of their lives, plenty of time for love to have formed. His mother might think she could help, but he highly doubted she'd understand unrequited love within a marriage. Or how to fix his other problem.

"It does," she mused, breaking Elijah of his thoughts.

"No." He narrowed his eyes on his mother. Why was she even out here? "Say, what has you escaping Caroline's party?"

She idly shook out her dark blue skirt. "I'm not escaping. I just came out for some air."

A bark of his laughter passed his lips. "Is that your story?"

"As much as it is yours that the look on your face has nothing to do with Lady Amelia," she said, lifting her eyebrows at him.

He lifted a finger. "I never said that."

"Mmmhmmm." She pursed her lips and cast him a doubtful look.

"As a matter of fact, I was thinking about Amelia. In an indirect way."

Mother crossed her arms, her brown eyes twinkling with all sorts of mischief. "And?"

"I was thinking of how I'll word my request to Alex to have him speak to Caroline about borrowing some gowns for Amelia until her wardrobe arrives later this week." He'd sent a message to her father, requesting her things be sent to Watson Estate, post haste. But that would still take some time for them to arrive, just as it would take some time to get a seamstress out to make her a new wardrobe.

Mother reached up and tucked a tendril of her auburn hair behind her ear. "I see. Well, I suppose I could help you with that."

Chuckling, Elijah shook his head. "You'll do anything to escape Caroline's party, won't you?"

"And you'll do anything to avoid telling me what put that expression on your face," she retorted.

"Indeed," he acknowledged. It might be rude to admit to one's mother that he wasn't going to tell her the information she'd requested, but it'd be an outright disrespect to lie to her.

"I'll go see about Amelia now," Mother murmured. She twisted her lips as if she were debating whether she should say anything more. Finally, she said, "I know no grown man wishes to use his mother as a confidant, but I want you to know that I might be able to help you more than you might think."

He doubted that, but wouldn't be so cruel as to tell her so. "Thank you, Mother. If you'll just see to it that Amelia is properly attired until something more permanent can be arranged, I'd greatly appreciate it."

"Very well."

Elijah waited for his mother to walk off then slipped in the side door. Amelia would probably prefer him not to be around while discussing her wardrobe and now that he didn't have to seek out Alex, he could try to puzzle out the coded missive he'd received along with Henry's missive yesterday.

Only because Caroline was hosting one of her nearly unbearable house parties, filled with games of pall mall, charades, and the most excruciatingly boring game of them all: lawn chess, Elijah would be able to spend time in the library without being interrupted by Alex who likely spent as much time in the library studying scientific tomes thick enough to injure a man were he to drop one on his foot as he did in his wife's bedroom. It was to Alex's good fortune indeed that his wife had the same unnatural interests. Elijah shuddered at the thought. How fortunate he was that Amelia had normal interests.

Elijah pushed open the door to the large room that was three walls of solid books and one wall of floor to ceiling windows that flooded the room with plenty of sunshine.

He reached into his breast pocket and removed the folded parchment that he'd hidden in this coat yesterday when he'd first visited the cabin after sending Amelia off to spend time with Caroline and the other ladies. He fell into a chair behind the oak table and unfolded the note.

Where I be
There I pray
That He be there

Right beside
Thy maiden fair

What the blazes did that mean? Mindlessly, he drummed his fingertips along the top of the table and stared out the window. Sometimes—like right now—he wished he'd have never met that rugged stranger down by the shipyards. If he hadn't he wouldn't be in this mess. Or the one created by this mess.

He sighed and turned his eyes back to the words scrolled across the paper. He hated cryptic messages. Especially those of the poetic variety. Like Henry, he'd always preferred it when given an anonymous tip written out in simple English. Riddles and rhymes were for those in the nursery, not grown men of seven-and-twenty.

Unfortunately, the fellow who'd been sending them anonymous tips about the prostitution ring he'd been investigating felt different and sent all of his correspondence in the form of senseless riddles.

The hair on the back of Elijah's neck stood on end. Soft almost inaudible footfalls were coming down the hall. Slowly, he folded the missive and tucked it back into his breast pocket just as the door to the library creaked open.

"Oh, it's just you," Elijah muttered when his eyes collided with his twin.

"Indeed." Henry said nothing more as he walked across the room and fell into the black chair opposite Elijah. "What's your plan?"

Elijah frowned. "I don't have one yet."

"I wasn't talking about your evening with Lady Amelia," he said with a quick grin.

"Just Amelia," Elijah corrected.

Henry's blue eyes danced with laughter. "Oh, I didn't realize she'd given up her courtesy title." At Elijah's silence, Henry added, "Or are you just expecting her to?"

Elijah threw his hands into the air. "I have no idea what that blasted female plans to do."

"You mean besides torture you?"

"Exactly."

Henry crossed his ankles and leaned back in his chair. "Does she know?"

Elijah studied his brother. "I'm sure she knows *something*."

"I see," Henry said slowly. "And would that something be that you're not the dashing prince she'd always thought you to be but an arse instead?"

"No, I believe she's always reserved those particular feelings for you. And rightfully so."

Henry shook his head. "I still don't understand why."

"Because you were always the one being impolite."

Henry knit his brows. "Pardon me? What did you just say?"

"I said you were always the one who was impolite to her."

"No, I wasn't." Henry scoffed. "In my recollection, it seems to always have been you who was impolite. Why just this morning, you said—"

"Forget what I said this morning," Elijah snapped. "You tricked me into saying it."

"No, I didn't. You allowed yourself to get distracted."

Elijah snorted. "Yes, and Alex never meant to let Sir Wallace best him at chess, he just got distracted."

Henry grinned ruefully. "I still can't believe it. And probably wouldn't had I not seen that with my own eyes. But that was bound to happen eventually. As Alex used to tell us when he bested us, nobody can win all the time." He shifted in his chair. "But Alex's win at chess isn't what we're discussing. I want to know why you think it's me who's always been impolite to Amelia when it's you who used to run away from her, dismiss her foolish claims of being in love with you, and now you've gone so far as to humiliate her —"

"That was unintentional," Elijah interrupted. "Had I known

she was still behind me, I would have chosen my words with a little more care."

Henry looked doubtful. "As I said, you were distracted. But why?"

Elijah ducked his head. He might have perfected the stoic expression, complete with a clamped jaw and cold eyes, but Henry knew him too well to believe Elijah was unaffected by his words. "I am married now," he said at last. "It would stand to reason that I'd be distracted from time to time."

"But you weren't always married."

Elijah bridled at his remark and its intended reminder of the hash he'd made of things the night before he married Amelia. "Did you happen to see the missive?"

"I did," Henry said, frowning. "What's your plan?"

"I don't have one."

"Why not?"

"Because I haven't had long enough to puzzle out the clue yet to know what my plan should be."

"You haven't?" Henry burst out.

"No."

"But you said this morning that you got it."

"And I did. When we passed the hunting cabin coming in yesterday, I saw that the window in the common room was open so I sent Amelia to spend time with the ladies so I could go retrieve the missive." Elijah pulled the missive from his breast pocket and tossed it on the table.

Henry groaned. "You've been spending far too much time with Alex. Any more and you just might best him at being the most obtuse gentleman in existence." He raked his hand through his hair. "What I meant was did you solve it, not retrieve it."

"Then you should have said that," Elijah retorted.

"I didn't think I had to," Henry grumbled. "But not to worry, from now on when I use a word that has more than one meaning, I'll be sure to clarify which meaning I intend."

"See to it that you do." He scowled. "However, I did get—both definitions—your other missive. The one about the fellow I apprehended in Brighton escaping."

"I haven't many other details on that. I'm to meet with a runner tomorrow to see what else he's learned."

Elijah sighed. "Back to where we were before, I suppose."

"Or further back," Henry commented. "Now, they know someone's looking for them."

Elijah's heart twisted. That just meant Amelia was more vulnerable than he'd originally thought.

Henry reached for the paper he'd left in the cabin for Elijah yesterday and unfolded it. "I spent three hours yesterday trying to solve this damn riddle."

"I'd spent an entire three minutes trying to solve it before you had to interrupt."

"Perhaps you'd have had more time if you hadn't spent your time dreaming of Amelia," Henry said with a chuckle.

Scowling, Elijah grabbed the paper from his brother's hands and turned it around so he could read it. "It isn't what you think."

"I'm pretty sure that it is."

Elijah lowered the left corner of the paper a fraction. "Damn," he muttered, meeting his twin's eyes.

"Have you told her?"

"No, on both accounts."

"On both accounts?" he echoed, knitting his brows. A moment later his eyes flared wide, then returned to normal; the color in his cheeks heightening, presumably at just being informed that not only had Elijah not told Amelia the truth about himself but that he'd been unsuccessful in bedding her, revealing to her the truth about herself. "I see."

"I doubt you do." Elijah sighed and dropped the paper he held to the table. "I can't tell her one without revealing the other."

"So then..."

"I just need to do my duty and bed her as soon as possible."

"Yes, well, I don't need *those* details, thank you."

Elijah straightened his silver cufflink. "Then we're in agreement because I hadn't planned to share them."

"Have you been putting it off on purpose?"

"Bedding her?"

Henry nodded. "She is our childhood friend. I can see where it might be difficult to...er...perform."

Elijah twisted his lips and crossed his arms. Had it been anyone else—even Alex—who'd just insulted his abilities, Elijah would have laid him out. "As it would happen, contrary to what you're implying, I have no reservations about consummating the marriage. She does."

"Perhaps she doesn't fancy the idea of sleeping with *you*."

"I've already guessed as much," he muttered. "For as much as she used to claim she loved me before we reached our majority, she sure has no interest in me now."

"Oh?"

"I thought you didn't want details," Elijah reminded him, forcing a grin.

"That depends. Details about you deflowering Amelia I could do without. Details about how Amelia denies you sound most interesting."

Elijah snorted. "You would be the one interested."

"Anyone would." He flashed Elijah a grin. "Especially if they knew the details of your past together."

"Yes, well, her fascination for me is no more, I'm afraid." He turned his head a fraction to the side and idly scratched his cheek. "No matter what I do, she pushes me away."

"She does?"

"She does." Elijah put his elbow on the table and then leaned his cheek against his palm. "Whenever I try to kiss her, she turns as cold as those marbles we saw in Venice. When I touch her, she jerks and moves away. Or pushes me away," he added, thinking at how she'd shoved him away earlier this morning when he'd touched her. "It's almost as if I repulse her."

"Perhaps you do."

Elijah did his best attempt at a snarl. "She can't possibly find me repulsive. She was about to marry Lord Friar, for pity's sake."

"That doesn't say much about you then, does it?"

"No. I suppose it doesn't."

"Perhaps that's for the best."

"For the best that my wife has more interest in winning boons and eating cake than wanting to be intimate with me?"

The left corner of Henry's lips tilted up. "Is that so?"

"Never mind that. The fact is, I've married an Ice Queen, and short of hell itself, nothing seems to warm her up."

"Now *that* could certainly be a point in your favor. At least she'll never take a lover."

"Indeed," Elijah forced himself to say. He hated the way his agreement to such a stupid statement felt on his tongue. She might not love him, but she'd positively devastate him if she took a lover. He sighed and picked up the paper he'd set down a few moments before. "Now about this..."

"I don't know why you deny it so," Henry said, seeming to be reluctant to quit their former conversation.

Elijah's fingers tightened on the paper he held, crumpling the edges. Henry knew. Whether it was his glib tongue or perhaps something far more subtle, Elijah had somehow revealed himself to his brother and for a reason he couldn't explain, being vulnerable right now was the last thing he wanted. "Stop," he warned in a low tone. "I have no further wish to talk about the icicle I married."

"Mayhap you just need to seduce her."

Elijah ground his teeth. "Don't you think I've tried that already?"

"No. I envisioned you just telling her to take her clothes off and get under the covers."

"Do you have feathers filling your skull? I told you earlier that she turns cold at my kisses and pulls away from my touches."

"Then you're doing something wrong," Henry said simply, knocking the sides of his leather boots together. "I might regret asking this, but—"

"Then don't ask," Elijah barked, slamming his hand, and consequently the parchment, on the table.

"—how exactly are you touching her?"

"With my hands. The same part of your body that will soon be holding a pistol at the opposite end of a field from me if this conversation continues."

Henry threw his hands up into the air. "Someone has to give you advice. You seem to be unable to get the task done."

"And what makes you an expert about such matters? Unless I missed something, I didn't see you sneaking off to any brothels, either."

Henry neither confirmed nor denied his charge as he brought all four legs of his chair back to the wooden floor with a sharp snap. "Forgive me. I was just trying to help you lose your virginity before you reach an age where your concern won't be if your partner is willing, but if *you're* able."

~Chapter Twelve~

"Oh, there you are," Edwina said to Amelia as she sauntered down the hall to where Amelia was standing outside the library where Elijah and Henry were inside discussing her with no cares or morals. "You're welcome to go in there if you'd like."

Amelia cleared her throat. "I already did," she lied. She gave an exaggerated sigh. "As it would happen Alex and Caroline don't keep many books that would hold my interest."

"No?" Edwina asked with a grin. "Do you not find grasshoppers and honeysuckles as fascinating as those two do?"

Amelia's lips bent into a watery smile. "No. I'm afraid I don't."

"Surely we can find *something* that does." She looped her arm through Amelia's. "Come, I'll show you where I hide the novels."

Amelia dug her heels into the carpet. The last place she wanted to go was into the library where Elijah and Henry were discussing her. Or more specifically, bedding her. Embarrassment flooded her as the snippets of phrases she'd overheard sounded in her head, *"...I've married an Ice Queen and short of hell itself, nothing seems to warm her up...My wife has more interest in winning boons and eating cake than wanting to be intimate with me...I have no wish to further talk about the icicle I married..."*

Tears sprang to her eyes. How dare he have the audacity to speak of her in such a way? Even if he had no love for her, she was still his wife. Did that not command even a kernel of respect? Just enough not to go around and talk to his brother about the intimate side of their marriage? Shame and rage boiled inside of her. What must his family think of her that Elijah thought so little of her to say those damning remarks about her?

She blinked back the hot tears and noticed Edwina's head was cocked to the side in interest; her dark brown eyes, studying Amelia's face. Edwina broke eye contact for just a moment, long enough to peek through the cracked door and into the library. When she met Amelia's eyes again, they were full of compassion.

Edwina gave her arm a gentle squeeze. "Come with me," she whispered.

Amelia allowed Edwina to lead her to a private sitting room farther down the hall.

Once inside, Edwina was the first to take a seat and then patted the cushion next to her.

Numbly, Amelia sat down.

"Is my brother being beastly again?" Edwina asked without ceremony.

Amelia sputtered with laughter. She had no idea why—perhaps it was her tone, or the blunt question that brought back memories of when Regina would catch Elijah and Henry being 'beastly' as she put it and invited her in for tea to talk about it, or mayhap it was just that her emotions were beyond her control—but for whatever reason, she couldn't help but laugh. "Yes. Yes, he is."

Edwina wrapped her arm around Amelia. "Would you care to talk about it?"

How could she? There wasn't anything she could tell her without having to explain far more than she ever wanted to tell another living soul. "I can't."

"And if I told you a secret about me?"

"Even then," Amelia whispered, leaning her head against Edwina's shoulder. She knew Edwina could be trusted. She also knew Edwina wouldn't be the kind to scorn or shame her. But for some reason it didn't feel right burdening Edwina with a problem so large neither could attempt to fix it.

"I've never seen you so upset," Edwina commented a minute later, genuine concern lacing her voice. "How about if I speak to him about whatever it was he was talking to Henry about in the library—remind him of his manners."

Amelia shot up. "No, you mustn't." She cleared her throat. "That's to say, I really don't want to get you involved."

"So then you're going to speak to him yourself?"

Oh, she had plans to speak to him all right. But not about what Edwina might think. "I intend to handle the situation, yes."

"Not by ignoring it, I hope."

"No." She'd ignored certain things for too long as it was. She had no intention of ignoring what she'd heard him say about her in the library. "Please, don't fret, Edwina. I'm not the docile creature everyone thinks me to be."

"I never said you were," Edwina countered, frowning.

"I wasn't talking about you. I was saying that more for my own sake." She sighed. "See, as you might have already guessed, Elijah and I...well, see, er..." How did she explain the circumstances of her marriage to her sister-in-law who seemed to be convinced they'd run off to Gretna Green to marry?

"Are just friends?" Edwina suggested softly.

"That, too," Amelia agreed automatically. There was no use in denying it.

"Have an in-name-only marriage," Edwina guessed again.

Amelia's face flooded with heat. "That, too," she said again. "But it's more than that. See...uh...it wasn't because of any great love either of us had for the other that we married." That was true enough. "It was more that he was doing me a favor."

Edwina showed no sign of shock or pity. "I see."

"And it's because of that favor that I've become so...so—" she waved her hand through the air— "well, a spineless, ninny." She dropped her hand into her lap and took a deep breath. "But not anymore. He may have done me a favor by sparing me the humiliation of being jilted and becoming a pariah, but that's no excuse for what he's done."

"And you plan to tell him this?"

"No," Amelia said, shaking her head. For the first time she could remember in the immediate past, a genuine smile took her lips. "I have other plans for him."

~Chapter Thirteen~

It took every ounce of strength Elijah possessed not to beat his head against the table. He'd been staring at the same blasted five lines for more than four hours and hadn't come close to understanding its meaning.

"Perhaps we're thinking about it too hard," Elijah said, spearing his fingers through his unkempt hair.

Henry unfastened the cuff of his sleeve and rolled it up toward his elbow. "Or perhaps you've been thinking about the wrong thing."

Elijah sneered at his brother then turned his attention to where he'd discarded his coat and cravat more than two hours ago. "I have no desire to discuss my relationship with Amelia again."

"Interesting, that wasn't what I was suggesting," Henry mused. "I was merely suggesting that you're only looking at the words that rhyme, not the whole of the riddle. But since you brought up Amelia—"

"No," Elijah barked, straightening in his chair. "I'm done speaking to you about her."

"That's all right. I hadn't planned to ask you anything more about her."

"Then why did you say anything about her?" Elijah asked, exasperated.

"I didn't. You did."

Elijah put his head in his hands and groaned. Marriage to Amelia was going to be the death of him. "Well, forget I said anything," he muttered.

"I can't now. You've already brought her name into this conversation."

"And I beg your apologies for doing so. Now what was it you were saying?"

Henry put his hand over the letters that had been scratched on the parchment. "Go."

"Go where?"

"Go to her, Elijah. It's becoming quite clear that you're unable to think about this until you...you..." He cleared his throat. "Just go."

"And do you think you can solve this while I'm away?" he scoffed. Henry might be better at making his expression unreadable and separating his feelings from his tasks, but Elijah had always been the one to find the clues and solve them. Except this time, dash it all.

"No." Henry snorted. "I couldn't even solve the last one."

Elijah nodded slowly, the words of the last missive sounding in his head: *under and over the cliffs and clover.* It took him all of five minutes to realize that a person of interest would be found at Lord Nigel's scandalous costume party in Dover where the party's guests could choose to engage in activities on the ground floor or in the basement. That was simple to puzzle out. This nonsense about praying and a lady fair? Not easy at all.

"Elijah, go," Henry urged him again.

"And say what to her?"

Henry's eyes narrowed on Elijah's. "I never said you had to actually tell her anything. Just go...you know."

A sharp bark of laugher passed Elijah's lips. "If it were that easy, don't you think I'd have done it already?"

"As I said before, the problem must lie with you."

Elijah abruptly slid his chair from the table with an ear-piercing screech as the four legs scraped against the stone floor. "I cannot wait until the day you have a wife. I've no doubt your interactions with her will be quite fascinating to watch." He shoved to his feet and scooped up his discarded coat and cravat. "Perhaps I'll finally become as interested in science as Alex seems to be and spend my days observing how the two of you get along."

Henry grinned. "Perhaps you ought to do just that. You might learn something."

"And what would that entail? How to be allusive and indifferent toward one's wife?"

"You seem to have that particular lesson down perfectly," Amelia said, gliding into the room through the open door.

Elijah's gaze snapped in her direction. There was no way to mask the surprise on his face this time. Despite the blood that was draining from his face faster than Henry's prized horse Knight could run, he straightened and inclined his chin. *Just what exactly had she heard?* "Surely you don't find me to be a snob, do you?" Elijah said with far more grace than he felt.

Amelia snorted and ran her gloved hand over the top of the mahogany bookcase closest to her. She looked rather fetching in one of Caroline's green morning dresses. "Actually, I do." She adjusted her glove and dropped her hand at her side. "But my opinion is of no account, really."

Yes, it is. More than you might think. "And why would you say that?" he forced himself to ask.

She shrugged. "Caroline has asked—"

"I don't care what the blazes Caroline asked," Elijah snapped.

Amelia's eyes widened, but she said nothing.

"I beg your pardon," Elijah said in a much calmer voice. Mindlessly, he dug his toes into the bottoms of his shoes, refusing to do anything more to let her know how unsettled he was by her accusation. Did she really think *he* was a snob? He wouldn't argue with her thinking Henry was one, but him?

"It's of no account. I wouldn't expect anything less from you?"

Elijah's body tensed. "What's that to mean?"

Amelia waved her hand through the air in an annoyed manner. "Please, forget I said anything." Though her words were pleasant enough, Elijah sensed her meaning was not.

"Are we even speaking of the same thing?"

"Probably not," Henry said helpfully.

Elijah scowled at his grinning brother. "Amelia, what are you talking about?"

She pursed her lips. "I'd say that was a rather rude question, but once again, I shouldn't be surprised."

Elijah stared at her dumbfounded. He'd never thought himself a simpleton—

"Then perhaps you're wrong," Henry said with a chuckle. He dropped his voice to a stage whisper, "You really need to stop mumbling under your breath when you're distressed."

"Indeed," Amelia agreed, smirking.

A small wave of relief washed over Elijah. At least Amelia was finding some sort of amusement in the situation. "Amelia, my sweet— What's that look about?"

"Nothing."

"It's not nothing," he argued. "You look—" The image before him could not possibly be put into the right words to do justice for the way she looked. Her lips were puckered—not pursed—but actually puckered, and not in a way that might suggest she was about to kiss him. Her hands were on her hips and her eyebrows were nearly to her hairline. She was a sight to behold, to be sure. "Well, I can't describe it exactly, but you have a look about you."

"Nauseated," Henry said.

Elijah resisted the urge to kick his annoying brother. "Pardon?"

Henry twisted his lips. "Since when did your vocabulary—and your mental abilities—become stunted?" He shook his head and shifted in his chair. "No matter. What I was saying is she looks nauseated."

"Nauseated," Elijah repeated softly, at a loss.

"Yes, and I would be, too, if you kept calling me 'sweet'," Henry said with a grimace.

"Would you care to leave?" Elijah asked his brother.

Henry leaned back in his chair, bringing the front two legs off the floor a good six inches. "No. I'm rather enjoying this conversation."

If not for the slight twitch of Amelia's upper lip, Elijah would have used force to get his irritating brother out of the room. Instead, he ignored him and turned his attention back to Amelia. · "Does it bother you when I call you sweet?" Why was he even asking that? It didn't matter one iota if she liked being called a term of endearment by him or not, the more pressing question was—

"No, I suppose not." She exhaled. "But it's what I've come to expect from an arrogant, pigheaded, addled gentleman such as yourself."

Cough, cough, cough, hack, hack, hack. "Excuse me," Henry choked out between coughs. He used his palm and banged it against his chest.

Elijah turned sharp eyes over to where his brother had just been overcome by a terrible coughing fit. "Leave."

Elijah's tone sobered Henry faster than a splash of cold water to the face. "Very well."

An eerie silence filled the air as Henry brought the front legs of his chair back to the floor, then stood and gathered his discarded coat, cravat and waistcoat. Even his booted steps as he retreated toward the door were muted—not by the softness of the carpet under his feet, but because Henry wanted them to be unheard. He paused briefly at the door, and whispered something to Amelia that was so soft and low Elijah couldn't have heard it no matter how hard he strained to listen.

Amelia's eyes lowered, and Henry whispered something else —making her cheeks color.

Elijah cursed under his breath, then opened his mouth to speak.

But he didn't have to. Just as wordlessly as Henry had lowered his chair to the floor and gathered his belongings, he quit the room, closing the door with an almost inaudible click behind him.

Now that he was alone with Amelia, he didn't know what to

say to her. Again.

"What did Henry say to you?" He asked for lack of anything else to say.

Something—fire, or perhaps rage, he might never really know—flashed in her silver eyes. "Should I add jealousy to your list of unbecoming traits?"

"Unbecoming traits?" he asked with a scoff. "Pardon me, madam, but it seems to me that it is you who's become unbecoming as of late."

Amelia's gaze didn't waver as she arched one eyebrow in a silent question for him to try to explain his stupid statement.

Unfortunately, Elijah's mind swam with words like arrogant, jealous, pigheaded, snob, becoming and unbecoming, rendering him nearly incapable to form a well thought out statement, such as the nonsense he'd said a moment before.

"Why do you find me to be an arrogant snob?" he blurted at last.

"Because you are one."

Elijah fought to keep the frown off his face. "No, I'm not," he said as evenly as his clamped jaw would allow.

"Perhaps you're right," Amelia agreed, a hint of sadness in her voice that matched the same sadness that was now visible in her eyes. "Perhaps *you* are not a snob, but you've certainly taken to acting like one recently."

What the blazes was she talking about? He hadn't acted as if he had little regard for her. He'd admit he'd been a bit impatient with her and had said things that were probably best left unsaid, but he had *not* been a snob. An image of his father flashed in his mind, reminding him that he was a gentleman, and as such, he owed her an apology for whatever he did or didn't do that had upset her. "Amelia, if I've said or done something to make you think I was talking down to you, I apologize."

"I see you've allowed yourself the usual loophole you're so fond of." Her statement was devoid of any emotion.

Elijah's eyes bore into her. "I've apologized, Amelia. What more do you want from me?"

"You did no such thing. You offered a hollow apology *if* I felt the need for one, and it was rather reluctantly given, if I might be blunt."

"Of course it was," he agreed automatically. "I don't think I actually owe you one."

"Of course not."

Elijah dragged a deep breath in through his nostrils to help tame his rising temper. She was pushing him to his limit. And she knew just how to push him there. But they were not children anymore. Throwing balls of mud at one another wasn't going to solve this. So why was she pushing him? Or was she? The slight frown on her face and the way her brows were knit together were enough to make him second guess his earlier assessment. Did she truly feel he owed her an apology?

Nonsense. He'd done nothing to apologize for.

"Amelia, I don't know what your game is here—" His eyes narrowed on her. "Oh, I see what you're doing." He took a step toward her. Then another. "You're good," he murmured, closing the gap between them. "You thought if you picked a fight between us that I'd forget about my promise this morning, didn't you?"

Color rose in her cheeks. "I did no such thing and if you think that I'll have intimacies with you here, in your brother's library, you are truly cracked."

He shrugged and flashed her a smile. "I hadn't planned on it, but now that you've suggested it..." He reached behind her, purposely grazing the outside of her ribs with his arm as he did so, and wordlessly slid the lock.

She stiffened instantly. "Will it be by force, then?"

That was it. The final stone had just been laid. His internal scale was to its tipping point. He'd had enough of her and her sharp tongue. Rage like he'd never experienced before pumped through his veins at such a rapid rate he could hardly think of what to say in response. Refusing to break eye contact with her, he reached his arm behind her and turned the lock with a click so loud even a deaf man could have heard it. "Out."

~ *Chapter Fourteen* ~

Amelia couldn't get down the hall and away from Elijah fast enough. She'd gone into the library with the intention of telling him that, per Caroline's request, everyone who would be attending dinner was meeting in the drawing room. Instead, she'd let her tongue get away from her and what had started out as hoping to put Elijah in his place had changed into wanting to provoke him just enough to unsettle him and then had quickly become her unintentionally provoking his temper.

Not that he was violent or cruel when in a temper, just the opposite, rather. He'd get quiet and his breathing would grow heavy, never once uttering a hint of what he was thinking about, unlike when he was mildly irritated and would grumble beneath his breath.

She'd only seen him truly angry once before. It had been about ten years ago, Henry had made some remark about Elijah's inability to hit a target with his pistol and instantly Elijah's eyes had grown as dark as the ocean, his lips had thinned into a tight line that left two white, perpendicular lines on either side of his mouth, and the vein in his forehead had protruded. Just a moment ago, his face had transformed the same way.

The words she'd last spoken played over in her mind and she nearly tripped over her own feet as she scurried down the carpeted hall as fast as her slippers could carry her. She hadn't meant to lob such an accusation at him, it had just come out. He'd walked over toward her with such purpose and intent, never an unsure or unsteady step, but each exact and with purpose. His face unyielding and unreadable. But she didn't need to read it, she knew why he was coming to her, he was ready to collect on his earlier promise. And why? Because that's all she was to him, an outlet for his primal urges. He'd practically said as much to Henry earlier this morning.

Indignation swelled in her breast. She wanted nothing more than to win this wager and flaunt her winning in his face; and of course politely remind him that as the winner she was forever free of his unwanted advances.

"Amelia."

Amelia's heart jumped in her chest. What did *he* want? She ignored him and kept making her way down the hall. He wouldn't want to make a scene any more than she did and if she could just get down the hall and to the staircase, she'd be safe.

"Amelia," he said again, suddenly at her side.

She pulled to an abrupt stop, whether out of aggravation with the man or just to see if he'd stumble a little when he matched her stance, she'd never tell. "What do you want, Henry?"

He gestured to the door behind him. "I'd like to speak with you for a moment."

"Why, so you can mock me?" She slapped a hand over her mouth with a quiet pop as soon as the words were out.

He shook his head. "No. Why would you think I'd mock you."

"Never mind. We shouldn't be going off alone anyway." And that was the truth. No matter how scandalous everyone else in this house might be, even they couldn't turn a blind eye to catching a newly married young lady alone in a distant room with her husband's brother.

Henry's chuckle brought her from her wayward thoughts. "They're all eating dinner by now, so as long as Elijah's absent, nobody will suspect anything. Anyway, this won't take long. Come."

She dug her heels into the carpet. What if he were just as amorous as Elijah seemed to be? Her blood turned to ice in a second. Physically they were the same: tall, broad shoulders, hands as large as chickens, but Elijah had always been the more gentle of the two, the first to her side when she'd been injured, the first to calmly talk her down when she'd climbed too high up a tree and got scared, the first to remember that while she might think she was of equal ability and strength to the two of them, she was really a lady. It wasn't that Henry had purposely tried to hurt her, but he'd required a reminder of his own strength from Elijah from time to time. She swallowed and folded her arms across her chest. "No."

Her hands grew clammy under Henry's unwavering stare. "You said you'd talk to me," he reminded her in a voice that brooked no argument.

She nodded numbly. Amelia remembered him whispering for her to come see him in the yellow drawing room when she was finished speaking with Elijah. She'd offered him a smile and murmured an agreement, but after Elijah had grown so angry with her and tossed her from the room, she had no desire to speak to anyone.

"There's no reason to fear me." His quiet words startled her.

"I don't fear you. I just don't know what to expect from you or anyone else anymore."

"I see." He shoved his hands into his pockets. "Life is full of uncertainty—especially when married into this family." He shot her a grin. "Perhaps if you will come talk to me for a few minutes, some of your uncertainty will be made certain."

Despite herself, a small burble of laughter passed Amelia's lips at his ridiculous statement. "I really shouldn't."

"Oh? And when has Lady Amelia ever been accused of resisting the temptation to do something she shouldn't?"

A dull ache formed in her chest. Ever since she'd made a horrible mistake with a masked stranger, that's when. Since then, she hadn't done a single thing a respectable young lady wouldn't do, except ride away from her own wedding with Elijah, but that had been unavoidable.

"Come," he said again, opening the large door just to the right of where she stood. "This will take but a few minutes."

She cast a quick glance over her shoulder then went into what appeared to be Alex's study. Glass jars with plants or insects lined the windowsill. She shuddered. On his desk, over the top of his open account ledgers lay several contraptions, some metal with dials, others had a strip of numbers in the middle. She almost chuckled. Nothing about Elijah's dark-haired, bespectacled older brother had ever changed.

Henry left the door open a scant three inches then walked over toward her and pulled out the chair behind the large desk. "This one is far more comfortable than the others," he murmured when she hesitated to sit.

Swallowing her unease at the possibility of being caught alone with him, she lowered herself into the chair, clenching her hands together as he made his way around the desk to sit across from her. She had a sudden urge to flee the room. To run back to Elijah and make sure he knew she hadn't done anything she shouldn't have with his brother. Bile rose in her throat. That would be the worst of it if they were caught. It didn't matter the scandal that might ensue, those were only words. But if Elijah had reason to believe she'd been untrue to him in favor of his brother, and she really was pregnant... It was unthinkable.

She jumped to her feet with such vigor the chair she'd been sitting in toppled backward to the floor. "I need to go."

"No, you need to listen." Henry gestured for her to sit back down. "If we're caught, I'll speak to Elijah, if you'd like. He'll know nothing happened between us."

That didn't make her feel much better, but she righted her chair and took her seat anyway. The unnerving truth was it didn't matter what Elijah thought of her anyway because it would never rival the feelings she had for him.

"Amelia," Henry started with what sounded like a sigh borne of frustration. "As you know, I'm a gentleman, not a lady."

"Yes, I can see that."

He shook his head ruefully. "You've certainly got the tongue of a Banks," he muttered under his breath. "What I meant by that is, while ladies are more eloquent with their words and more sensitive of others' feelings, gentlemen are not."

She bit her lip and nodded. He was about to say something completely blunt and tactless. Splendid. At least he'd given her warning, she supposed. "All right."

Henry reached his ungloved hand up to the side of his face and idly scratched his temple for a moment. "Gentlemen, such as Elijah, don't—" He twisted his lips and turned his head to the side as if he were in deep concentration, now tapping his fingers against his cheek. Suddenly he stopped, and his eyes lit with what she presumed to be a brilliant idea. "Think of it like this. Your skin is different from Elijah's. Yours is soft and delicate. His is like mine, coarse and callused." He lifted his hands to show her. "Say, you two were to walk through a rose garden together without gloves. You'd notice if your hand brushed against some thorns and would likely draw attention to the scratches it put on your skin. Gentlemen could brush up against those same thorns—"

"And not feel them," Amelia cut in flatly.

Henry shook her head. "No. They still feel them. They might not cut their hands as much because their skin is coarse, but they'd still feel the sharp thorns when they get scratched by them. The difference is, they won't draw attention to them. They'd rather pretend it wasn't happening and let everyone around them think nothing is hurting them."

Mindlessly, Amelia wrapped a fallen tendril of her dark hair around her fingers. "Why?"

"Because they don't want anyone to know."

She licked her lips. "No, I meant why are you telling me this?"

"Because you need to know."

Amelia rolled her eyes up to look at the ceiling for a moment before meeting his gaze again. "I must be as articulate as a gentleman today. What I want to know is what this has to do with Elijah."

"Everything."

"Everything?" she echoed.

He nodded his confirmation and drummed his fingers along the edge of his brother's desk as if he were contemplating just what he should tell her.

She sat quiet, waiting. She'd sit here as long as necessary for him to decide what to tell her—and then she'd wait a while after that in hopes he'd tell her more.

His long, blunt-tipped fingers made one final tap. "It's exactly as I said before. Elijah might seem impassive or unaffected when talking to you, but he's not. He just wants you to think he is."

"Why?" she blurted, heedless to whatever trite remark he might counter with.

"That's just how gentlemen are," he said with a shrug.

If the hangman's noose wasn't the punishment for attempted murder of a titled gentlemen's brother, Amelia might strangle the insolence right out of Henry herself. "Are you trying to be obtuse?"

He blinked at her the way his older brother Alex was prone to do when confused or caught unawares. "No," he said slowly.

"I'm sorry," she said. "I just don't understand."

"And you're calling me obtuse," he mumbled. He ran his hand through his hair. "What I'm trying to tell you is he's just pretending not to be affected, but he is."

"And you know this because you're a gentleman," her words were more of a statement than a question.

"And his twin," he confirmed. "There's very little one can hide from his twin."

His words made sense. Heaven only knew how many times she'd heard one of them finish the other's sentence or have a conversation without uttering one word. "What is it that he doesn't want me to know?"

"That, my dear sister, is for you to discover."

~ *Chapter Fifteen* ~

Elijah watched as the last orange flame in the three-candle candelabra on the table in front of him was put out by its own pool of wax, leaving the room in utter darkness. Several hours ago a storm had rolled in, taking with it every ounce of moonlight that might have been able to stream in through the window.

In the darkness, he continued to sit alone. Thoughts of his earlier conversations with Amelia played over in his mind. Since they'd been married, they hadn't had but one or two conversations that didn't turn sour, which was a stark contrast to the one or two that had gone sour in all the years they'd known each other before marrying.

How could repeating a handful of words before the archbishop change everything they'd had? He shook his head. He was no closer to solving this mystery than he had been after demanding she leave following her outrageous suggestion that he was not only capable, but intent on raping her. His stomach knotted and a surge of bile burned his throat. How could she even *think* him the sort who'd do that? Or was it because she thought he already had? The bile that had burned his throat now filled his mouth.

He grabbed one of the empty glass jars on the edge of Alex's desk and spewed the burning liquid into it, then used the back of his hand to wipe his mouth. He had to set things to right. But how? There wasn't any options available to him now that wouldn't bring about more questions—questions he couldn't answer.

He'd tried to avoid all of this just days ago. If he'd been successful, none of the feuds between them would have ever taken place.

Clenching his fists and closing his eyes, he dredged up the

memory of when he'd gone to see Amelia's father...

London
Last Week

"Mr. Banks, so good to see you," Jacob Brice, Lord Strand said, coming into the drawing room.

Elijah noted Lord Strand's smile wasn't as wide as usual, and the corners of his eyes hadn't crinkled the way they normally did when he grinned; his hands were clenched into twin fists at his sides and the ruby cravat pin he always wore was slightly askew. That could only mean one thing: he'd heard. Just what he'd heard, Elijah had yet to determine. But that was a challenge he'd gladly accept.

"It's good to see you, too, my lord," Elijah said, flashing him a grin. "I was hoping to speak to you about something important, if this is a good time for you, of course."

"Well..." Lord Strand threw a glance over his shoulder to the hall, then turned back to Elijah. "Just keep it quick," he muttered, falling into a leather chair by the fire.

"It's about Lady Amelia," Elijah started uneasily. "I heard she's to marry Lord Friar."

"For once the gossip mongrels got it right."

"Or did they?"

"Did they what?" the older man barked.

"Get the story right?"

Lord Strand's grey eyes narrowed on Elijah. "What's your game, boy?"

"I'd like to marry Amelia," he said, lacking any sort of finesse or moderation.

"No."

Elijah stared at him in shock. "No?"

"No," the man affirmed. "She's promised to Lord Friar at the end of the week. It would bring about an awful scandal if she were to cry off now."

Squeezing his toes together so not to grind his teeth, Elijah ventured, "Does she and Lord Friar have great affections for one another, then?" He wouldn't dare put voice to the real reason he suspected Lord Strand had accepted the man's suit, but frankly Lord Strand lacked the funds to eat more than gruel.

Lord Strand scoffed. "I'd wager a feline is fonder of a hound than she is of Lord Friar." He shoved to his feet and grabbed the fire poker. Poking at the log in the fire, he continued, "But it matters naught. They're set to marry in Brighton this weekend."

"There is still enough time to cry off," Elijah said softly.

A large spray of sparks flew through the hearth. "She'll not be crying off."

"Even if she had a better offer?" Elijah hedged.

"Even then." Lord Strand wordlessly placed the poker back in the stand and adjusted the screen, then crossing his arms, turned around to face Elijah. "Amelia wants this match, and you'll do nothing to stop it."

Elijah searched the man's stoney face. "Why?"

"That's none of your concern, young man," Lord Strand snapped. "I knew your father. A more honorable sort I have yet to meet." He shook his head sadly. "I'm assuming it's because of him, and the sense of honor and duty to protect those closest to you that he instilled into you that brings you here, but it'll do you no good. Amelia has already made her choice."

"And she chose *him*?"

Lord Strand hesitated a second. "Yes."

"No, she didn't," Elijah said flatly.

"Yes. She did."

"You might claim she did, but I know Amelia. She would have never agreed to such an ill-suited match."

Lord Strand's face grew red. "Now, see here, young man. My daughter might have dreamed up some sort of foolish notion of love as far as you're concerned, but that gives you no right to come in here and take away her chances of a good match."

"A good match? Surely you don't mean to reference Lord Friar when you use those words."

"He is an earl," Lord Strand said smugly.

"I see," Elijah said slowly. "My lack of title never seemed to bother Amelia before."

"Perhaps not," her father agreed. "But you've also never sought me out to ask for my daughter's hand in marriage before, either."

"The time was never right."

Lord Strand snorted. "You seemed happy enough to accept Amelia's affections for you for years now without giving her more than a few minutes of idle chit-chat in the corner and an occasional waltz, but never did you call on her or ask to court her, and now that she's about to marry another, you suddenly have an interest in her." He curled his upper lip up in disgust. "Disregard what I said earlier about your father instilling his gentleman's honor in you. It's nothing more than sheer, unadulterated jealousy that has brought you here today, isn't it?"

"No," Elijah clipped. "I'm not here out of jealousy. I want to marry Amelia because—" because he loved her and realized that he always had, but he couldn't marry her while he was still working for the Crown. It was too dangerous. She'd live her life as an oblivious walking target. Anyone who wanted to inflict pain on him would only have to take one look at them together to know the best way to hurt him was to hurt her. He couldn't do that to her.

"You don't have a good reason, do you?" Lord Strand placed his large hand on Elijah's shoulder. "It's all right, Elijah. You're still young. Another young lady will come along."

"I don't want another young lady," Elijah said through gritted teeth.

Lord Strand urged him toward the door. "Let her be, Elijah."

"And if I don't?" Elijah challenged.

"Then you'll wish you had," Lord Strand said, his fingertips digging into Elijah's shoulder.

Elijah pretended not to notice the vice-like grip the older man had on his shoulder. "Sir, other than not having a title and waiting a little longer than you may have liked, why do you find me so unfavorable in comparison to Lord Friar?"

Silence hung in the air and Lord Strand's grip loosened. "It's not something I can explain." He sighed. "She made the choice and I have to respect what she's done."

"What she's done?" Elijah echoed.

Something flickered in Lord Strand's eyes. "Her decision is to marry Lord Friar. It's done."

"Right," Elijah agreed, narrowing his eyes on the older man. He was hiding something. But what?

He didn't get the chance to ask when the door swung open and Amelia's older brother Philip strolled in, sneering.

"What are *you* doing here?" he asked without ceremony.

"Nothing," Lord Strand answered for him. "He was just on his way out."

Philip stepped aside and gestured to the door. "I'll see you out."

Elijah thought to protest, but quickly decided not to. With Philip in the room, his chances of getting any more information out of Lord Strand were nonexistent. "Good day, my lord," he said to Lord Strand.

"Good day, Mr. Banks," came the man's gruff response.

Elijah chanced one final glance at the man. His face confirmed the sadness his voice had indicated.

"You'll leave her alone if you know what's good for you," Philip whispered in his ear as soon as they were in the hall.

Elijah spun around to face the weasel. Thinner than a reed and the spotted face of a green boy, Philip Brice was the last person who should ever be issuing any type of threat. "And what about what's good for her?"

"That'd be Lord Friar," he said simply. "He's everything you're not."

"Yes, cruel and heartless," Elijah mused. "Oh, and he has a title."

"And a great deal of wealth," Philip added.

Elijah's muscles tensed. "Is that it? Is your father in need of money?" It was an impolite question, to be sure. One that could get just about any man called out, but seeing how Philip possessed less strength than it took to shoot a gun or hold a sword for longer than thirty seconds, Elijah didn't mind breaking the rules of etiquette.

Philip snarled. "No. It would be, it has nothing to do with Father being in need of money. Amelia consented to marry Lord Friar all on her own."

Her father had said as much, but he doubted it was the truth. It was widely known that Lord and Lady Strand's visits to London had become fewer and were often cut short. Not once in the last four years had they hosted so much as a breakfast. The undeniable truth was, they had no money. "Do you know why she accepted?"

"One can only speculate."

"Then speculate."

Philip gave a lopsided shrug. "There are many reasons young ladies decide to marry, Elijah. She could love him."

"Not bloody likely," Elijah cut in.

Philip's lips formed that unsettling smirk he usually walked around town wearing. "There are many things you might believe are unlikely when it comes to Amelia, but I assure you sometimes the truth is more absurd than those gothic novels that are all the rage."

"If you really believe she loves him, then you are a fool."

Two flags of bright red appeared on Philip's cheeks. "And if you believe love has to be involved for two people to commit certain acts, then you are the fool," he shot back.

Elijah took his meaning, Amelia had been compromised. "With Lord Friar," he nearly choked out in disbelief.

"Perhaps. Perhaps, not." He shrugged. "She really doesn't

know."

"She doesn't know?"

The clodpole shrugged again. "As I said, more absurd than a gothic novel."

No, not absurd. Asinine. How does a lady not know who she's shared intimacies with? Was such a thing even possible? Perhaps if she were a trollop in the seedy part of Covent Garden and a stranger approached her. Otherwise how would a lady not know her partner's identity? Elijah's innards twisted and the air was robbed straight from his lungs as understanding came over him: a lady wouldn't know the identity of a masked man at a costume party.

"Is she here?" he asked despite the lack of air in his lungs.

"No. She's staying with a relation until her wedding."

"Which relation?"

"I'm not sure," Philip said, looking down to inspect his fingernails.

It would only take two hits—Elijah to hit Philip, and for Philip to hit the floor—to end this nonsense here and now. Fortunately for Philip, he was spared a punch to the gut when his father reappeared. "Banks, go home. Philip, get in here. Now."

Elijah waited while Philip walked away. It didn't matter that Philip hadn't given him the information he needed. He still had two and a half days before the wedding was to take place. Brighton wasn't too terribly far or that large of a place. That should be plenty of time to find Amelia.

More than two days, was not enough time to find her and convince her to jilt Lord Friar, however. In fact, his time had been cut short when he'd been seeking information about Amelia's family in a tap room and had overheard a boat named *Jezebel* had been spotted down by the docks—

SLAM!

Elijah jolted in his seat as if he'd been struck by lightning. He looked around in the darkness; his skin tingled. Someone else was in the room with him.

"Alex, stop," his sister-in-law Caroline protested with a giggle.

"Someone's in here," Elijah barked.

Caroline let out a little shriek and someone clearly tripped. Alex muttered a curse as he fumbled in the dark for a match. He tried to light one of the candles on the table, but there was nothing left to light since Elijah had watched them all burn out this evening. Instead, Alex held the lighted match in the air between them, as if it were some great light source. Fire quickly consumed the little wooden stick and he put it out, but didn't let the lack of light deter him. "What are you doing in here?"

"Sitting."

Elijah couldn't see his brother's expression, but assumed he'd scowled. "In here? Right now?"

"Yes, I do believe here and now would be accurate."

"Why?" Alex ground out.

"I don't know. Why did you come in here?"

"To help me find a book," Caroline blurted before her husband could answer. She fumbled for something on the desk. "Now, that I have it, I'll go on up to bed."

"She does know that she took a quill and not a book, doesn't she?" Elijah asked when he was sure Caroline was out of the room. "Perhaps she plans to pen—"

"Yes," Alex snapped, ending Elijah's words. "She also knows this is her own home and she's welcome to go in any room she'd like, any time she'd like, and take from it any *thing* she'd like."

"I never said she couldn't," Elijah said. "But last I heard, one's bedchamber was more appropriate for the activity you brought her in here for, Amorous Alex."

"You have such a small imagination, it's astounding," Alex murmured, taking a seat. "Why are *you* here?"

Elijah didn't answer.

"Ah, I see. matrimonial troubles already."

Elijah doubted he did. Just as he struggled to believe his mother could offer him advice about his situation, he couldn't even imagine Alex offering him any good advice. Alex had been very fortunate, indeed to find a lady like Caroline. She didn't mind his love for science, nor the fact that he often missed subtle, and not-so-subtle, hints; and said things that were easily taken out of context. But nobody was ever offended by the latter—even Caroline.

When they'd begun courting, Alex had foolishly written down his courtship strategy as it if were nothing more than a science experiment. When she found out what he'd done, she hadn't developed a tongue sharper than a sword or turned into an Ice Queen. Instead, as far as he could remember, she'd never said anything to him about it at all.

"Caroline and I didn't always have an easy time of it," Alex said a moment later.

Elijah snorted. "That's not what I remember."

"That's because you don't know everything like you think you do."

Elijah shoved his hand into his pocket and ran his thumbnail along the edge of his gold pocket watch. "Alex, this is different."

"Is it?" The sound of a chair leaning backwards was the only sound in the room. "I know you think I say idiotic things because I don't realize what I'm saying, but that's not always true. I'll grant you it's true sometimes, but I've learned it's better to keep one's mouth shut than to say the wrong thing."

"Then take your own advice and stop talking now."

"I've hurt Caroline with my words before," Alex admitted as if he hadn't heard Elijah's former statement. "Purposely."

Thank heaven for sending the storm clouds to block the moon's light or else Elijah's slack jaw would have given himself away. "What?"

Alex brought his chair back to the floor with a soft thud. "I said I've knowingly hurt Caroline's feelings." He let out a deep breath. "The night you and Henry informed me that Caroline had known for some three weeks about what I'd done, we had a row. As usual, I misunderstood what she'd been doing and what she was saying that night. I got angry and left. The next day, she tried to speak to me about it and instead of listening, I let the hurt she wasn't even trying to inflict on me get the better of me and rattled off every hurtful thing I could think of. It only got worse from there," he added quietly.

Elijah thought back to that day. He vaguely remembered sitting in the breakfast room with Henry, Mother and Edwina, when in the middle of the meal Mother abruptly stood and closed the door herself, rather than directing a footman to do it. He'd thought it odd at the time, but had never given it any further thought.

"How did you repair things?" Elijah heard himself ask.

"I fixed her telescope," Alex said as if to suggest Elijah could do the same thing to mend his relationship with Amelia.

"While I'm thrilled that worked for you, I don't think it'll have the same effect for me."

"No, probably not." Alex's chair screeched back away from the table. "It wouldn't have worked for me, either, if I hadn't been there, ready to apologize and make things right when she found it."

"And what did you say when she found it?"

"The truth. All of it."

~ Chapter Sixteen ~

The sun always shone so bright after a storm it was amazing half the countryside hadn't been blinded, Amelia thought as she rapidly blinked her eyes to get used to the blinding light pouring into her window.

She lifted her left hand to shield her face and looked around the empty room. Dropping her hand, she sighed. Elijah must have decided to spend the night in his brother's home. That was for the best, really. She rolled to the side of the bed, put her feet over the edge, stretched her hands way up over her head and gave a hearty yawn.

"I can't imagine why you'd have such a need to stretch so much after having such a large bed all to yourself last night."

Amelia dropped her arms as if they suddenly weighed five hundred pounds each. "I made sure to stay on my own side last night. But since I woke up today in the same condition I went to sleep in, I'll be sure to sprawl out like a starfish tonight and every night hereafter."

"You be sure to do that," Elijah said with a quick grin. "We were better at being friends than lovers anyway."

She forced a smile. Although she'd wanted him to stop trying to get her into bed, his cavalier attitude about it stung. "Right you are."

Elijah walked into the room and over to the wardrobe. "Once you're dressed, I'll take you into Bath. We never did have that slice of cake I'd promised you yesterday."

Amelia's heart squeezed at the memory of what he'd said about her and cake yesterday. "No, thank you."

Elijah turned to face her, his blue eyes wide with what

appeared to be shock. "Did I just hear Amelia Banks forfeit her boon?"

"I'm not very hungry." That was a lie. She was famished.

"That's all right." He turned back to the wardrobe and pulled out a white shirt and red waistcoat. He laid them across the back of the chair closest to him. "After we walk around and visit the shops for a while you will be."

She opened her mouth to protest, but quickly closed it. He might have made an unflattering remark about her request for cake yesterday, but if Henry was to be believed, and there really wasn't a good reason to doubt him, she'd do well to spend the day talking with him—she just might discover what it was he was hiding from her.

"We could even get an ice if we see a vendor," Elijah continued, bending down to unlace his boots.

Amelia knew she shouldn't stare at his backside. She just couldn't help it. Would it be as hard and muscular as it looked? She tore her eyes away. What was wrong with her? Not two minutes ago she'd boasted about her win and that she was now free from his unromantic advances. So why now did she find herself even more attracted to him than before?

"Get dressed," Elijah said, handing her the lavender morning gown she'd borrowed from Edwina.

She took it from him, thankful that it'd only be a week or so before the modiste who'd come by yesterday afternoon would have some gowns whipped up for her. "Do you plan to leave?"

"No," he said, tugging his shirt over his head. "If you'll wait a moment, I'll help you dress."

Help her dress? "That won't be necessary," she rushed to say in spite of the way her cheeks burned.

Elijah pulled on his clean shirt then reached for his trousers. "In case it has escaped your notice, I haven't yet employed a lady's maid for you."

"Oh, so that's your plan?"

Elijah's movements stopped and his face hardened. "I don't like what you're insinuating, Amelia. And you'd do well to stop accusing me of being a depraved reprobate."

Amelia's heart slammed in her chest. "I never meant—" She broke off. How had her words been taken so wrong? "I was jesting with you, Elijah."

"Jesting?"

"Jesting," she confirmed. She set her gown on the bed next to her and fell backwards onto the soft mattress.

"That's a jest I don't find very humorous."

"I know that now, but I didn't mean for it to come out that way," Amelia mumbled, bringing her arm up to rest across her eyes. Why was it so hard to talk to the one person who'd once had the ability to put her at ease better than anyone else?

Next to her, the mattress dipped under his heavy frame as he lay down next to her. His warm hand found her cheek and turned her head to face him. "Why don't you explain it," he said in a tone far softer than the one he'd spoken in a moment ago.

"It's of no account."

"Sure it is." He brushed his thumb across her cheekbone, his jaw no longer clenched. "I want to know."

"It won't even be funny now."

He grinned. "All the more reason to explain it."

She knit her brow. Was he cracked? Who wanted to hear a jest when the moment for the height of the jest had past?

"I'm waiting."

"You're impossible," she said with a smile. "You'd said you were going to help me dress—play the part of my lady's maid because you hadn't hired one for me so I asked if that's your plan."

"Yes, I got that," he said in a tone that lacked any humor whatsoever.

She closed her eyes. "I didn't mean it *that* way. What I was implying was that since you're a younger son and have no title, you have to have a plan for your life. You're seven-and-twenty and haven't yet taken up as an officer or become a vicar, both of which are respectable things for a gentleman of your station. So since you haven't done either of those, I was jesting that you'd—"

"Planned to become a lady's maid, instead," he finished for her, a blank expression on his face.

***

What an idiot he'd been. He swallowed past the pound of gravel in his throat. "Amelia?"

"Yes?"

He searched his mind for the right words, but nothing came to mind of how to make amends for accusing her of something so distasteful.

"I told you it wouldn't be funny now," she mumbled, taking him from his thoughts.

"No." He reached for her small hand and held it in his. "It's not that. It was funny. Or it would have been had I not been such an arse to realize it."

She stared up at the ceiling. "It's all right. It seems we've both been guilty of such these past few days."

He nodded against the mattress, companionable silence filling the room. He released her hand, then moved his so they were palm to palm and entwined his fingers with hers. It had been years since he'd touched her ungloved hand, and yet it was still as soft as he remembered.

"Will you forgive me?" he whispered after some time had passed.

The slight movement of her fingers between his was the only indication he had that she'd even heard him at first. "You're not the only one who's been beastly," she said softly a moment later.

He brushed the pad of his thumb across the back of her hand. "Shall we start over?"

"No." She turned back to look at him, a small smile on her lips. "Your brother hasn't yet discovered how to travel through time, thus making starting over impossible."

He grinned at her logic and traced the edge of her jaw with the index finger on his free hand. "All right, since starting over is an utter impossibility, how about if we both try to atone for our recent beastly behavior and have a nice visit to Bath today?"

Her lips twisted as if she had to think really hard about her answer. "I'll agree, but only on one condition."

"Which is?'

She pulled her hand from his and sat up in one swift motion. "You must get rid of *that*."

Elijah's eyes followed Amelia's outstretched finger to a little wooden box with a thin sheet of glass over the top, and he began to chuckle. "I think I can manage to get rid of the box."

"And the creature inside," Amelia said, pulling a comical face.

"No, he stays."

"Oh please, Elijah; last night while I was getting ready for bed I saw what's in there and nearly swooned."

He snapped his fingers. "Ah, but you didn't."

Amelia shook her head ruefully. "No, I managed to keep my wits about me, but only because that thing was behind the glass."

"That thing has a name," Elijah said in the most serious tone he could muster. "His name is Mr. Henry Hirsute."

"Well, Mr. Henry Hirsute needs to find a new residence."

Elijah shook his head sadly. "I have nowhere else to take him and he'll die if I just let him go. Tarantulas weren't made to endure the weather this far north." Elijah glanced over at Mr. Henry Hirsute. He'd found him on the England-bound ship the last time he'd come home from South America. In the summer months, Elijah had to place his box by the window to help keep it warm and in the winter months, he'd wrap blankets around it and move it close to the hearth. He was actually surprised the critter had lived this long.

"If he can't survive the cold, then why did you bring him here?"

"I thought he'd make a good pet."

"Then get a hound."

"I've had one before," he said with a dismissive flick of his wrist. "They eat too much."

"I see," she said slowly. "And just what does Mr. Henry Hirsute eat?"

"Cockroaches."

Her silver eyes grew to the size of Mother's favorite tea saucers, just the way he'd hoped they would, and her hand went to her throat. "Cockroaches?" she breathed, her lips curled up in disgust.

"Would you like for me to show you?"

She shook her head with so much vigor her loose coiffure started tumbling down. "No, but that is just all the more reason to get rid of your friend."

"Because he eats insects?"

"Yes, and because the particular insects he likes to dine on often have friends of their own that like to come into places they are not invited."

He chuckled at her reasoning. "He can eat other things, and often does." He reached over onto the table and picked up the glass jar he usually kept insects in to feed Mr. Henry Hirsute. "While he prefers cockroaches, I have no more desire to touch them than you have to see them, but he'll happily eat grasshoppers, too." He frowned at the jar in his hand. It was empty. "Apparently, I need to go catch some more for him."

"Outside?" Amelia croaked, drawing her knees close to her chest and wrapping her arms around her legs.

"Unless you know of somewhere else."

"Actually, I do," she said with a small giggle. "Alex's study has enough insects for Mr. Henry Hirsute to eat like Prinny for a week."

"Indeed," he agreed. "Say, how would you know that?"

She swallowed audibly. "I...uh...went in there yesterday."

What reason in the world would she have to go in there?

"And?"

She shuddered. "There were jars of insects lining the windowsill."

"Did you enjoy looking at them?" he asked just for no other reason than to see her shudder again, an action which unbeknownst to her made her pert breasts jiggle in the loveliest way.

"About as much as I enjoyed seeing Mr. Henry Hirsute last night."

"That much?" He set the jar back down. "He's really not so bad. He's soft and fuzzy. Would you like to touch him?"

"Would you like to learn to embroider?"

"Oh, all right." He flashed her a hopeful smile. "Perhaps in time you'll grow to love Mr. Henry Hirsute the same as I do."

"The chances of Henry—both of them—having a love match are greater than your chances of convincing me to touch that."

Elijah let out a low whistle. "My chances are worse than I thought." He took to his feet and looked around the room. "But, in the unlikely event that Henry *does* have a love match, I cannot say fare-thee-well to Mr. Henry Hirsute. You might change your mind and decide you want to pet him."

"The two events are not related, Elijah."

"I know." He picked up the box and walked it into the common room where he set it on an end table, then scooted it in front of the large window on the east side of the room. He walked back into the bedchamber and said, "Just because your touching Mr. Henry Hirsute isn't dependent on Henry making a love match, doesn't mean I can't try to convince you to touch him again."

"*Try* is the most important word in that sentence."

He lifted his left shoulder in a lopsided shrug. "That's all right. One may never know for sure if he doesn't try." Elijah walked over to her and picked up her gown. "Now, let me see if I can *try* to get you into this gown so we *can* go to Bath and have an enjoyable day together."

~Chapter Seventeen~

Elijah was a surprisingly good lady's maid.

Never once did he knot her tapes or struggle to get them tied. His fingers were deft and quick as he fastened the row of buttons that ran up the back of her dress.

"All done," he whispered in her ear.

The skin on her neck turned to gooseflesh at the roughness in his voice and the nearness of his warm body to hers. He smelled spicy, of sandalwood and his lips were so close to her she could feel his breath against her skin.

Reluctantly, she took a step forward. She wanted nothing more than to melt into his arms and longed to let him hold her tight. But that wasn't his way. He didn't see her as anything but a friend, and that wasn't the way friends acted toward each other—only lovers. Hastily, she picked up her bonnet and tied it on, then scooped up her reticule and craned her neck to look out the window. "Is that carriage for us?"

"No. I thought we'd walk to Bath. I just asked Damon to pull it over here so we could say goodbye to the horses before we began our journey."

Amelia pursed her lips, but it did no good, her laughter still escaped. "Forgive my stupid question. I think this gown is so tight it is cutting off the flow of blood to my brain."

Elijah's eyes did a slow sweep of her, sending a new round of chills over her body as his gaze lingered at her chest and hips. "Do you want to take it off?" he asked hoarsely, his face growing bright red. He cleared his throat. Then again. "What I meant is if the dress is too tight, I can help you into another if you'd like."

Ah, there was the impartial Elijah she'd married. "No. I'm sure

I'll get accustomed to it." She smiled. "Besides, as we walk around, it might become a bit looser."

"Until you eat the ca—" He closed his mouth with a sharp snap.

She laughed. "Yes, we might have to forgo the cake after all."

"That's not what I—"

Amelia pressed her fingers to his lips to halt his words. "I know you didn't mean it that way."

He pulled her hand away, but didn't let it go. "Are you sure, because it sounded—"

She covered his mouth with her other hand now. "Stop. We both promised not to think poorly of the other today." She lifted a single eyebrow. "Or have you decided to renege already."

Beneath her fingers, his lips turned up into a lopsided grin. "Never," he said against her fingers. He pulled her hand from his lips and was now holding them both. "But just so you can't say I didn't warn you, if you press your fingers to my lips again, you'd better be prepared for the consequences."

"Which are?"

He showed no sign of noticing how her voice had hitched on those two words, merely bent his head and pressed a kiss just below the edge of her glove on each wrist, then released her hands. "Do it again and you'll find out."

Her breath caught and she curled her fingers into her palms, the skin on her wrists still burning from where he'd kissed her as if he'd touched her with a branding iron instead of his lips. Suddenly overly warm, she snapped up her fan. "If we're to walk all the way to Bath, we'd better start now or we won't make it there and back in time for Caroline's costume ball on Friday."

"You really think it would take us a day and a half to walk ten miles to Bath and another day and a half to walk the ten miles back home?"

"Of course. Have you ever tried to walk in a pair of ladies' slippers?"

"Would you believe me if I said I had?"

She wagged her finger at him playfully. "Trying on your mother's shoes when you were four doesn't count."

He brought both of his hands up to rest on his cheeks in a show of what she presumed to be feigned embarrassment. "How did you know about that?"

"Henry."

He dropped his hands back to his sides. "I should have known," he muttered. "As much as I hate to disappoint you and your dreams of walking to Bath, the carriage is waiting and the horses are starting to sound impatient."

"You're the one who keeps delaying our departure by chatting."

He reached forward and shoved a lock of her fallen hair into the edge of her bonnet. "There's no crime in a man chatting with his wife, is there?"

"Only if he enjoys it."

"Then we must cease at once," he said between clenched teeth, his eyebrows shooting halfway up his forehead. He made a show of looking over each shoulder and out the window, then leaned close to her and said in a stage whisper, "Good. I don't think anyone saw us."

Amelia swatted playfully at his shoulder. "If you ever find yourself in need of employment, I'd suggest you look for a post as a lady's maid because you'd be a horrible spy."

"Me? A horrible spy?" He darted his gaze over her left shoulder and then her right as if he were slyly examining their surroundings.

"The worst ever," she said, trying to suppress her laughter.

He slapped his palm against his chest with a resounding thud and gasped. "Surely not. Have you met every spy?"

"No."

"Then how would you know I'm the worst ever?" he questioned, throwing his hands into the air; his eyes alight with laughter.

His facial expression and hand gestures were just too much! "You're absurd."

"Absurd? You're the one who suggested I become a lady's maid."

"And can you deny that you wouldn't enjoy the job?"

"I think that would depend on whose lady's maid I was."

She pulled on her overcoat. "No need to tax yourself with worry about finding a desirable lady to work for," she said, plucking up her scarf since it was still a little cool outside this time of year. "I'll be sure to write you a very high letter of recommendation."

He leaned close to her ear as she wrapped her scarf around her neck. "Could you be sure to address said letter to yourself?" Then, before she could recover her wits enough to form a response, he was gone.

***

Elijah threaded his fingers though his hair, then gave it a quick tug. What was he doing? He'd told her this morning he was content to just be her friend and then he'd gone on to make several inappropriate remarks and even kiss her.

He took in a deep breath; then another. He needed this. Fresh air, that is. Amelia had only been staying in the cabin with him for a few days and already it smelled of her. And frankly, the smell was enough to intoxicate a man and impair his judgement. He kicked a rock with the toe of his boot and watched it roll a good ten feet away, stopping only when Amelia arrested it with her slipper-clad foot.

Shamelessly, he let his eyes move slowly from her feet up. He swallowed uncomfortably. What he could see of her gown between her unbuttoned overcoat, it clung to her almost like a second skin, hugging her in all the right places. He reluctantly dragged his eyes away before he could surrender to his impulse and touch her, destroying any shred of trust he'd managed to build today.

He sobered instantly. He couldn't give her the truth like Alex had suggested—not yet anyway, but he could show her that he was worthy of her trust and good opinion. She'd know soon enough that she wasn't increasing, if she didn't already. His face heated. Most gentlemen knew next to nothing about female matters. Elijah's father, however, ensured his sons knew more than most. Alex probably didn't mind the knowledge, and likely felt the need to inform him of any discoveries he'd read about on the topic that might have come after Father had studied it. When the time came for Elijah and Henry to be informed, neither could get out of the room fast enough. Just now though, he was grateful for the knowledge because at least he didn't have to ask carefully worded questions to ensure she knew at least that particular truth.

"Are you going to take me to Bath for a slice of cake or stare at me all day?"

"I'm still waiting for you to get into the carriage," Elijah said without hesitation. He offered her his arm and helped her into the carriage.

"I haven't been here in what feels like ages," Amelia marveled a short time later as the carriage rolled down Milsom Street.

"That's not true. I saw you dance at one of the local assemblies a few years ago."

"You did?" Her brows drew together in confusion. "I don't remember you there."

"I was there but a few minutes," he said dismissively. That was true enough, and all she needed to know. He *had* been there only a few minutes. That was all it took for him to realize the fellow he'd been seeking wasn't at that particular assembly. He'd found him a week later in Cambridge. He shook his head to clear his thoughts of the menaces of society. It did no good to dwell on them. Once the two involved in the prostitution ring were brought to justice, he'd be done with his work and could relax into a quiet country life, perhaps as a lady's maid. Most preferably Amelia's lady's maid.

He closed his eyes and leaned his head back against the red velvet squabs of Alex's carriage. No gentleman wanted to be a lady's maid—that required he help her redress, and that was the last thing he wanted to do. He leaned his head to the right a couple of inches, then abruptly brought it to the left, hitting it against the hard inside shell of the carriage. Stars burst in front of his eyes, and just as quickly they disappeared. Dash it all. Hitting his head against the wall didn't knock any sense into his head anymore than it knocked out the image of helping Amelia undress. The truth was, he had no business thinking about her in such a way. As history had already shown, in three short days at that, she did not appreciate his advances, and he'd do well to remember that.

"Are you all right?"

Elijah straightened. "Hmm?"

"Your head."

Mindlessly, Elijah raised his fingers to his head where he now found a knot quickly forming. "Oh, it's nothing. We must have hit a bump."

She didn't look convinced, but he didn't care. He'd rather take his chances of running barefoot next to a bush infested with adders than admit he'd been thinking of undressing her. "Are you sure," she said, reaching up toward his head.

He moved his head back to evade her touch and put his hand out to stay hers. "I'm fine. I promise."

She pursed her lips and turned her head to look at him from the corner of her eye. "You'd better be. I'd hate to have to return early with you pleading a headache."

"Not to worry, I wouldn't dream of cutting our time short today."

~ Chapter Eighteen ~

Amelia misstepped. Something about the seriousness in his tone had caught her unawares. It had been deep and silky, purposeful.

She forced a shaky laugh. She was being ridiculous. His tone had been no different than it always was. She was just more acutely aware of him today for some reason. His scent and presence both seemed more commanding. His body radiating with a heat she couldn't ignore.

"Where to first, my dear?" he asked, startling her from her senseless thoughts.

"Er... I don't know." She looked around at the two rows of buildings that lined the street. To the left was a bookshop and a confectionary. Neither interested her. To her right was a museum and a modiste. Neither of those held any appeal, either. Further down was a bathhouse. She flushed. There was absolutely no way she'd enter one of those with Elijah. There was also a small theatre and an assembly hall, either would be a safe choice—were it evening and either of them actually open. "Hmmm. I don't know."

"Then shall I pick a place?"

She cast a nervous glance at the bathhouse, praying he wouldn't pick there. "I suppose." She wagged a finger at him. "But if it's somewhere inappropriate, then take this as your warning."

A sly grin took his lips as if he were challenging her. "Your warning has been heeded, Mrs. Banks." He offered her his arm and led her down the street.

With each step she took, her feet grew heavier. She shouldn't have chanced a glance down at the bathhouse, now he was going to take her there for sure.

"Come," he encouraged when her steps began to slow just enough to make him nearly trip over his own feet.

"I—I don't think so."

"You'll like this," he promised.

She gave him a sharp look. "I have no reason to believe that's true, and neither should you."

His grin didn't falter. "You won't know unless you stop digging your heels into the ground like a stubborn mule and come along."

They seemed to have caught the attention of two young ladies strolling down the street, one of whom had lifted her fan and was whispering to the other behind it. They both giggled. Amelia gritted her teeth and picked up her pace. There was no need to cause a spectacle.

"Very good," he murmured. "We'll be there in just a moment."

"Ooof," she gasped, running into his side when he abruptly turned to the left, just feet before they reached the bathhouse. "Where are we going?"

"Down the street."

"Oh."

He slowed his steps. "Was there somewhere else you had in mind? The bathhouse, perhaps?"

She lightly tapped him in the ribs with her elbow. "I have no desire to go there and you know it."

"No, I didn't. I assumed as much, though." He resumed his stride, then slowed down half a block later. "Ah, here we are."

Amelia lifted her hand to block the sun, but still had to squint to read the sign: IAN'S TOP CLASS GLASS. "What is this place?"

"What does it look like?"

"A shop that sells odd-shaped things made out of glass."

"Close enough." He dropped his arm and reached for her hand, the action oddly intimate. "Come, I'll show you."

Amelia went with him inside. As she'd guessed by the large irregularly-shaped bowls in the windows, and the sign of course, this was a glass shop. But not just any glass shop. It would seem that Mr. Ian specialized in unusual and rare pieces. "Why are they all so different?" she asked, running her index finger along the edge of a translucent pitcher.

"Do you not like that each is unique?"

"Actually, I do." She picked up a watery-blue vase with a top that flared out and curled. "I like it very much indeed."

He picked up a large bowl that had a small base with tall sides that came out at a considerable angle, leaving the opening of the bowl considerably larger than the base. "You don't see these too often around here," he murmured.

"What, a bowl?"

"A fruit bowl," he corrected, setting it back down. "When I traveled to America, most of the homes I went into had these in the middle of their dining tables."

"Why?"

He shrugged. "Their custom, I suppose." He picked up another and handed it to her.

Reluctantly, she let go of his hand so she could hold and inspect the fruit bowl he'd handed her. It had swirls of green and blue at the bottom and was a dark red fading into orange at the top. She ran her gloved fingers over the smooth surface of the bowl.

"The swirling color is made by heating pieces of other glass and melting them into it."

She stared at the beautiful bowl in her hand because she didn't dare look at Elijah lest he realize she hadn't a clue what he was talking about. "I see."

"Not yet, but you will."

Her eyes shot to his. "I'm sorry, but what did you just say?"

"Not yet, but you will."

She rolled her eyes. "Always the jester, aren't you?"

"I try. I'd hate to have disappointed anyone by not carrying on the Banks tradition."

"Oh dear," she said, feigning shock and bringing her right

hand up to her mouth. "If the Banks family legacy of humor rests on your shoulders, I fear the trait shall die."

He smoothed her brows and took her hand in his, giving her a small, affectionate squeeze. "Don't worry, my dear, sweet Amelia, with you as the mother of my children, the trait shall live on. There might be a small hiccup now, but it *will* continue on."

Amelia couldn't stop herself from grinning at his horrible theatrics. "You really might have to be a lady's maid," she whispered, not taking her hand from his, though she should. It wasn't proper for a couple to be showing such affections in public, even if they were married. "Your acting rivals your spying ability."

"Some might say those two occupations are one in the same," he said softly. Abruptly, he let her hand go and raked his hand through his blond hair. "But enough about my natural abilities, let's see what yours are."

"What natural ability would that be?" She lifted her chin a notch. "We both already know I can run faster, climb higher, and hold my breath underwater longer than you."

"Is that so?" he drawled, looking decidedly unconvinced. "And how are you at blowing glass."

"Better than you, I expect."

Elijah opened a steel door and gestured for her to go inside, making her quickly regret the words she'd just said. He fully intended to have her blow glass—whatever that was—and she didn't have a clue. She opened her mouth to protest, but he shot her a quelling look.

"Come over here and I'll show you what to do."

She folded her hands in front of her and watched as Elijah stripped off his gloves and coat and loosened his cravat, letting it hang loosely around his neck. He grabbed a pole and opened a little door to a chamber that held the hottest fire Amelia had ever been near.

"You're all right," he murmured, his face so close to hers she thought he might kiss her. Instead, he placed his hand on her shoulder and guided her in front of him.

Amelia didn't know which was making her skin burn with heat: the two thousand degree fire behind the iron doors in front of her or the nearness of Elijah.

"That's it," he murmured in her ear, his lips so close to her skin she could actually feel them brushing the shell of her ear. The muscles in his bare forearm flexed as he helped her lift the long metal pole with a ball of burning glass on the end and carry it from the fire to a skinny metal table. "Now roll it."

Amelia wanted so badly to reach up and dab the moisture from her forehead. Because he was a gentleman, and it could be overlooked when gentlemen stepped outside the bounds of propriety, Elijah had discarded his coat and gloves and rolled his shirtsleeves up to his elbows before casually draping himself over her for the sake of offering her help; and because she was a lady, she was still swathed in every stitch of fabric she'd left Watson Estate wearing.

Pushing aside the heat that was flooding her skin and the violent urge she had to press her shoulders against Elijah's chest, she slowly rolled the long pole across the table with the fireball hanging off the end.

"We have to go slow or the bubble inside might break."

Amelia nodded numbly and continued to help him roll the pole across the table. "It doesn't look so hot."

"No. We need to put it back in the fire again." He helped her lift the pole and bring it back to the fire, and it was a good thing he did or she'd have surely dropped it, for the pole itself must have weighed a good twenty pounds. Or so she guessed by the way his forearm nearly doubled in size from flexing his muscles when he lifted the pole. He carefully guided the ball of glass into the circular opening in front of the fire and held it in there but a minute. "Let's roll it again."

Together they rolled the pole along the top of the table for a few more minutes.

"All right. I think that's good enough for now." He lifted the pole into the air. "Now blow."

"Blow? Blow where? On the glass?"

A chuckle rumbled in his chest. "No. Blow in the end of the pole."

"But it's dirty."

"And so was my face when I was a boy, but you had no problem putting your lips to that."

Were anyone around to hear him say that, she'd have denied it. But since she'd just been close to a roaring fire and had a little taste of what Hell might be like, she didn't want to risk going there to save her pride in front of him alone. "Very well. Could you lower the pole?"

Wordlessly, he lowered the pole to her lips and held it for her as she did her best to blow.

"Softer," he said quietly. "Just a little."

She tried again, but nothing happened.

"Let me show you." He took the pole from her and lifted it to his mouth, and blew a slow, steady breath into the end that made the glass ball double in size.

"Amazing," she said in awe.

"Isn't it?" He motioned with his head for her to take hold of the pole again. "I want you to hold this down and roll it like we've been doing, all right?"

"A-all right." She licked her lips. "Where are you going?"

"Over here." He walked to the end of the pole and picked up a rounded piece of iron with a crude wooden handle and brought it underneath the ball. "Start rolling." When she did, he moved the iron curve as she moved the pole. "This is to help it maintain shape," he said as if he'd read the question on her mind.

She rolled it a few times and stopped when he pulled the piece of iron away and came to stand behind her. "The fire?"

"See, I knew you'd be a natural."

"Knowing that we have to stick it in the fire again doesn't

seem like it makes me a natural."

"Believe what you want—" he guided the pole into the fire— "but *my* wife is a natural, so be careful what you say about her and in what tone you say it in."

For a reason she couldn't explain, she was rather pleased with his possessive words about her. She waited patiently while the glass heated again. Then instead of leading her back to the table, he nudged her to the right. "Now where are we going with it?"

"Somewhere else. I have to add in an extra step now and then so you don't best me with your astonishingly good glass blowing abilities." He led her to a table where there was a row of metal bowls lined up and then lowered the hot bulb of glass into the first one. "Slate grey, the same as your eyes."

Amelia's heart slammed in her chest and emotion clogged her throat. Who knew his picking such an ordinary color could affect her so? "How does this add color?"

He lifted his left elbow as high as he could without letting go of the pole. "Go down there and see."

She released the pole and ducked under his arm, then walked down to the end of the eight-foot pole where he was "dipping" the glass bulb into a bowl of tiny pieces of grey glass, making some of the little pieces stick to the bulb in a way that reminded her of sprinkling salt or pepper over a meal. There were little flecks of glass all over the hot piece of glass on the pole, but it didn't cover it. Strange. "To the fire again?"

"Not yet. More shaping." He waited for her to come back over to him then helped her walk the pole back to the steel table. "This time I'm going to roll it for you, but I want you to blow in the end."

She nodded once, uneasy. What if she didn't do it right and ruined the whole thing?

"You'll do just fine," he assured her, spinning the pole.

Amelia bent her knees and brought her lips to the end of the pole and softly blew while Elijah held the curved iron and kept the pole rolling, in place this time instead of across the table and back.

"All right," he said, lifting the pole. He helped her return to the fire to gather more hot glass. "Let's go shape it again."

And they did; twice more. Then they went back to the row of bowls filled with colored glass. "Blue this time."

He lifted his gaze from the burning ball of glass on the end to meet her eyes. "I was enjoying the grey."

"And *I* will get to enjoy seeing the blue swirled together with the grey."

The left side of his mouth tipped up and he visibly swallowed. "All right. Blue it is."

She made him dip the bulb into the bowl of blue shards again until she was satisfied the amount of blue—to match *his* eyes—equaled the amount of grey he'd already blended in, then helped roll and shape again.

"How in the world do you know how to do this?" Amelia asked more as a distraction from his closeness and the sensations he stirred in her rather than genuine curiosity.

He blew a long, deep breath into the glass, making the bubble inside grow significantly. Pleased, he removed his mouth. "My father."

"Pardon me?" His father had been a baron, not a craftsman. Surely he hadn't asked Cook to heat the fires in the kitchen high enough to mold glass.

Rolling out the pole, he said, "My father used to tell me that a gentleman needed a special talent. Something unique and unusual."

Memories of his father flooded her mind. Nearly as scientifically bent as Alex and always the perfect gentleman, she had a hard time believing he'd convince his son to break the rules of Society and learn a trade. "Why?" she asked at last, unable to stop herself.

"To woo the young ladies."

A peal of uncontrollable laugher erupted from her mouth. Those were *definitely* his father's words. No disputing that. "And what are your brothers' talents?"

He got some more glass from the fire. "I have no idea. I don't think either actually has one."

"Are you saying you're the only son who listened to his father."

"Yes, ma'am." He walked down to the end of the pole and this time instead of picking up one of those rounded cast iron pieces he'd been using to form the bulb as she rolled it, he picked up what appeared to be a thick cloth of some sort. "We're almost done," he murmured, motioning for her to keep the pole in place as she rolled it. "The other two might have *some* sort of talent, but neither as interesting as this one, wouldn't you say?"

"For once, Elijah Banks, we are in perfect agreement."

He scoffed. "We've agreed on things before."

"That's right. We both agreed that Henry cheats at draughts."

He blew one last breath into the pole, then picked up a pair of tongs and used them to do something to the top. "We've agreed about other things, too."

"Such as?" she murmured, watching intently as he expanded the glass near the top of the bowl just enough to stretch it out equally all the way around but not break it from where it attached to the end of the pole. His talent was beyond interesting. It was fascinating.

He dropped the tongs and picked up another tool which he then scraped along the "neck" of the glass just below where it attached to the pole but above where he'd just made the glass flare. He dropped that tool and picked up a pair of dirty, brown gloves and a wooden block. "I need you to hold the pole as tightly as you can."

"All right." She gripped the pole as best she could and watched in amazement as Elijah placed one gloved hand under the bowl, gripped the wooden block with the other, then brought the piece of wood down against the glass with a quick snap, breaking their creation from the end.

He held it up and inspected it. "Now we just need to heat the rim, then place it in the oven over there to cool."

"How long does it take to cool?"

"Usually just a day, but with how large this bowl is, I think it'd be best to wait two." He looked over Amelia's shoulder. "What do you think, Ian?"

"I think that piece will be staying here, is what I think."

"Not this time," Elijah said, heating the rim and smoothing out the glass. "This one belongs to Mrs. Banks."

The old man scoffed. "You've never wanted to keep one before. You always let me sell them. And for a fine coin, I might add."

Elijah shrugged. "I never had anyone in mind to give one to before. Now I do."

Mr. Ian looked at Amelia and lifted his bushy brows. "I can see that. A beautiful bowl for a beautiful young lady, and all that." He twisted his lips. "You younger fellows are all the same."

"Oh, and how's that?" Elijah asked, opening the door to the cooling oven.

"Besotted."

~Chapter Nineteen~

Guilty as charged. Elijah was most certainly besotted, but now was not the best time to admit to such.

"We'll be back day after tomorrow for the bowl." Elijah narrowed his eyes on the man. "And it had better be here."

Ian waved him off. "You know I'd never steal from you."

"I know that." Elijah unrolled his sleeves and secured his cuffs. "I also know you might try to convince me to sell it next time I come in."

"That, I can promise."

Elijah shrugged on his blue coat and offered his arm to Amelia. "I don't know about you, but I'm swiftly becoming gutfounded. Shall we go see about some cake now?"

"That'd be wonderful."

Elijah paused. Why was she hesitating? "It's not a punishable offense to eat a piece of cake. Or two."

"I know, but I'm not feeling very well."

Her cheeks did look flushed and her hair was plastered to the front of her forehead. He assumed that was just because it was hot in here, not because she was feeling ill. "Do you need to go lie down?"

"No, I think some fresh air will help. But I don't feel like eating cake right now."

"Forget about the cake, let's go for a walk." He opened the back door to the shop and helped her out. It was the fastest way out. He cursed himself. He should have known not to bring her there. It was hot and musty, not to mention cramped. "Would you like to take a small picnic down to the pond?"

"We didn't bring a hamper."

"And if we had?"

She shrugged. "Then I guess we could go on a picnic."

"Excellent." He pointed to a little white brick building up the street. "It's the best restaurant in Bath. We'll see if Marge can make us up a picnic hamper."

"Mr. Banks," a robust woman with bright red cheeks hollered when they entered. She came around the table and waddled over to them. "My, ye look more handsome than the last time I saw ye."

Elijah made a show of kissing her hand, just as he always did, hiding his grin when she blushed. "It's good to see you again, too." He turned to the side and gestured toward Amelia. "Marge, I'd like for you to meet my wife, Lady Amelia Banks. Amelia, this is Marge, she is the cook in this fine establishment."

Marge's cheeks flushed a darker red. "It's so nice to meet you! It's about time this one took a wife." She lowered her voice to a stage whisper and said, "Between yous and mes, I didn't think he'd ever find a young lady to settle on. I was gittin' worried, I'd have to marry him meself."

Amelia grinned at her, sending a jolt of desire straight through Elijah. He loved seeing her happy. Genuinely happy, not forcing herself to be. And for some reason, she'd found great humor in Marge's words and he didn't dare take that away from her.

"Tell me, dear, is e bein' a good husband?"

Before Amelia could answer, and lead them into an uncomfortable conversation for all, Elijah spoke up. "We've come for sandwiches."

"Takin' yer bride on a picnic, is ye?"

"That was my plan. But first we need the sandwiches."

Marge screwed her face up and wagged a finger at him. "Ye best not be forgettin' yer manners now or ye'll be gittin' a few extra ingredients on yer sandwich."

Elijah's lips turned up in disgust. There were few things he hated to eat more than horseradish and cabbage. Both of which Marge knew he hated. "I'll be good, I swear it."

"Very well," she said, wiping her hands on her apron. "Why don't ye and yer lovely bride sit o'er there and wait. It'll just be a few minutes."

Elijah pulled the chair out for Amelia before taking a seat himself. "This won't take too long." Her face was still flushed and her hair was beyond repair. From the corner of his eye he saw Mr. Goodman, a reputable messenger from the area, sitting in one of the tall chairs at the counter. He'd suspected it was Goodman who'd left the random missives for him at Watson Estate, but knew better than to question the man about whom they'd come from. Likely, he didn't know and if word got back to the original sender that Elijah had been sniffing around for information, the messages might stop coming. And that was the last thing he needed. "Wait here, I'll be right back."

Amelia nodded and fiddled with the strap of her reticule.

"Goodman," Elijah said by way of greeting, clapping him on the back.

The other man jumped nearly a foot in the air, his green eyes wide with curiosity, or perhaps panic? He'd always been a bookish sort. He wore old, scuffed-up spectacles and always had a tome thicker than a brick with him when not out carrying messages. He usually kept to himself, never speaking unless spoken to. And even then, he'd use the fewest amount of syllables possible to answer.

"Two lemonades, please," Elijah called to Marge.

"Aye. I'll put them in yer hamper."

Elijah glanced back over at Amelia. She didn't look any better now than she had when they left Ian's. She needed to go home. "I'll take them now. I don't think we'll be going on a picnic today. Just bring the food over to us when you finish." He made his way behind the counter and walked back to the ice room.

"What do ye think yer doin'?" Marge demanded.

Elijah flashed what he knew to be his most charming smile at her. "Getting my wife some lemonade." He picked up two glasses and quickly filled them with the cool lemonade from the silver pitcher she stored in the ice room.

"Well, as long as it's for yer wife."

Elijah grinned at her again, then picked up the two glasses and walked out of the kitchen. He caught Mr. Goodman's gaze and nodded to him as he took the glasses over to Amelia. "It shouldn't be much longer," he said, taking his seat. "I told her we'll just eat here and go home, but while we wait, you should drink this, it will help you feel better."

With no regard whatsoever to any sort of manners befitting a young lady of her station, Amelia wrapped her fingers around the glass so tightly her fingertips turned white, then lifted it to her mouth and took three large gulps before setting the now empty glass down.

He'd never admit this to her, but he was rather impressed with the way she'd consumed her drink. It was enough to make any boy jealous. But he also knew she hadn't done that in an attempt to best him or issue a challenge. He picked up both of their glasses and switched them.

Amelia darted her pink tongue through her lips and reached for the glass he'd given her. "Thank you."

"I'm sorry."

Amelia's hand froze, the glass halfway to her lips. "Pardon me, did you say something?"

"I said I'm sorry," he repeated hoarsely. He hadn't meant to make her unwell. He'd just wanted to have a peaceful and enjoyable day with his wife, not make her ill.

"For what?"

He blinked. "For not noticing you weren't feeling well sooner and taking you out of there." Had he been paying a bit more attention to how she might be feeling and not so concerned with impressing her with his talents (or enjoying the way her body felt pressed against his, if he were to be completely honest), he could have gotten her out of there sooner and she wouldn't be ill.

She didn't respond. At least not with words. Her eyes were

wide with wonder, her head cocked slightly to the side, and her eyebrows knit together. She looked almost as if she'd just witnessed a dog walking down the street, standing upright on his hind legs and was trying to puzzle out how such a thing was possible. Unfortunately, for how much time he'd spent reading people's facial expressions in an effort to know what they were thinking or planning, he hadn't a single idea what would make her look that way.

"Why are you staring at me that way?"

"Because I just witnessed a miracle." She set the glass of lemonade back on the table with a soft thud. "That, or the heat from that room has baked my brain."

He grimaced. "I hope not."

"I do, too. The prospect of witnessing a miracle is far more preferable."

"And what miracle would that be?"

"You just issued an apology without the word 'if'."

Elijah stared at her, dumbfounded. "How is that a miracle?"

"A miracle is a rare and inexplicable event that happens only by some sort of higher power, and that seems to fit the description of your apology."

"No, not a miracle. Sincere."

"Aha!" Her silver eyes sparkled with amusement. "I knew you'd never meant any of those other apologies."

"Do you blame me?" He withdrew his handkerchief from his breast pocket and wiped up the ring of water her glass had left on the table before she got her gown wet. "My mother used to make me apologize for the silliest things."

"Silliest things, you say? I don't seem to recall finding it silly when you tied a stick in my hair."

He couldn't help but laugh at the memory of seeing her stand up after one of her many impromptu picnics she insisted on bringing out to him and Henry only to find a long, thick stick swaying from the end of her braid.

"Or what of the time when I was fifteen and Henry asked to see my book and removed a page while you plagued me with ridiculous questions about why my eyebrows were a little darker than my hair and if I was sure my hair was naturally this color?" She grabbed a fallen lock and brought it before her face. "And how could I have possibly turned my hair this color?"

"I don't know." Elijah shifted in his seat. How many times as a boy had he considered her hair such a mundane color as brown, or even worse: mud brown. Neither of those adjectives did her beautiful hair justice. It was a deep, rich mahogany. And truth be told, his fingers itched to touch it. "If we were so beastly to you, why did you keep coming around?" He swore under his breath. He had no right to ask her that. She'd told him the answer to that so many times back then and it was for his own selfish reasons now that he'd asked her again. Just once more to hear her tell him that she loved him then, even if she didn't now. His stomach knotted; painfully so."Never mind."

She offered him a wobbly smile and looked just past his left shoulder. "I suppose I thought you two teasing me all the time was better than having no friends at all."

The way her lower lip quivered as she said those words tore at his heart. How could he have been so careless and cruel to her? Instinctively, he reached across the table and took her hands in his. "Amelia, I'm sorry. So very sorry. I—I—I—" He racked his brain for the right thing to say, but nothing seemed adequate. He'd never dreamed he'd actually hurt her. "I never meant to hurt you. Please know that. I only did those things because— Are you crying?" he choked. Gads this was worse than he thought.

She shook her head, but said nothing; her eyes glistened with unshed tears.

He had the strangest urge to reach across the table and pull her onto his lap. He wanted to hold her and reassure her that he hadn't meant any harm. What had once started out as boyish behavior had one day turned into something else. Wait. He scanned her face. Her eyes were red with two rivulets of tears streaming from the corners now, her cheeks were red, and her lips were moving as if she were fighting to hold her composure. Odd, she wasn't sniffling... "You're having me on!"

Amelia pulled her hand from his and wiped her eyes with the tips of her fingers. "Yes, I was, and if I made you feel even a speck of remorse, then it was worth it!"

"Oh, you're good."

"Thank you." She brought her hands to her sides and grabbed both sides of her skirt and pulled it to the side a bit and dipped her head, as if to do a mock curtsey.

I love you. He wanted so badly to say it. It was little things like besting him and then boasting about it that made him love her all the more. Instead, he craned his neck as if by doing so, he'd be able to see Marge in the kitchen. "I wonder what's taking her so long."

"She had to go out back and harvest the cabbage for your sandwich."

Yes, indeed, he was the besotted fool Ian claimed him to be who loved his wife to distraction.

~ Chapter Twenty ~

Amelia placed her hand on her stomach in a futile attempt to make it settle down. All around her, finger foods were consumed, tea was poured and all the ladies of Elijah's relation chatted.

But Amelia wanted none of it. She just wanted to go lie down and pray when she woke up her monthly flux would have started. As it was, she'd been having all the signs of the impending condition without the most crucial part.

Tears welled in her eyes. That could only mean one thing.

"Are you feeling all right, dearest?" Edwina asked, coming to sit next to her.

"Of course," she lied.

Edwina's brown eyes softened. "Is there something we might be able to do to help?"

At those words, the entire room grew quiet. Eerily quiet, to be exact.

Amelia fidgeted. All eyes were on her now. "No." She sighed. "It's a female complaint, I'm afraid."

A couple of ladies nodded their understanding and offered her a polite smile before turning back to their tea.

Edwina wasn't so easily put off. "Come, let's go chat."

Amelia hesitated. The last thing she wanted to do was draw more attention to herself, but the determined look in Edwina's eyes gave her little choice so Amelia made her excuses to the room as Edwina looped their arms together and led her out of the room and down the hall to the library.

"You owe me, you know," Edwina said without preamble as soon as she shut the door.

Amelia's eyes widened. "Owe you? What do I owe you for?"

"Saddling me with the nickname of Weenie," Edwina said

144

with a stoney face and a bit of a frown.

Amelia sputtered with laughter. "I didn't do that. You did that to yourself."

"I'll grant you I might have overreacted a touch, but it was because of you and your mispronunciation of my name that it came to be." She made a face to show her utter disgust for the nickname her brothers called her.

"Sorry, Edweeena," Amelia said, trying not to laugh. Amelia would never forget the day Edwina had first joined her brothers outside to play. She'd been five, six at most, and had insisted her brothers allow her to join their game. They wouldn't of course. Amelia had brought over a picnic that day, and trying to emulate the way Regina had always treated her, Amelia invited Edwina to join her for a picnic instead. Unfortunately, she'd just popped a blackberry in her mouth when she said, "Edwina, won't you sit down with me?"

"My name's not Edwina," said the little girl with golden curls and a pretty pink dress as she put her hands on her hips and stamped her foot. "It's pronounced Edweena."

Like older brothers were wont to do, Elijah and Henry had laughed at the absurdity of Edwina's reaction and Amelia had been mortified, rushing to assure her she'd only mispronounced her name because she'd been eating. That only made the girl's older brothers laugh more. One of them, Amelia would never know which, because she was too flustered to pay attention, said, "Settle down, Weenie, we all know—"

His words were cut off when a little waif of a girl ran into him, tackling him to the ground. From then on, she rarely heard any of her brother's call Edwina anything other than Weenie. She'd wondered once or twice over the years if the nickname hadn't come from something else, something that had happened before this incident due to the strong reaction Edwina had had. But never mind what the real story was or exactly how Elijah and Henry explained such an unusual nickname to the rest of their family, as far as Edwina was concerned, it was Amelia who'd been responsible for the awful fate that had befallen her.

"Would you like me to tell Elijah to stop?"

"No. It's far too late for that." She smoothed her long, blue skirt. "But you can make it up to me another way."

Amelia's stomach would have roiled if it hadn't done so already. She didn't like where this was going. "What do you want?"

Edwina's face softened, genuine concern now evident in her brown eyes. "Just tell me what's wrong."

"I already did," Amelia said between clenched teeth. "I'm having a female complaint."

"No, you're not."

Amelia snorted softly.

"You're not *just* having female complaints," Edwina amended. "I've known you longer than anyone else here, excluding my mother and brothers. You were like the sister I never had when we were younger, Amelia. I used to dream of being as witty and clever as you and besting my brothers." A wistful smile took her lips, then vanished. "I know something isn't right. Just tell me what it is and I'll see if I can help you."

"You can't." And that was the truth.

"You don't know that if you don't tell me," Edwina pointed out. She clasped her hands in front of her. "Did something happen on your outing with Elijah yesterday?"

Yes. She'd fallen more in love with Elijah, a man she could never fully have. "No, nothing like you're thinking."

Edwina lifted her brows. "And how do you know what I'm thinking?"

It was hard for Amelia to see Edwina as anyone other than the little sister of her only playmates. But she *was* a lady now, and a married one at that. How ironic the once young girl Amelia had given her old dolls and frocks to was now the more experienced of the two. "I don't know what you're thinking," she said at last.

"I didn't think you did." She found a spot on the settee and patted the cushion next to her. "Anything you tell me won't leave this room."

Oh, her secret would leave this room. Perhaps not today, but soon enough. Amelia sat down and took a deep breath. Who could she trust if not her own sister-in-law? She took another deep inhale. Perhaps telling Edwina would be a good thing. She'd had a child not so long ago, she'd know what to expect. Not to mention, she was Elijah's sister. Amelia might have played with him more as a child than his sister had, but likely Edwina knew him better and might be able to offer her help.

She bit her lip. Was it worth the risk of losing Edwina as a trusted friend? Because that was a very genuine possibility. Edwina might like her well enough now, but when she learned the truth, and how it would affect someone Edwina loved, would she dismiss Amelia? It was a risk, one she needed to take. Keeping it to herself was going to kill her.

"Earlier," she started, fidgeting, "when I said I had a female complaint, I might have been misunderstood."

There, she'd said it, and now she was too nervous to even wrap her hair around her finger, let alone look at her sister-in-law's face! Would Edwina laugh and dismiss her statement, claiming it was far too early for her to know if she'd conceived Elijah's child? Or would she speculate and come to the correct conclusion? If she did, would she cut and scorn her? It wouldn't be anything less than Amelia deserved.

"Are you certain?" Edwina's voice reflected her eyes: no condemnation or pity, only compassion.

Her stomach was unsettled. Her breasts felt swollen and sensitive. Her emotions went from one extreme to the other so fast she was certain she was a good candidate for Bedlam. All the signs that she was pregnant were there and the one indicator that she wasn't had yet to make an appearance. Tears stung her eyes, blurring her vision and she nodded. "Fairly certain, yes."

Two gentle arms came around her. "It'll all be all right, Amelia, I promise."

How could she make such a promise? She couldn't. For as much as Edwina wanted to be reassuring, Amelia couldn't be reassured.

"Does Elijah know?" Edwina whispered in her ear.

Amelia shook her head, unable to speak.

"It'll be all right, Amelia, I know it will be. Elijah isn't the kind —" Her words died on her tongue, replaced with a gasp as her body tensed.

Amelia didn't want to look. But she had to. She had, no *needed*, to know who'd just happened upon them and overheard her biggest secret.

Slowly, she turned her head and almost had an identical reaction to Edwina, only she did more than gasp and tense, all of her blood drained to her toes.

Henry.

She didn't know why, but for some reason it seemed worse that it would be Henry who might have overheard than if Elijah had. Of course it wouldn't have been ideal for Elijah to have heard that way, but at least he'd have heard and her secret would be revealed. Now, even more people knew than she'd intended and she'd be forced to tell Elijah tonight, Henry would demand it.

"Weenie," he said quietly, crossing his arms. "Your husband was looking for you. I assume Alex wants him to play chess again or some such nonsense and he's looking for you so he doesn't have to play."

Edwina lowered her eyes in a silent apology, then released her hold on Amelia.

Instinctively, Amelia reached for her friend and patted her arm as if now she was the one reassuring her that it would all work out. Perhaps not the way that Amelia once dreamed everything would be, but now there would be no more uncertainty or suspense.

The two ladies exchanged a look, then Edwina quietly slipped out of the library, leaving the door slightly ajar.

"Henry."

"Amelia."

Amelia clasped her hands in front of herself, not sure what to say.

"Would you like to sit by the window? The settee over there is far more comfortable than the one here by the door."

His words were anything but an invitation, but neither were they a coldhearted demand. There was certainly something unusual about him today.

Without a word, Henry uncrossed his arms and fell into a chair not far from where she'd just moved. "Has my brother done something to upset you?"

Amelia started. Not only had he not asked her what she thought he might, his tone had been softer than usual. "P-pardon?"

"Elijah. Has he done something to you or did the two of you have a quarrel?"

"No." What on Earth was this coxcomb talking about?

Henry stretched his long legs out in front of himself and crossed his ankles. "And have you thought any more about what I told you the other day?"

Amelia snapped her brows together. What *was* he talking about? Oh. Elijah's supposed secret. "You mean that he blows glass?"

Henry looked at her as if she'd just grown a pair of horns. "No."

She forced a shrug. "That's the only secret I learned about him yesterday."

Scowling, Henry said, "That's all you learned?"

"Yes. We spent the entire day together, Henry. Don't you think if there was a secret to uncover about Elijah, I'd have ferreted it out?"

"If you spent all day together, I'd think you would have," he mumbled. "Just give it more thought and try again."

She scowled. What did he think this was, a business opportunity for her to ponder over? "No, Henry, I haven't given it nearly as much thought as you think I should have. Quite frankly, I don't think he has a secret. I honestly believe he'd have told me if he did."

"Oh, he would have, would he?" He scoffed. "Everyone has a secret, Amelia. One they want to keep buried. You just need to dig a little deeper to uncover it."

"And what is *your* secret?"

His lips thinned and it appeared he had no intention of answering her, then in a voice barely above a whisper, he said, "I used to be insanely jealous of my own brother."

"Because of his title?"

"No. I never cared about that." Henry fiddled with his cuff. "Actually, it was about you."

She pointed to herself. "Me?"

He nodded once, still playing with his cuff. "You used to chase after Elijah and shower him with your attentions. I guess—" He shrugged as if that were a perfectly acceptable way to end a sentence.

"But you didn't like me," she pointed out, her mind still racing, trying to puzzle out how in the world he could have possibly been jealous. "You used to tell Elijah all the time how you had all the luck between the two of you because you didn't have me on your heels."

"I know."

"You—you also used to throw snowballs at me harder than you did at him and even put a dead fish in my picnic hamper."

"I know. That's how a boy tries to get a girl's attention," he said, meeting her eyes again.

"But why?"

"I already told you, I was jealous that you only paid attention to him."

Good grief. This was a conversation she'd never dreamed of

having. "Yes, I understand that part. But how was tricking me into eating a worm or hiding my shoes on top of the conservatory supposed to gain you the right kind of attention?"

"How does chasing a boy all around the lawn, screaming like a gypsy that when you catch him you're going to kiss him gain you his favorable attention?" He slid his right leg up and rested his ankle on top of his left knee. "I think you've found your answer."

"Why didn't you just tell me?"

"Would it have mattered if I had?"

She closed her eyes. It had been because Elijah had been the one who allowed her to join their games without too much of a fuss and had taken her side against his brother that she'd initially gravitated toward him. But it had been his similar sense of humor and their ability to hold a conversation that had kept her attracted more to Elijah than Henry. Henry was as handsome as Elijah, but he was far too cryptic and quiet, and nearly unapproachable at times where she was concerned. It wasn't that he acted as if he didn't like her, he just seemed indifferent toward her when she was in the room. Yes, indifferent, that was a good way to describe it.

"That's what I thought," he said quietly. He smiled. "It doesn't matter, Amelia. My interest in you is the equivalent of your interest in me: we're just friends. That's all you and I can ever be, and not just because you're married to my brother, but because that special spark isn't there between us." He raked his hand through his hair and swallowed uncomfortably. "I was at your wedding, too. I could have just as easily been the one to convince you to run off with me. But that's not what either of us would have wanted, was it? While I had some strange sort of jealousy for Elijah being the object of all of your affections, I realized sitting in that sanctuary, that's all it ever was. I didn't actually have feelings of the romantic variety for you."

"Well, thank you, Henry; this is just the conversation every young lady longs to have. So eloquent and flattering."

He looked as impassive as he always did. "I'm not the best

with words, you should know that by now. So ignore the not-so-flattering parts and think about the others."

"Must you always talk in riddles?"

"No, I don't have to. But it's more fun this way."

Of course he'd think so.

"Just think about what I said. Everyone has a secret—even Elijah."

"Why don't you just tell me what it is then," she hedged.

He stood. "It's not my secret to tell."

"Does that mean..." she started hopefully.

"Does that mean what?"

Her face flushed. Leave it to Henry to make her say it. "My secret, is it safe?"

Henry quirked a brow. "I wasn't aware that I knew any secret of yours."

"Yes, you do."

"Ah, that secret." He leaned in close as if he were about to make some profound statement that she alone were fortunate enough to hear. "Amelia, that secret isn't a secret at all—"

The blood rushed from her head and the room spun. It wasn't? "Does Elijah know?" she blurted.

He rolled his eyes and gave a shake of his head. "No. He's probably the only one who doesn't, though."

Amelia's already unsettled stomach lurched. She was going to shoot the cat. There was no way to hold it in. Franticly, her eyes searched the room for something to retch into, her heart was pounding so hard it just might leap out of her chest.

"Are you all right? You look as if you're about to spew."

Any other time Amelia might have done her best to give him an icy look for being so vulgar in her presence. But the truth was, she *was* about to spew and if she didn't find a receptacle quickly enough— No. She wouldn't even entertain the thought.

"Truly, it isn't the worst fate in the world to be in love with one's husband."

"What?" she choked out. Surely she hadn't heard him right over the roar of her blood pounding in her ears.

Henry reached over and slid a chamber pot out from behind a tall potted plant, then handed it to her. "I never thought you were one for theatrics."

"I'm not. It's just...well, what exactly did you hear?"

"That Weenie is still blaming you for her nickname all these years later; and still trying to use it to her advantage, I might add."

Amelia scowled. "Anything else?"

"No."

Amelia's grip tightened on the side of the porcelain she held. Was he telling her the truth or was this the way he kept people's secrets safe, such as Elijah's? She released her death grip on the chamberpot. It didn't matter. If he was willing to keep her secret, then it was as good as if he hadn't heard it. And that was one thing to be said about Henry. He might come across as distant and boorish sometimes, but he always kept his word.

She placed the chamberpot on the floor beside her and stood up. Brushing out her skirt, she said, "Very well. I shall speak with Elijah tonight."

"Good. It's about time."

She sucked in a sharp breath. "What is that to mean?"

His lips tipped up in the same lopsided smile Elijah had—except his didn't make her heart race and her blood boil. "Just that it's time the two of you talked. You both might learn something."

~Chapter Twenty-One~

"You need to go find your wife. Now."

Elijah snapped his head up to face his brother. "What the devil took you so long?"

Henry found a seat on the leather divan. "I was having the most fascinating conversation."

Elijah scowled. "With whom?"

"Your wife."

Elijah's scowl deepened. "And what did the two of you discuss?"

"You."

Elijah jabbed a finger at his chest. "Me? What the devil for?"

Henry grabbed a pillow and set it at the far end of the divan, then rested his head on it as if he were truly about to take a nap right here and now.

"Well?"

Henry clasped his hands behind his head. "Why don't you go ask her yourself?"

"Because I'm asking you," he bit off. Amelia and Henry had never gotten along as well as he and Amelia had, and while he knew Henry didn't have any ill feelings for Amelia, he'd often wondered if perhaps the same might not be true regarding Amelia. Considering how coldly Henry had always come off where she was concerned, it wouldn't be without warrant that one might think so. "What did you and my wife talk about? You didn't upset her, did you?"

"*I* didn't."

"Are you implying that I did?"

Henry crossed his ankles and shifted to get more comfortable.

"Perhaps inadvertently." He sighed. "You really need to do your duty, Elijah. If not for her sake, then at least for everyone else's."

Elijah bit back a vile curse. "Who did she tell?"

"Edwina."

Relief coursed through him. "Edwina won't tell anyone. Lord knows enough gossip has flown about her own husband that she's more likely to jump onto a bed of rusty nails with her bare feet than gossip." He crossed his arms and lowered his lashes. Perhaps he should just tell her the truth. All of it. She *was* owed it, after all. No. If he told her she might get herself into danger. His heart constricted. He had to keep her from knowing. But just until the men were apprehended, then he'd retire and could tell her. But not until then.

"Edwina might not tell, but it doesn't mean that she wants to be burdened with such a large secret."

Elijah loosened his cravat. "Don't worry about that. I'll take care of it."

"Nonetheless, you'd do well to put Amelia's mind at ease before she confides in someone else."

Elijah's grasp on the coded paper he held tightened. Dash it all if his brother wasn't correct. If she'd told Edwina, she might not hesitate to confide in someone else or ask questions about what to expect while she was increasing. Panic mounted in his chest. He *had* to do something. Sadly there was nothing to do. He'd made her a promise and though his breaking it would be for her own good (and there was no need to lie to himself, he'd enjoy making love to her), he just couldn't bring himself to break his word to her.

"Confound it all," he muttered in frustration. Elijah extended his foot and kicked his brother in the boots. "Don't you be thinking of going to sleep over there. We still have this missive to puzzle out together. I'm ready to catch these two and be done with it."

"All right. Read it to me again."

"'*Where I be/ There I pray/ That He be there/ Right beside/ Thy maiden fair.*'" Elijah dropped the slip of paper. "It reads more like a warning than a clue."

Henry opened one blue eye. "A warning?"

"Yes. I still don't understand all of it, but the author of this note writes he with a capital H. It's been a while since Mr. Fink first taught us about pronouns, but aren't they all supposed to be lowercase?"

"Except when referring to God."

"That's exactly what I was thinking. Also, he mentions praying to Him," he added beneath his breath. That should have been enough to give it away the first time he read it. *Since when had he become as obtuse as Alex, missing everything that's obvious?*

"Since you married Amelia and became frustrated that she didn't fall right into your bed."

Elijah grabbed the pillow from under Henry's feet and threw it at his head. "That's enough. Now, let's think about this some more." He frowned. "All I have is that he's praying that God will keep someone safe. But who?"

"Doesn't it say *thy maiden fair* in the last line?"

"Yes, but I don't think that's meant literally—"

"It also didn't occur to you until today that the H in he was capitalized."

Elijah crossed his arms. "Oh, and you'd already solved that little mystery, had you?"

"No. But I don't claim to be a mastermind, either."

"No. You prefer to let my brain do this type of work while yours dreams about horseflesh."

Henry sat up. "This isn't my fault, Elijah."

"Isn't it? If I remember correctly, it was you who agreed to take this mission. Mr. Robinson had told us we were finished and all charges would be dropped after we helped end the illegal whiskey coming to Exmouth from France. We could have been done with all of this and living respectable lives, but you voluntarily took on this task."

Henry's face grew dark and shuttered. "It was hard to say no, considering what we saw in India."

Snatches of memories of their time in India flashed in Elijah's head. Young girls, some Indian, some from England, France, Spain or anywhere else in western Europe, all far too young to make decisions for themselves, had been forced into the life of prostitution. Barely dressed and covered with rouge, these young girls would walk the dirty streets, trying to find a paying customer. "And that's why I didn't stop you," Elijah said hoarsely.

"Stop blaming me for what happened with Amelia."

"Well, if you'd done your job, we wouldn't be in this mess."

Henry scoffed. "I'm not the one who took her upstairs at Lord Nigel's house."

Elijah's face warmed. "You're right, you weren't. But neither were you there to help me apprehend both men in Brighton."

"Because I didn't know they were going to be there, Elijah. I went with you to Brighton to help you find Amelia. How was I to know Twiddle Dee and Twiddle Dum were going to try to smuggle a boat load of girls off from the docks in Brighton that night?" Henry said defensively. He blew out a deep breath. "Has marriage made your brain evaporate?"

"This isn't about my marriage, Henry."

"Then what is it?"

"It's about the fact that taking this assignment was your idea and you never seem to be around when you're needed."

The muscle in Henry's cheek ticked. "That's not true."

"Yes, it is," Elijah burst out. "You wanted to take on this task and have left all the work to me."

"Oh, is that what you think I've done?" Henry demanded, his blue eyes sparkling with fire. "How quick it is that you forget about the information I've discovered regarding the escape and murder or the fact that I was the one dropping hints and searching for clues about the identity of the man who owns *Jezebel* while you were carrying Amelia upstairs and seeing her to bed. I might prefer a clear directive over puzzles, but that doesn't mean that I haven't been present when needed, Elijah."

"Yes, well, I prefer clear directives, too. Unfortunately, that is not what we got this time," Elijah fired back.

"A clear directive? Is that how you think of an agreement for a free trip from Dublin to Lancashire aboard a steam packet at one in the morning, when we could have just spent the money to stay another night and come home on a passenger ship the next day?"

Elijah tensed. "Why must you remind me of that?"

"Because you seem to enjoy reminding me that we wouldn't be in this mess if it wasn't for my agreement to help capture the two remaining men involved in the prostitution ring."

"Well, is it true?"

Henry ignored him. "Would we even be having this conversation if not for what happened with Amelia?"

No, they wouldn't. It might have been due to Elijah's young and careless decision to board a steam packet filled with one hundred barrels of whiskey heading for England's shores that made them work for the Crown in the first place. When the ship had been captured, the two brothers had almost gotten away, stopped only by a burly man who'd seen two more men fall off the side of the boat than bullets had been fired. Those two extra men had been Elijah and Henry. They swam, staying under the water as much as they could until they found a little cove about a mile away. There, waiting for them was Mr. Robinson.

He'd offered them a choice: the gaol for smuggling whiskey or work for the Crown for ten years. The decision was easy: become a spy. Fortunately—or perhaps unfortunately depending on which day you asked—the two had always been assigned to the same mission due to their ability to communicate with mere looks.

Elijah took a deep breath. "No, we wouldn't be having this conversation if Amelia wasn't involved. But you never had to come along. On the steam packet from Ireland I mean."

"I know." Henry's voice was softer than before. "But I did for the same reason you agreed to help with this one."

"Help, not solve myself," Elijah reminded him with a faint smile. He drummed his fingers on his knees. "I'm assuming this has to do with a church."

"What has to do with a church?"

Elijah gestured to the note on the table in front of him. "The chap who wrote this mentions praying, and by his other word choices, such as 'there', it makes me think he's talking about going somewhere."

"And the most logical place to go and pray is a church," Henry finished for him. He grinned. "See, I'm helping."

Elijah shook his head. Never mind that not two seconds ago Elijah had been the one to mention the church.

Henry leaned forward and put his elbows on his knees. "Do you think he means the next exchange will take place at a church?"

Elijah pursed his lips. "I suppose it's possible, but that isn't very helpful."

"The location of where the exchange is to take place isn't very helpful," Henry said in a tone dripping with sarcasm.

"Not if you don't know the town, you coxcomb. There are dozens of churches that line the coast. It could be any one of them."

Henry nodded slowly. "Perhaps since he doesn't give us a new city, we could assume he's still speaking of Dover?"

"I don't think so. Surely they wouldn't plan another—" He stopped abruptly. His last encounter with the men wasn't at the party in Dover, but in Brighton. Only, they hadn't had any clue leading them to Brighton. Elijah had just happened to overhear someone talking about the *Jezebel*, and recognized that as the name of the boat. "All right, say he's speaking of Dover."

"He's speaking of Dover."

Elijah shot him a pointed look.

Henry threw his hands in the air. "You're the one who said 'say he's speaking of Dover'. I was just following your command. I wouldn't want you to think I'm not as dedicated to solving this as you are."

Instead of strangling the insolence right out of Henry as he was tempted to do, he turned back to the note. "It can't be Dover. There are at least two churches in a city that large. Were there one that was widely known, his clue would have been enough. But since there isn't one that is more well known than the other, nor a clue where to find said church, then I don't think he's speaking of Dover."

"What about a church around here? I'm sure there's a church in Bath or even Dorset."

"I don't think so. We're not on the right side of the country. All of the girls have been sent across the Channel to the continent to be transported. It's the fastest way out of the country and to the continent."

"But they have to gather the girls first," Henry said simply. "If they'd have relied on taking girls from only the coastal villages, they'd have been caught before now."

"You have a point. This could be a gathering place, not necessarily where they're loading them on the boat." He frowned. "But that could be anywhere. Just because he sent the missive to us here, doesn't mean it's a church near here. He just knows we're staying here."

"All right so what's the first church you think of when you hear someone say they're going to church?"

"St. Gregory's in London," Elijah said automatically. "But there's not a grasshopper's chance in Mr. Henry Hirsute's cage that they'd be foolish enough to meet there."

"No, they wouldn't."

Silence filled the room. Over the past eight years, they'd help return stolen goods, shut down illegal import and sale of whiskey, and even tracked down dangerous criminals. At first, they did it to stay on this side of the Tower of London. Then after a while, it became fun. There was a sense of danger and intrigue. Then of course came the thrill of apprehending the criminal. They'd been able to travel the world. Asia, Europe, Africa, even the Americas hadn't been off limits for someone with connections such as theirs. But after their last stint in France which almost got Henry killed and shut down a major whiskey smuggling operation, Mr. Robinson had said they'd served long enough and were free to leave if they wished it. Oh, how Elijah wished it. He'd always wanted to marry Amelia and each time his directives took him back to England his first priority was to go see her.

He'd had mixed feelings about her still being unmarried. In a way, he was glad because it gave him hope that one day she'd be his wife. At the same time, he wished for her the happiness that being married would provide, but that he couldn't offer her. He was under the direction of the Crown and could be made to leave whenever they were ready to send him away or for whatever mission they needed complete. He was theirs to command about and having a wife who he couldn't be there to protect was unthinkable.

Mr. Robinson releasing them, however, changed everything. He'd planned to court her this Season. Try to win back the feelings she'd once had for him. But when Mr. Robinson approached them with the task of finding the two gentlemen who were leading up a private sex slave operation, Henry couldn't be stopped. And neither could Elijah. Just as Henry had boarded that steam packet from Dublin that cold night, Elijah couldn't fathom letting Henry do this alone. They were brothers. Twins. They worked better together, and after extracting a promise from Henry that this would be the last time, they went to see Mr. Robinson for the details.

It should be simple enough. Two gentlemen were taking young girls from England and transporting them to the conti— Elijah felt the muscles in his face fall. Two *gentlemen*. "He's not talking about a literal church."

"Pardon?"

"When Mr. Robinson came to us about taking this mission, he said *gentlemen*, not just men."

Henry frowned. "That could be any lord, his brother, son or cousin."

"Specifically, if he's a vicar or a bishop."

"Or the archbishop," Henry added.

"That's not possible."

Henry crossed his arms. "He might be a Man of God, but that doesn't mean he isn't capable of being a criminal."

"I know that. Remember Lochlan Campbell who was poisoning members of his own kirk with the communion wine?" Elijah shook off the thought. "What I meant was that the archbishop couldn't have been in Brighton that night because he married me and Amelia the next night at Templemore's estate."

"He could have ridden there overnight."

"Would you ride your horse that far at night?"

"I might if I was on the run," Henry argued. "Besides, nobody said he rode there on his own horse. He could have taken a carriage."

"But he wouldn't have done that. Not if he wanted to help release his friend."

Henry crossed his arms. "Nobody said your hostage had an accomplice to help him escape."

"They didn't have to. The bloody constable was shot in the head and his keys were stuck in the cell's lock."

"Didn't you read the report? There was also a trail of blood from the fellow's cell to the chair the constable was found in. The constable very well could have been close enough to the cell for the criminal to have reached through the bars, grabbed his gun, shot him, then taken his keys and unlocked his own cell."

"But then why was he in a chair?"

"To make it look like someone else had been there to help," Henry said with a shrug.

"But why?"

"I don't know, so we'd look for who murdered the constable?"

Elijah shook his head. Sometimes Henry's logic was just too

much. "I see what you're suggesting, but why would that benefit him if we're searching for them both already?"

"Because we have to actually catch them in the act of transporting those girls in order to try them. If there's reasonable proof of murder, however, that's all that's needed to send them to the gallows."

"So you think he framed his friend?" Elijah said flatly.

Henry nodded. "He was probably unhappy that his partner had abandoned him."

"Well, that still doesn't tell us anything useful to discovering his identity."

"You could have had one of their identities had you not beaten him so badly."

Scowling, Elijah said, "He left me no choice. When a masked man comes at you firing his gun, instinct replaces logic and asking his name and making his acquaintance is the last thing that seems to matter."

"Yes, but you didn't have to leave him bloody, swollen, and unrecognizable," Henry teased.

"And how would I have known who he was by looking at him? It wasn't until five minutes ago when I realized he was likely to be a gentleman that I thought there might be a chance that I've met him before. Prior to that, he was just another nameless criminal who needed to find the justice he deserved."

"Very well. What shall we do now?"

"I don't care what you plan to do—" Elijah took to his feet, the sun was sinking lower in the sky— "I plan to do exactly what you told me to do when you barged in, I plan to go find my wife."

~ Chapter Twenty-Two ~

Amelia awoke to the sound of a creaking door. Slowly she sat up, then frowned. Where was Elijah? Gripping one of the bed posts, Amelia stood and walked to the bedchamber door. She'd left it slightly ajar so she could hear him when he came in, but she'd still wanted to block out the sunshine that now flooded the living room because of Mr. Henry Hirsute's new spot under the open window.

She opened the door a bit more and poked her head out. "Philip?"

Her brother who'd been holding a piece of parchment abruptly put it down and smiled at her. "Amelia, it's good to see you." He lifted one of his eyebrows. Last time she'd seen him his face had still been bruised and cut, but it looked almost back to normal now. "Won't you come out here and greet your brother properly."

Amelia flushed. She'd taken off her morning gown and stockings and had taken a nap in only her shift. "I'd rather not. But next time, I will."

"Ah, the blushing bride," he said, fisting his hands at his sides. "Say, is your husband in there with you?"

"No, he's right here," Elijah said, swinging open the front door.

"Mr. Banks, so nice to see you here."

"Is it?"

"Of course. You are my sister's husband, after all."

Elijah grunted. "Is there a reason you're here?"

Philip licked his lips. "Actually there is. I've come to see that Amelia's wardrobe was delivered."

"It wasn't." Elijah crossed his arms and cocked his head to the side. "I find it a little strange that *you'd* come all the way here to see after a lady's wardrobe."

"Yes, well, she is my sister."

The two men exchanged looks. "Why are you really here, Philip?" Elijah's voice was as hard as his face appeared.

"I need a favor."

"From Amelia?" Elijah asked.

Philip nodded.

"No."

"Elijah," she hissed. It wasn't that she had any great desire to do a favor for her brother, but she didn't like him speaking for her. "Philip, my answer is no."

"Why not?" Philip demanded of her, ignoring Elijah's presence altogether.

Amelia turned her head down a little, lifted her eyebrows, gritted her teeth and then shook her head, as if to communicate to him the disaster that had happened the last time she did a favor for him.

"Oh, it wasn't so bad," Philip goaded. He gave his head a small nod in Elijah's direction. "It seems it worked out quite nicely."

Amelia didn't dare chance a look at Elijah. No matter. He probably resembled a statue with a clamped jaw and cold, unreadable eyes. "The answer is no."

"Amel—"

"She said no," Elijah said in an icy tone.

Philip pressed his lips together, color growing in his cheeks. "Very well, then." Without another word, he stalked out of the cabin.

"Did you and my brother have a quarrel," Amelia asked.

Elijah snapped his head around. "Not a genuine quarrel, more of a disagreement."

"About?"

"You."

Amelia sucked in a sharp breath. "Me?"

He nodded once. "I...er..." He twisted his lips and raked his hand through his hair. "I can't explain it."

She opened the door to the bedchamber, heedless to her state of undress. "Sure you can," she said softly. What could Elijah and Philip possibly have disagreed about concerning her?

"No. I probably shouldn't." His voice was thick.

"Shouldn't? So then you can, you just don't want to."

"You are correct."

She crossed her arms. "Why not?"

Elijah swallowed visibly, an action she hadn't seen from him in a long time. "Because he didn't want me to marry you."

***

Elijah realized his mistake as soon as he'd said it. But he just didn't care. Seeing her thus: in nothing but her transparent chemise with her arms folded under her full breasts in a way that pushed them up so far they half spilled over the lacy top of her garment sent all the blood that should be in his head straight to his groin, his pretense of being a marble statue gone. He wasn't one and he was no good at portraying one, besides. Nor did he want to be one with her. He might not want to let on to how vulnerable he was to her, but erecting a shield only made things worse.

"You wanted to marry me?"

Elijah nodded. *I didn't want you to marry Lord Friar.* The words resounded over and over in his head, but he couldn't force himself to say them, even if they would keep her inquiries quiet. Instead, he took a step toward her, then a second, and a third.

"Why?"

Because I didn't want you to marry Lord Friar. The voice inside his head yelled louder for him to say those words, to staunch her questions and perhaps spare his own pride and feelings. "So I could do this."

Her breath hitched, and he would have smiled at her if he hadn't just pressed his lips against hers.

She leaned her head back. "Wh-what are you doing?"

"Kissing you," he murmured, taking her lips in another kiss.

To his surprise and great relief, she didn't protest and kissed him back. He lifted his hands to cup her face, savoring the way her soft lips moved beneath his. Risking being rejected by her once again, he parted his lips a fraction and drew her bottom lip in between his. She gasped his name and he murmured hers, too lost in her lips to want to stop kissing her.

Suddenly her hands were up on his shoulders, but she wasn't pushing him away; rather she was clutching him tightly to her. He gently raked her lip with his teeth, then soothed it with his tongue, her grip tightening on his shoulders and her lips parting more. Slowly, so not to startle her, he pushed his tongue into her mouth. She tasted sweet, like fruit and cream. He swept across her mouth, exploring her cheeks, tongue and even her teeth. He brushed his thumb against her cheek, silent encouragement for her to do the same.

As if she were unsure, she slowly slid her tongue into his mouth to tangle with his for a moment. His mouth left hers, trailing openmouthed kisses all the way to her jawline then behind her ear where he placed a single kiss just behind her earlobe. She sighed and leaned her head to the side, granting him full access to the side of her neck, which he gladly kissed.

Praying she wouldn't freeze up on him like she had in the past, he moved his hands to the top of her chemise. Taking her left shoulder strap between his thumb and forefinger, he eased it closer to the edge of her shoulder, following its path with his parted lips. He kissed the last inch of skin at her left shoulder, then repeated the action on the right, his excitement growing ever stronger as her skin grew warmer and more flushed with each of his kisses. When he reached the edge, it took all the self control he possessed to resist the urge he had to release both straps and let her chemise fall, revealing her fully to him. But he couldn't do that. Not without permission. Not without knowing this was what she wanted.

"Amelia," he rasped.

"Yes?" Her grey eyes were wide and her pink lips swollen.

He swallowed past the gravel in his throat. "May I?"

***

May I? Why was it that all of the important questions were so short, and yet would change their entire lives together? She searched his blue eyes. They were darker than usual, hooded even; and most certainly intent. His face looked hard, but not in the same impassive way he'd looked all of those times when he'd approached her before. This time his jaw was clamped and that elusive vein on his forehead that only came out in intense moments of emotion was protruding a bit. He looked uncertain and vulnerable and most importantly: interested.

The idea that he could be interested in her thrilled her and sent a wave of excitement flooding over her. Followed by a wave of uncertainty. She was nearly certain she was carrying another man's child. Of course she could tell him all of the sordid details afterwards, but would he forgive her? Would he be angry with her when he went to take her innocence only to find she wasn't chaste? No. She couldn't let him find out that way he deserved to know now. She closed her eyes to keep in the stinging tears that seemed to come more frequently than the post.

"Elijah, I must tell— Oooh." She snapped her eyes open to make sure she wasn't dreaming that Elijah had grown too impatient waiting for her decision and decided to offer her more encouragement, as if just feeling his warm mouth on the crest of her barely covered breast hadn't been enough.

"Just yes or no," Elijah murmured against her breast. Not taking his mouth from her swollen breast, he sank to his knees, then closed his mouth around the hardened peak and gently nipped it with his teeth.

A strange feeling shot through her. Then another when his tongue passed over where his teeth had just been. He pulled away and looked up at her. She'd never seen genuine desire in his eyes before, but recognized it immediately. Keeping his gaze locked with hers, he carefully slid down the other side of her chemise, the soft fabric like a gentle caress over her swollen breast and against her hardened nipple. With a swallow loud enough to wake even the heaviest sleeper, he kept his eyes trained on hers and moved his mouth next to her now exposed breast.

Hot desire shot through her as his open mouth moved over her breast. Then suddenly it felt like fire had been poured into her veins when he found what he'd been searching for. His wicked tongue flicked across the tip. Once. Twice. Then he pulled away, his hands lifting her chemise back into place.

Panic washed over her. What if this was the only chance she'd ever get? What if he rejected her or only bedded her because he was between mistresses and didn't want to bother with a bawdy house after she told him the truth? This could be the only chance she'd ever have to have him like this and curse her black soul, she wanted it more than she'd ever wanted anything before, the consequences be damned.

"Yes."

Elijah froze, his hands back on her shoulders, his fingers loosely holding onto the straps he was about to release.

Wordlessly, he took to his feet again, the hungry look in his eyes stronger than before. With a slowness that made Amelia's heart hammer so wildly in her chest that she was surprised it hadn't beat right out, he lowered both sides of her chemise. The fabric, followed by Elijah's intense gaze, glided over her sensitive skin, arousing her more, if such a thing were possible. He swallowed and his Adam's apple bobbed in his throat just as he lowered it enough to reveal her full breasts. His hands stopped moving the garment lower for a moment as his eyes drank her in thus far.

Her breasts swelled under his watchful gaze. He dropped to his knees again, then ever-so-slowly, he continued lowering her shift to the floor. "You're more beautiful than I'd imagined," he said as he took to his feet; his voice hardly more than a broken whisper.

Amelia furrowed her brows. Was that an insult or a compliment?

As if he'd read her mind, he said, "That's a good thing." Then he leaned forward and pressed a kiss between her puckered eyebrows, then at the top of her nose, then in the middle of the slope of her nose. He kissed all the way down until their lips met again.

Her hands reached forward on their own accord. He was moving too slow. If she didn't start taking his clothes off, they might be interrupted and reminded of dinner. That was the last thing she wanted. She slipped the buttons free first his coat, then reached inside and unfastened his cravat and waistcoat. He broke their kiss and stepped back just long enough for her to push his coat and waistcoat off his shoulders, remove his cravat and pull his shirt from his trousers. As if now *she* were the one moving too slow for his liking, Elijah yanked his shirt over his head.

His skin was bronzed as if he'd spent a considerable amount of time outside without his shirt. He'd been to the Mediterranean and many other exotic places, she should have expected nothing less. His skin was tight against the protruding muscles in his chest and the twin row of ripples that went down his stomach. In the middle of his chest was just a sprinkling of curling, light brown hair. Instinctively, she reached up and touched him, reveling in the way his muscles leapt beneath her touch. She glided her hands over the plane of his chest and to his broad shoulders, down his sides and across his stomach, there wasn't a part of him she didn't want to touch, all the unusually shaped scars that littered his abdomen included. Simultaneously, his hands found her body, too. They skated down her from just beside her breasts to the flare of her hips, up her back then slowly back around to cup her full breasts.

He squeezed, not hard, but not in a way that made it tickle. Perfect. His hands slowly caressed her breasts as his lips set out to find hers again. This time his kiss was more demanding, urgent.

His tongue swept through her mouth and his hard body pressed hers. She lowered her hands down to his waistband. Would it seem too forward of her to unfasten them? His thumbs brushed her pebbled nipples and she instantly knew the answer: no, he wouldn't mind at all. One. Two. Three. She slid the buttons through their holes, releasing the fall of his trousers.

He broke their kiss and removed his hands, his breathing ragged and his face slightly flushed. He bent down and tugged at the laces in his boots until they were just loose enough for him to step out of. He took off the first and tossed it to the ground with a thud, then did the same with the next. When his eyes met hers again, that savage look was still there, thrilling her to no end. He reached for her hands and placed them back where they'd been at the top of his waistband. "Continue. Please."

No more words were needed. She slipped her hands just inside the top of his trousers, and gave them a gentle tug. They came down just an inch or two. Revealing only the dips of his hips, just enough to frustrate her.

"They're stuck," Elijah rasped.

"Yes, I see that, but on what?" She'd undone all of the buttons. She ran her hands along the outer edge of his waistband, perhaps they were stuck on his hips and needed help coming down—

Elijah's fingers closed around her wrist then moved her hand down the front of his trousers.

Shock, then curiosity, took hold. Longer than her hand, thick and hard, she'd never touched anything like it before. Holding that part of him against his body, she gave his trousers another tug. Ever-the-gentleman, Elijah took mercy and helped her with the other side, then when they'd fallen to the floor, he stepped out.

She blushed. Her hand was still on his...er...body part. She abruptly let go, eliciting a small sound of vexation from Elijah. She smiled at him. Who knew *she'd* ever have this affect on anyone, especially Elijah. She reached forward and took his hand. "Come."

He waited for no further invitation and followed her to the

bed. He helped her climb in and then was there beside—then on top of—her in a matter of seconds. He positioned himself to lie between her parted legs and brought his mouth back to her chest where he tasted and kissed her. She arched into him, offering him as much of her breast as he could take. He didn't fail her, he covered one with his mouth and the other with his hand, squeezing and shaping it. She gasped his name and her fingers found his silken hair, sinking into it and holding his head against her breast. His lips closed around her nipple and his fingers around the other. Each time he licked or lightly squeezed her there, she had this strange, yet exciting sensation in her abdomen.

His mouth moved lower, down to her hip, licking a hot trail with his tongue as he went. He drew up to his knees, his other hand now finding her recently abandoned breast. In tandem, he explored them both while his mouth continued its exploration of her hips. He placed a kiss just in the dip of her hip, then on the point of her bone, then just above. She shivered.

Just when she thought she could stand no more, he began to kiss a path up the middle of her stomach, then through the valley of her breasts and all the way back to her lips. He released her breasts and repositioned himself again, this time lowering his body to rest on top of hers. He rolled just off to the side a bit and reached between them. Something broad brushed her most private flesh, exciting her in a way similar to what she'd felt the other day when Elijah touched her there. She flushed at the shameful memory, but all shame and embarrassment was banished from her mind when he brushed her again and another small wave of pleasure shot through her. Then, something pushed at her opening. She tensed, her fingers clutching his hair so tightly she feared she might pull some out. With one swift motion, he thrust in.

Her body jerked in response. That had hurt. Why, she didn't know, but it had hurt. She brought her hands to his shoulders. "Could you wait a moment, please?"

His eyes widened. "I'm sorry, Amelia. I should have warned

you," he said thickly.

"No." She shook her head violently against the pillow. "I just hadn't expected it to hurt."

He dropped a kiss on her lips. "It won't next time."

She certainly hoped it wouldn't, but couldn't be too hopeful. It had hurt this time and it wasn't supposed to, after all. She moved her hands to his shoulders, giving them a little squeeze. Their eyes locked, his were asking a question, and she hoped he could read the answer in hers.

With a terse nod, he began to move again. Slow and easy at first, then a bit quicker and more deliberate. Her fingers dug into the warm skin of his muscled shoulders as he drove into her. With each thrust, her skin grew warmer and her abdomen contracted as small sparks of excitement shot through her.

Elijah bent down and kissed her lips and then her chin, and then over to her breast. When he found the crest, her body bucked on its own accord. He moved to the other, lavishing the same attention on it. He lifted his head, his eyes so dark blue now they almost looked black. His breathing was heavy and with each thrust became louder, more labored. Then suddenly a savage grunt that sounded as if it were ripped from his chest filled the air and his body stiffened, then collapsed on top of hers.

He murmured something against her hair, but she didn't hear it, nor did she mind so much. She was perfectly content to hold him this way. She brought her hand up to sweep back the blond hair on his damp forehead.

"Don't move, I'll be back," he said a few minutes later. He moved to stand up, separating their bodies.

She felt bereft in his absence, like part of her was missing. He came back a moment later with a basin and a handkerchief. She swallowed. What would he say when he didn't find what he was looking for? Terror washed over her. He might not have noticed before, but he'd certainly notice now.

He took her right leg in his hand, and instinctively she flexed the muscles to keep them together. "Can you move your legs apart for me a little more?" He squeezed her leg, presumably to help her understand what he wanted.

Taking a deep breath, she did as he'd asked.

"There's not much, don't worry," he murmured, wiping the cloth between her legs.

That did *not* put her mind at ease. There was a reason there wasn't much. Wait. If there wasn't much, then there was *some*. Nervously, she sat up. What was down there? Perhaps her stomachache and sensitive breasts had just been a sign of her impending monthly, she thought hopefully as she craned her neck to see if perhaps that was what he was seeing.

It couldn't be. Her monthly had never been quite so...bright before. But that didn't make sense. She'd woken up with her gown crushed and the bodice gaping, and no actual memory of what had happened. Was it possible the stranger had left her chaste, after all? How could that possibly be? Perhaps she'd fallen asleep and the stranger had lost interest; or perhaps he'd been caught before something happened; or discovered she was a lady; or had some sort of male trouble, she'd heard a few of the old matrons discuss special herbs before. A million questions cycled through her mind, and all would have to go unanswered because she didn't even begin to know where to seek her answers. Whatever had happened, she didn't dare question it. She was far too grateful that Elijah had been her first and would be her only. She looked up to Elijah. He didn't look quite so well, his face had gone pale and his eyes were downcast.

A sudden sense of shame came over her and she clamped her legs back together. His eyes shot to hers. "Amelia?"

"You don't need to do this, I can take care of it."

He shook his head. "It's my honor to do so."

A shaky laugh passed her lips. "Are you cracked? An honor?"

He shook his head. "Not at all. Many bridegrooms think it's an honor to do this."

All right, so *many* bridegrooms were cracked. "Why?"

"Some feel it's their duty and a way of paying penance for the pain they've caused. Others like to do it as a means of showing respect for the wonderful gift their wife has given them."

She swallowed past the emotion in her throat. "And you?"

"For both."

"How unfortunate there isn't something similar for a wife to do to a husband." She forced an uncomfortable laugh. "Not that it'd matter, I suppose."

He dropped the handkerchief into the water. "Why not?"

She shot him a doubtful look and moved over so he could crawl into the bed next to her. "Gentlemen are never virgins on their wedding night."

"You think so, do you?" He lay back against the pillows and gathered her into his arms. "And if he were, would you take his word for it?"

Amelia stilled. Did he mean to imply... "Were you?" she blurted; too nervous to look at his face, she studied his chest hair instead.

"Yes, my dear Amelia, it was *you* who divested me of my virginity."

She would have laughed at his tone and ridiculous statement if not for the excitement she'd felt that what they'd done together was new for both of them. But it didn't make sense. He'd traveled the world over. Surely, he'd felt the need for some female companionship as her mother once explained her father's frequent visits to London. "Why?"

He kissed the top of her head. "You're the only one I wanted."

~ Chapter Twenty-Three ~

"Do you have any plans today?" Elijah murmured.

Amelia's eyes fluttered open. "Don't we need to go to— Oh dear, we missed Caroline's dinner, didn't we?"

"I'm afraid so," Elijah said, running his hand up and down her arm. He loved the way her skin was so soft and smooth compared to his. "I'm sure we could make her breakfast or her luncheon today if you're so keen on dining with my family."

She traced the muscles in his chest. "It's not that. I just feel awful that I've missed almost every day of her party."

"Don't. We weren't even originally invited guests, remember?"

She grinned at his logic. "Actually, *you* were."

"Only because I live here. And once you came to live here, you were invited, too." He ran his fingers through her hair. "Tonight is the costume ball. We'll attend that. Today, however, you are all mine."

Amelia grinned up at him, sending a jolt of desire straight to his groin. She came up on her knees, causing the sheet to fall from her body and expose her delicious body to his very hungry gaze.

He shifted. He couldn't take her again. He'd felt so guilty after what he'd done last night, he couldn't do it again. He hadn't come into the cabin yesterday bent on seduction. Just the opposite. He'd heard she'd retired and had come to check on her. But then...and then afterwards, a crushing weight of guilt had come over him. He'd had no right to take things so far without offering her the truth. She'd deserved the truth, and yet, he hadn't given it to her. He nearly snorted. It wasn't until after he'd decided not to bed her until he could explain everything that she was finally willing. And now there was a giant lie between them.

The way she'd stood before him yesterday like a siren, leading him home was too much for his resistance to bear. He'd wanted her and in a moment of clouded judgement, he'd acted without thinking.

She moved to straddle him, bringing her supple breasts within mere inches of his lips, the temptress; and then looped her arms around his neck for stability.

"Actually," he started, skating his hands up and down her back. "I wanted to take you on a picnic today."

"You did?" she murmured before kissing him.

He closed his eyes he deserved to be tempted and left wanting, that's exactly what he deserved, but she didn't deserve the same. "Amelia." He opened his eyes and tucked a lock of her silky hair behind her ear. "We need to start walking soon if we're to make it to Bath for our picnic."

"And if I don't want to go on a picnic," she asked between kisses.

"There'll be plenty of time for this later," he promised, praying he was right and she wouldn't hate him when she learned the truth. "But for now—" he rolled her onto her back and came to lie on top of her, her firm breasts pressing against his chest— "we're going to go on a picnic together and you're going to enjoy it."

She nipped his lower lip. "Oh?"

He repeated the gesture. "Yes." Mustering every ounce of strength he had, he crawled out of the bed and away from her warm body. "Is something the matter?"

"No," she said quickly, too quickly.

Elijah followed her line of vision. "A curious sort, are you?"

She flushed. "Well, you looked your fill at me yesterday," she reminded him.

Placing his hands on his hips, he said, "Feel free to do the same."

"No, thank you." She sat up. "I've seen enough."

He looked down at his erect phallus and frowned. "Is there

something not to your liking?"

"Your cockiness," she said smartly.

"Well, as long as it's my cockiness that's put you off and not my—" He shut his mouth with an audible snap, embarrassment and a small dose of shame creeping up his face. She might be his wife, but she was still a lady. "Sorry. As you know, I am my father's son."

"It's of no account, Elijah. I'm not always the proper young lady gentlemen desire. I have heard a few scandalous whispers behind some fans."

"Oh?" He lifted his eyebrows. "Do tell."

She laughed. "No. You wouldn't believe what I've heard even if I did tell you."

He shrugged. "You'd be surprised what I'd believe. I've heard plenty of gossip while in London myself." He reached forward and helped her to her feet. "Shall we dress and go on our picnic?"

"Only if you'll play the part of my lady's maid again."

"It'll be my pleasure."

And it was. It was a great pleasure to roll on her stockings, and a great disappointment to see her shift go back on. He tied her corset and helped her into her gown.

"Are you sure you've never kept a mistress? Your lady's maid skills are quite good," she said, admiring herself in the mirror.

"I'm positive." He dragged on his trousers, then his shirt. "Every country has a different way they find fashionable. I've dressed in many types of garments." That was true enough. As a spy, he always needed to blend into the crowd around him, no matter what they wore. He couldn't count how many times he and Henry needed to help each other dress in some of the most bizarre costumes—even in corsets once or twice. He finished dressing and helped her gather her reticule and bonnet. "Do you mind waiting here for a minute? It looks like Mr. Henry Hirsute is in need of another grasshopper. It'll just take a minute."

She glanced over to the wooden box with the glass lid that Mr.

Henry Hirsute lived in and shuddered.

Elijah laughed. "I would invite you to come with me, but I thought you'd prefer to wait with the critter behind the glass."

"Indeed."

"I'll be right back." Elijah stepped outside and walked about ten feet away. He bent his knees, his eyes scanning the grass. Aha. He cupped his hands together and caught him. Closing his hands to keep him from escaping, he walked back inside and dropped him in the top of the box. "Are you ready now?"

"More than you'll ever know."

He chuckled and reached for her hand. They walked to the main house where Amelia joined the ladies in the drawing room while Elijah ordered a picnic hamper.

"Have you learned anything more?" Henry asked, stepping out of the library and into the hall.

"No. Have you?"

Henry shook his head. "Are you still angry with me?"

"No. Really you haven't done less than your share. It's not as if you knew to be there in Brighton. We never had a clue that directed us there." He exhaled. "I just hate that Amelia's involved."

"And why is that?"

Elijah looked at his brother as if he were addled. Then he realized it wasn't that his brother didn't understand why Amelia's involvement bothered Elijah but why *she* was involved in the first place. Unease settled over him. "I have no idea. If I ask her, then I have to admit I was there and saw her that night." He shrugged. "I found her in the library looking through papers. Perhaps she found a way into her cousin's party and when she realized how dangerous it was, she wanted to leave and was looking for something to write with to send a message." At least that's what he'd assumed she was doing that night when he found her and he still hoped that's all she was there for.

"Something about that doesn't add up," Henry commented. "I promised Caroline I'd play lawn games for an hour today and I overheard that you're taking Amelia on a picnic, so I won't keep you, but I'll keep thinking about it."

"If you make a grand discovery and you're not too terribly injured by the whole ordeal, please let me know."

Henry twisted and puckered his lips and partially closed his eyes. Elijah had come to think of this as his "you think you're being humorous, but you're not" look.

Elijah clapped him on the back as he passed and continued to wait for the hamper to be brought to him.

Once he had the hamper and the carriage was readied, he collected Amelia and helped her into the carriage.

"How were the ladies this morning?" he asked, climbing up into the carriage.

She moved over so he could sit next to her. "Like they always are. Chattier than magpies, as your Aunt Carolina would say."

Elijah wrapped his arm around her and pulled her close. "Do they not include you?"

"They do. Or they would," she amended. "I just don't like to talk."

"I know." He'd always found that a little strange about her. When he'd glimpsed her from across the London ballrooms, he'd always noticed she was always listening. Very few times had he actually seen her chat. Perhaps that's why he was drawn to her when he'd seen her during her first Season. Not that he was one to dominate a conversation, but he was sure she had *something* to say, and even if nobody else did, he wanted to hear it.

Of course, she'd blushed and been reluctant to talk to him at first as back then rumors wildly circulated that she held a *tendre* for him and refused to consider anyone else, waiting for only his proposal. He'd tell her that it was just a young girl's fantasy, to marry her girlhood playmate, and would encourage her to let other gentlemen pay court to her. At the time, his actions had been innocent and what he believed to be in her best interest. He never dreamed that one day it would be him who was in love, only to have waited too long.

But that's what happened. With each ball or assembly he saw her at, he became more attracted to her smiles and craved more conversation with her. He'd jokingly suggest she allow a completely unsuitable fellow to court her only to see her nose scrunch up and hear her list his faults, to which Elijah would always try to parry back with how a negative attribute such as having foul breath from his tobacco was a good thing because it meant he'd spend the majority of each ball outside with his cheroot instead of collecting his obligatory dance with her.

He'd half-heartedly suggested himself as a candidate two Seasons ago. She'd laughed and said, "I couldn't marry you. You're my friend. If we were to marry, I'd never get to be a mother."

He'd wanted to refute that. To tell her then and there how much he desired her. But he couldn't. He was in the middle of a mission and the last thing he needed was to get her tangled up in the mess.

"Besides," she'd continued. "I'm no longer a young girl who believes she's known her true love all along. He's out there. I just have to wait for him to come to me. Unless I die first."

He'd chuckled at her jest, his heart lifting, at least there *was* a chance for him to woo her.

"Are you all right, Elijah?"

Elijah jumped. "Oh, sorry. Just a bit of woolgathering."

"It must be some heavy wool," she teased, stroking his cheek with the back of her finger.

"The heaviest sort."

She looked like she wanted to press him for more details, but he was saved when the carriage came to a halt at the park Elijah had asked the coachman to take them to.

"Here," he said, leading her by the hand to a grassy spot by the water. "We can even sit on the log and put our feet in if you'd like."

Amelia's eyes grew wide. "Take our shoes and stockings off, out here?"

He made a show of looking around. "I don't see anyone who'd care. Oh wait—" he craned his neck forward and squinted— "I think I see a toad in the distance he might be scandalized."

"That or try to nibble our toes," Amelia said as she kicked off her slippers.

Elijah tried not to stare as she rolled down her stockings and pulled them off. "You should have waited until you were already sitting on the log before removing your slippers. I don't image the bark will feel good under your bare feet."

Her throaty laughter filled the air. "Perhaps it'll scratch *your* feet, but I'm sure mine will be— Ouch!"

Elijah jerked his head up from looking inside of the picnic basket to see what had hurt his wife. "Did you step on something?"

"No. This hit me." She held up a little red apple.

Together, they lifted their eyes up to the tree they'd been using for shade. "Well, I never."

"Never what?" she asked, grinning. "Got sense knocked into you with an apple?"

"Guess not." He returned her grin. "Wait. What are you doing?"

She didn't bother to look up from where she was now walking around half bent over looking for apples. "I'm looking for fruit for our fruit bowl. Aren't we supposed to pick it up today?"

Elijah had nearly forgotten about the bowl. "Yes. But you don't have to collect apples, Amelia. We can get some fruit from Cook."

"Nonsense. You made the fruit bowl, *I'll* supply the fruit."

Elijah walked over, bent down, and snapped up the apple she was reaching for. "Correction. We made the fruit bowl together, so I'll help you collect the fruit." He bent forward and pressed a quick kiss to her lips then moved over to pick up another apple. "Perhaps tonight during Caroline's ball, we can sneak out and go to the orangery and collect some of Alex's oranges."

"Why would we have to sneak out at night to do that? Does

Alex not like people taking his oranges?"

"No, he doesn't mind." Elijah snapped up two more apples. "But if he catches us, *we'll* mind; and the price we'll pay will not be worth the fruit."

"Still has to explain the science of everything, does he?"

"Indeed." Elijah walked over to the picnic hamper and set his apples inside. "I think we have more than enough, love." He bit his tongue, but it was too late, he'd already said it. He chanced a look at Amelia, she looked frozen as if she didn't know what to say. He offered her a smile and gestured to the picnic hamper.

"You're right." She walked over to him and deposited her apples into the hamper. "I think we have more than enough."

"Just so. But when we run out, we can go visit Alex's orangery." He winked at her.

She blushed like he hoped she might. "I look forward to it."

"And what about having lunch with me?"

She walked over to the fallen log that extended out over the water and started making her way across. Halfway across, she stopped and flashed him a smile. "Hopefully I won't have to be looking forward to it much longer."

Chapter Twenty-Four

The picnic was wonderful with the tall shade tree, the cool water covering them to their ankles, the gentle breeze, the delicious food, and most importantly the company. Three days ago, she'd have never imagined they could be both friends and lovers. But last night had certainly changed her opinion of that. Her skin grew warm just thinking about it. Perhaps when they got inside, he'd hold up his earlier promise of 'later'.

Or perhaps not.

"Elijah, why isn't the glass on Mr. Henry Hirsute's cage?" she nearly shrieked, on the verge of hysterics as she entered the little cabin where they were staying.

"I didn't know it wasn't." Elijah stepped around her and went to the cage. "Damn," he muttered.

"Damn? Damn what? What are you damning, Elijah?"

He shot her his best smile. "It would appear Mr. Henry Hirsute has decided to go on another travel adventure."

Amelia shrieked. She didn't give a hang if that made her a ninny. There was a fuzzy spider on the loose, and it could be anywhere! Screaming like a madwoman, she ran through the cabin to jump on the bed, stepping only on her tiptoes as she went. She wasn't going to put her whole foot on the floor until Mr. Henry Hirsute was back in his prison cell.

"You think being on the bed will keep you safe?"

Amelia shivered. "It won't?"

Elijah shrugged lazily. "I don't see why it would. He can crawl up just as easily as he can crawl across a flat surface."

Amelia jumped to her feet. "Elijah, I swear if I see that filthy scoundrel, I'll kill him."

Elijah chuckled and peered behind the bureau then under the wardrobe. "Must you call him a scoundrel? It's not as if he's the greatest debaucher in all of England."

"No," she said with a sniff. "He's worse."

Shaking his head, Elijah lifted the overhanging bedsheets and searched underneath them for his errant pet.

"Why did you have to keep him?" Amelia asked again.

Elijah frowned. "I couldn't let him die, could I?"

"No, but you could have at least let his namesake adopt him."

"You're in a rather humorous mood today, aren't you?" He lifted one of the bed pillows and looked underneath.

Amelia's skin crawled. If that dratted menace had shed even one hair in this bed, she'd be taking up residence in the main house. "Why can't you give him to Henry?"

Elijah heaved the loudest sigh she'd ever heard. "I don't think that's wise. What with how upset he was when Mr. Fuzzinelli died."

"And just who was Mr. Fuzzinelli," she asked though she doubted she really wanted to know.

Elijah placed his hands around her ankles, searing her skin straight through her stockings. "A distant relative of Mr. Henry Hirsute's."

"Enough said." She darted her gaze around the room to see if she spotted the soon-to-be dead visitor. "Why did you name him after your brother, anyway?" she asked, hoping conversation would distract her enough to calm her nerves.

"I thought to name him Harry Hirsute, but that seemed too redundant because hirsute already means hairy, So naming him Harry Hirsute seemed to put too much pressure on him to keep his hair. What if he were to start losing it?" He shook his head, his eyes wide as if he were feigning some sort of great outrage. "Besides, Harry by itself is just too popular of a name."

"Yes, because everyone names their pet tarantula Harry," she said on the verge of hysteria again. She hadn't spotted the vile creature anywhere which left two options: one, it was in the common room, or two, it was hiding and waiting to make its grand reappearance later—most likely at a time when Elijah wouldn't be present. "Elijah, I'm telling you now, if I see Mr. Henry Hirsute and he's not in his box, his new name will be Mr. Elijah Expired."

"All right, but that means you have to come down here and help me look."

Just then, *something* touched her calf and she squealed like the little ninny Elijah and Henry used to claim her to be. "Something touched me! Mr. Elijah Expired just crawled on my calf!"

"Hmm, I guess I'll have to look into that for you," Elijah said cool as can be, slowly lifting her skirt. He handed her the fabric to hold and slowly skimmed his hands up her calves, his eyes never leaving hers.

Were the circumstances any different, she'd melt into a boneless heap at his touch. He slowly rolled down the top of her stocking, then leaned forward and placed a kiss just behind her knee. "Elijah, now isn't the time," she choked. "Mr. Elijah Expired touched me. You have to find him now."

"Yes, Mr. Elijah touched you," he agreed, caressing her calves. "Mr. Elijah Banks, that is. Your friend Mr. Henry Hirsute has been safely curled up in the bottom of his box this whole time. I must not have shut the glass all the way, but he never got out."

All the muscles in her body relaxed. "Why didn't you tell me that sooner?"

"I'd planned to." He moved his hands up to rub her thighs, inching ever closer to where she ached to have him most. "But when I saw you stand up on the bed like this, I decided not to miss the chance to do this." Just then, two of his strong fingers pressed against the sensitive flesh between her legs in the most delicious way.

She released her hold on her skirt and her hands flew to his shoulders for balance as his probing fingers continued their exploration, now adding a third to the fray. Her knees buckled and his strong hands moved to catch her.

"Lie down."

She heeded his ragged command, too excited for his touch not to.

Elijah removed everything but his shirt and trousers then climbed in the bed next to her, his lips immediately finding hers. She kissed him back and gasped when his right hand covered her breast and began shaping it. Elijah took advantage of her parted lips and pushed his tongue into her mouth.

She sighed his name. She loved kissing him and exploring his body. He broke their kiss and brought his lips to the plane of her chest, his fingers frantically working to lower her bodice. Were it her own gown, she'd have demanded he rip the fabric and end her torment immediately. Instead, it excited her more that in his state of want and need, he wasn't quite as nimble as he'd been getting her into the gown.

Suddenly the unmistakable sound of fabric tearing rent the air. But Amelia didn't care, Elijah's kisses along the tops of her breasts put the thought straight out of her mind. He grabbed the top of her corset, and gently pulled it down below her breasts, which he then touched and kissed, leaving no part of them untouched.

He pulled his face away from her skin, his breathing heavy. He rolled onto his side and grabbed fistfuls of her heavy skirt, lifting it until the hem was halfway up her thighs, then slid his hand between her legs. She parted her thighs to give him better access—which he greedily took. His strong fingers picked up right where he'd left off a few minutes ago, gently massaging her tender flesh.

He found a particularly sensitive spot and her hips involuntarily bucked. Wretch that he was, he had a wolfish grin splitting his face. But she didn't care. Not when he was stirring these sensations inside of her with his deft touch.

He shifted his hand and slid two fingers inside her. Her gaze shot to his. What was he doing? Was he supposed to touch her like that? As if sensing her unasked questions, he lowered his lashes and began moving his fingers in and out. At first, he moved slow, building a small series of contractions in the pit of her stomach. He thrust in again, a little faster and harder, sending a spray of fiery sparks through her. He did it again and her hips lifted to meet his thrust this time.

He shifted so he wasn't lying on top of her, leaving only his upper body covering hers as he continued his thrusts, which were growing more rapid and increasingly more addicting with each one. She was moving, too. Wanting to take every bit he had to give her, she moved her hips to match each of his thrusts. Something was mounting in her. Something hot and foreign, wild and exciting. Something she desperately wanted to discover.

Beads of sweat rolled down Elijah's face. But he didn't stop or slow his movements. Just then he dipped his head and sucked her nipple into his mouth, adding just enough fuel to her inner flame that she thought she might combust. And then she did. Waves of fiery pleasure washed over her, shattering her body into what felt like a thousand pieces that floated away.

Elijah slowed his thrusts in time with the slowing of the waves of euphoria overtaking her.

A moment later, she opened her eyes. Elijah had his head propped up on one hand looking down at her. She'd blush if he were anyone else seeing her thus. But for some reason seeing him look at her this way after they'd just shared such intimacy didn't feel embarrassing or shameful. She loved him and it was rather obvious he cared for her, too.

She licked her lips and rolled onto her side to face him. With the same torturous slowness he liked to use with her, she trailed her hand down his chest and abdomen to cup his erection.

He closed his blue eyes for an extended blink, then took her hand from where it rested and brought it to his lips. Kissing the tip of each of her fingers, he said, "Not now. That was for you."

"What of you?" she questioned in what she hoped was a seductive voice.

He pressed a row of kisses across her knuckles. "Don't worry about me, just—"

***

Bang! Bang! BANG! "Elijah, open up! I need to talk to you now. It's urgent!"

Elijah's blood shot through his veins. He'd never heard Henry shout like that. He cast an apologetic glance to a startled Amelia and then ran to the front door. "What is it?"

Henry ignored him and rushed into the cabin. Then, without a word, he shoved something into Elijah's hands.

Elijah's eyes scanned the words written on the missive.

16C Call Street. Bath. Eleven.

Elijah locked gazes with his brother. "Something isn't right."

"I know," Henry said quietly. "That's why I wanted your opinion. It's not a puzzle."

"No. Nor is it his custom to send missives so frequently."

Henry shrugged. "I don't know about that. He might just be getting impatient." He took the missive from Elijah's hand. "It gives a location: Bath. He might have known we were in the area and wanted to get this over with tonight."

Elijah nodded. That made sense. There was no need to let any more girls be sold into prostitution. But still, something was off. "Let me see that again."

Henry handed him the note. "The handwriting is different," Elijah murmured, frowning. Why hadn't he noticed that the first time? Likely because he'd been so distracted by Henry's shouting and the note's content. "The letters in the past have been formed perfectly, and all the Cs have had that extra swoop at the top."

Henry frowned. "The man was clearly in a hurry, Elijah. If he didn't bother to make his clue cryptic with arithmetic equations and rhymes, he probably didn't care too much about writing it in a hand to please a dandy."

"I concede." He began folding up the missive and froze, his eyes narrowing. "This isn't from him. I know it."

"Oh? Is the wax seal not in the precise place he's put it in the past? Or perhaps it's a different shade of red. Burgundy instead of crimson?" Henry asked, his voice dripping with sarcasm.

"No, you coxcomb. The others had wax that was flat, almost as if someone had flattened it with the bottom of a candlestick holder. This one was stamped with a signet ring." He turned the paper around so his brother could see it. "It's light but you can still see the bottom half of a crest there in the wax." It was just enough that they might be able to identify it if they could compare it to a picture, but as it was, there wasn't enough there to recognize just whose crest it was.

Henry took the paper from Elijah's grasp and cursed under his breath. "Damn. How did I miss that?"

"Because you lack the attention to details I have."

Henry snorted. "I could say something in response, but since I have a feeling we're about to spend the next few hours locked in Alex's library poring over *Debrett's* like two giggling debutantes on the hunt for a lord, I'll refrain."

"I'd say you're capable of using your mind for something other than dreaming about horseflesh after all." He cast a glance at the closed bedroom door and handed Henry back the paper. "Let me get Amelia to the house so Caroline, Edwina and Mother can fuss over getting her ready for the costume ball tonight. I'll meet you in the library in thirty minutes."

"Very well. I'll go to the stables and see if anyone knows what type of building is at this address."

"Amelia," Elijah called, coming back into their bedchamber.

"What's wrong?"

Elijah forced himself to ignore the look of confusion on her face. "Oh, you know Henry, he has a flare for the dramatic that's only outmatched by an actor on Drury Lane."

"No, he doesn't. What's wrong?"

"Mother has threatened to look for a wife for him at the ball tonight," Elijah said thickly. He *hated* lying. Especially to Amelia. But it would be the last one. Ever. Tonight, after they apprehended the men involved he'd tell her the entire truth and never utter another lie to her as long as he lived.

"Gracious. I had no idea he was so opposed to matrimony." She looped her arms around his neck, came up on her toes and then pressed her lips to his. "Perhaps he'll enjoy it more than he thinks if he gives it a chance."

"Have you forgotten who we're talking about?" he murmured against her lips. Unable to resist their temptation, he kissed her again.

"He's not as bad as I originally thought. Some lady might even enjoy being married to him."

"Yes, if she likes sarcasm and insolence," he agreed, dropping his head to kiss her neck. He forced himself to stop. Tonight, he promised himself. Tonight he'd tell her every one of his secrets then make love to her until they were both too tired to move. "I think it's time you go join the ladies and start getting ready for the ball."

"Do I have to?" She slipped her hands under his shirt; her fingertips brushing every edge and hard plane. "I'd much rather stay here with you tonight."

His heart leapt. He'd rather stay here with her, too, but he couldn't. "I'm sorry, Amelia, but we have to attend. This is very important to Caroline."

She sighed. "All right, I'll go."

"Good." He helped her repair her gown well enough to go to the main house and start getting ready for the ball.

Elijah walked her across the lawn to the house, savoring every step along the way. He loved spending time with her. He was a lucky fellow, indeed.

He led her upstairs and helped her find where the ladies were chatting it up in the drawing room. Of course when he left, they were all chatting about having the *perfect* costume for Amelia. He grinned. How fortunate he was to have a large family who welcomed Amelia as if she'd been the lost family member they'd always been searching to find.

Content that she'd be taken care of, he went to the library.

"Have you found anything?" Elijah asked.

Henry shook his head, but didn't bother to look up from the table. "No." He turned the page. "Why must everyone put swords or a horse on their coat of arms?"

Elijah chuckled and sat down next to him. "Because rabbits and flowers aren't nearly as powerful."

"You're a true jester, Elijah, aren't you?"

"I try," he said dryly. He peered over at the nine crests on the page closest to him. He studied each of them, then glanced at the wax seal, hoping for a match. Not in the top row. Nor the second. He sighed. "It's not any of these."

Henry flipped the page and in silence they both scanned their sides of the page. Nothing. Henry flipped the page again. Nothing again.

"What do you propose we do when we find it?" Elijah asked.

"Call the constable to arrest him. Then torture him until he gives up the names of everyone else involved," Henry suggested.

"So then we're in agreement, the author of *this* missive is involved?"

Henry nodded. "You were right earlier. About the handwriting." He turned the page. "While you were taking your precious time kissing your wife goodbye, I compared the writing on this one to the writing on the others we've received. There were differences that couldn't be accounted for by haste. The one who sent clues never used punctuation at the end of sentences or commas. This person used both." He turned another page. "The other fellow crosses his Ts and Fs up at an angle, this chap goes straight across. Even in a hurry, he'd still make the same movement."

"All right, but what reason would someone have to give themselves away?"

"That's the part I don't understand, either," Henry said on a sigh. "My guess is that the one who wrote this won't be there tonight."

"No," Elijah agreed, dread washing over him. "And neither will we if we don't find out who this crest belongs to." Dash it all, he'd hoped to be done with this nonsense tonight; but even the greenest of those who worked for the Crown knew better than to go anywhere on an anonymous tip that raised more questions than it answered.

"It's not in here," Henry said, closing the book with a thump.

Elijah leaned his head back and pressed his fingers against his eyelids. The sun had fallen from the sky more than an hour earlier. Caroline's costume party would start in less than an hour and whatever was going to happen at 16C Call Street tonight would happen without them in a little under two.

"What if the ring is old?"

"Yes, I imagine it is," Elijah mumbled.

"No, I meant, the title and crest could be dormant," Henry explained.

Elijah whipped his head around to look at the only shelf in the library that didn't hold some sort of science tome. "Is that the only copy of *Debrett's* we have?"

Henry scanned the shelf. "It appears so."

"I wonder if Mother has her old copy."

"Why would she?" Henry asked, coming back to the table. "She said she never cared for the Season and her marriage had been arranged. She wouldn't have needed a copy."

"No, but perhaps she kept the one issued after she became a baroness."

Henry snorted. "Have you met our mother? I don't think she ever gave a fig about being a baroness."

Elijah stood. "Nonetheless, if there is an older version to be found in this house she'd be the one to have it." Mother may not have been so high in the instep as to shoot icicles at people who didn't address her with the proper respect due her rank, nor did she enjoy participating in Society overmuch, but she was a bit sentimental; and if Elijah had to guess, she'd kept a copy because it had listed his father as the Baron of Watson.

A swift set of raps halted Elijah's steps to leave the library.

"Enter," Henry bade.

Their grey-headed, bespectacled butler opened the door. "Master Henry, it would seem Curtis is downstairs, asking to speak to you." The twist of his lips left no doubt what he thought of a stablehand seeking an audience with Henry.

Henry and Elijah exchanged a look. "Very good. I've been waiting to see him."

Elijah tried not to chuckle at the way the butler's eyes widened just a hint before recomposing himself. Snatching the missive from the table, he stuffed it into his breast pocket and set out to find his mother.

~Chapter Twenty-Five~

Amelia looked ridiculous. Her gown was made of a light blue silk with a high waist that formed a point. That part wasn't so bad, but then had come feathers for her hair in various shades of blue and green and a bright white mask that tied behind her head. According to Elijah's outspoken cousin, Brooke, Lady Townson, she looked like a princess. According to Amelia, she looked like a fool.

Oh well, the good thing about costume balls was that nobody knew who anyone was and usually everyone else looked just as ridiculous. Or not. She scanned the drawing room where she, Regina, Caroline, and Edwina were all waiting while the others finished getting ready. Regina had on a regal gown worthy of a queen. Caroline wore solid black with black lacy gloves and a matching fan. She certainly looked like a seductress. Edwina had worked the hardest on hers, and had sought some help from her Aunt Carolina in fashioning a gown that would have been the height of fashion in Charleston back when Aunt Carolina was a young debutante.

She glanced at Edwina again. She really needed to talk to her, to clear up her...er...earlier statement. Now certainly wasn't the time, but it *was* important that Amelia clear up any confusion. She still hadn't started her monthly, but had noticed that while her breasts were still sensitive and her emotions were a little off, she wasn't nauseous. Perhaps in her worry over it, she'd made herself sick and convinced herself of symptoms that weren't really there. That was silly, of course, but possible considering the young ladies she'd heard of who took to the waters in Bath more frequently than they bathed in their own homes. All of their ailments couldn't possibly be real, could they?

A soft knock stole Amelia from her wandering thoughts.

"Yes," Caroline called, appearing as confused as Amelia felt. Why would any of the other ladies knock before entering Caroline's private sitting room?

"Is everyone decent?"

Amelia's heart fluttered with excitement. She knew that voice.

Caroline winked at her. "You'll just have to wait to see your wife at the ball, Mr. Banks."

"Caroline, this is not the time. I need to come in, is everyone decent?"

The fluttering abruptly stopped, panic taking its place. His tone was strained, holding a similar edge that Henry's had held earlier. She got up and walked over to the door. "Is everything all right?" She hadn't meant for her tone to be so shrill, but his unkempt hair, rumpled clothes and stoney, impassive face had set her on edge.

"Yes." He peered over her shoulder. "I need to speak to my mother for a moment."

Amelia looked to Regina and then turned back to Elijah. "I think we need to speak first."

Elijah hesitated, but then took a step backwards.

"What's going on?" she asked when they were out in the hall together and she'd closed the door to Caroline's sitting room.

"I need to speak to my mother," he said as if he'd lost all other words in his vocabulary.

"Yes, I heard that. Why?"

Elijah took a breath. "I need to ask her if she has a copy of *Debrett's*."

Amelia fought to contain her mirth. "You're not helping your mother find Henry a wife by looking up daughters of the titled, are you?" she asked, smoothing down the front of his coat. Her finger brushed something stiff by his pocket. When he bristled, she moved her hand to cover it. "You don't have a piece of foolscap with possible brides listed, do you?"

He covered her hand with his. "No."

Her humor fled. "What are you hiding, Elijah?"

He clamped his jaw, but didn't release her hand.

"I know you're not above ripping pages out of books, you know," she whispered, trying to hide her smile as she inched her fingers toward the opening of his pocket.

"I know. But that's not what's in my pocket."

"Then just let me see it."

His hand tightened. "No."

"Elijah, much tighter and you'll hurt me."

He relaxed his hold a bit. Not a lot, but just enough for her to reach into his pocket and pluck out the note.

She closed her fingers around it and stepped backwards out of his reach. "Is this a letter?"

"No," he barked, taking it from her.

Her hands flew to her hips. "Then why does it have a seal?"

"Because it's private."

"Then it is a letter," she countered.

"No."

She narrowed her eyes on him. "Then show it to me again."

"No."

"Now, Elijah."

Something flashed in his eyes. "I'll explain everything later."

He couldn't have hurt her more if he'd slapped her. What was so important he couldn't explain it to her now? "What are you hiding from me?"

"Nothing," he bit off.

"Then show me the letter."

"It's not a blasted letter, Amelia. It's just a missive."

She crossed her arms. "Is there a difference?"

"I consider letters to be a lengthy compilation of someone's feelings—which this is not. A missive is just a short note giving a directive or soliciting one's opinion on a simple matter."

"I still don't see the difference between the two," she muttered. Perhaps it was some sort of nonsense that only gentlemen understood. "All right, then let me see the missive."

"I don't have time—"

"For me?" she finished for him, anger now mixing with the hurt from before.

He grumbled something then unfolded the paper and quickly turned it toward her then away so fast she hadn't had time to actually read it, but had seen it was in fact a very short, to the point piece of correspondence.

"Why do you have a *missive* with the Kirkham seal on it?" she asked after he'd tucked it back into his pocket.

Elijah's eyes widened and his hand stilled. "What? Whose seal?"

"The Kirkham seal."

"Kirkham?"

"Perhaps not." She shrugged. "That's just what it looked like."

Elijah pulled the paper out of his pocket and handed it to her. "Is that the seal you thought it was?"

"Yes." She nodded her head. "That's Philip's seal all right."

***

Elijah's gut clenched. "Philip?" he echoed in disbelief.

Amelia nodded and then chuckled. "Although he's normally not so sloppy with how he stamps it. Quite the opposite, in fact. He's usually very careful with how he stamps it to make sure the receiver can see its every line and groove."

Unless he didn't want anyone to recognize it. "I didn't think your father had any lesser titles."

"He didn't. Not always, anyway." She reached up as casual as could be and readjusted one of those hideous feathers sticking out from the top of her hair. "Mother was the only child of Baron Kirkham. When no male relative could be found after his death, his title went unclaimed."

"And then?"

Amelia shrugged. "Philip always hated that he didn't get a lesser title as other earl's sons who waited until they inherited, so after years of Philip's begging, Father finally petitioned the Crown to have Kirkham assigned to him. It took a while and a lot of convincing, but the prince finally approved, considering Father had no lesser titles already and that Kirkham *did* pass to a male relation."

Elijah nodded numbly. So much about the last clue made sense now. The clue about church was right there: kirk; and even why it was worded *thy maiden fair*, the person who wrote it clearly knew Elijah had married Lord Kirkham's sister. His heart twisted, Amelia. Instinctively, he wrapped his arms around her and brought her against him, those dratted feathers tickling his nose.

"I cannot wait to have my own wardrobe again," she commented when he released her.

A memory from yesterday sparked in his mind, but he couldn't come out and ask her about it. "Isn't that what your brother came by for yesterday?"

"He said something about it," she agreed, her brows furrowing just a little. "But I don't remember what exactly."

"Do you not think that was his real reason for coming?" he hedged, hoping she wouldn't suspect *his* real reason for asking.

"No, I suppose not. He was too interested in a favor."

Elijah squeezed his toes in his shoes and took a deep breath. He couldn't afford to give himself away or say too much here. Amelia really might be in danger. "What kind of favor?"

"I don't know," she whispered, her voice terribly uneven. "Look for some sort of paper?"

"What sort of paper?"

"I—I—don't know." She took a ragged breath. "He once asked me to find a piece of paper in my cousin's house, but I don't know what I was looking for. I think he wants me to look again."

A lead weight settled on Elijah's chest. There was no denying it, Amelia was involved in this somehow. He didn't know why or to what extent, and doubted she did, either, but she was involved and he'd do everything humanly possible to protect her and keep her safe. "Listen to me, Amelia. I have to go get dressed for the ball tonight. I want you to stay with my mother. Do you understand? Do not leave her side until I come back."

"Why?"

"Do you remember the time you climbed to the top of the big oak on the south border of Watson Estate and I told you to just stay there and not to move?"

"Yes. There was a giant wasps' nest on one of the branches."

"Right. But you didn't know it and had to trust me, remember?"

She nodded.

"I need you to trust me again, Amelia. Please don't leave my mother's side until I come back for you."

Amelia folded her arms. "On one condition. You had better tell me *everything* I want to know tonight."

"Tonight, I promise." He kissed her hand then led her back inside the sitting room.

~ Chapter Twenty-Six ~

A thousand questions ran through Amelia's mind. The least of which was why Henry was standing in front of her asking to escort her down to the ballroom.

"Where is Elijah?"

"He was having trouble with his costume and didn't want you to have to wait to go downstairs," he said loud enough for everyone in the room to hear. He held his hand out to her to help her off the settee.

There was something hard in his hand that he shoved into hers. Her fingers closed around it: a note. Excitement coursed through her. What did it say?

"Read it later," Henry whispered, offering her his arm.

She scowled at him. She knew that. She took his arm and allowed him to escort her down the stairs. "He does plan to attend, doesn't he?" she whispered.

Henry nodded. "Yes. He'll be here."

Because Amelia and Regina had waited for Elijah's return, the ball had begun a half an hour ago and already there was a crush of people. All around the room colorful skirts swished as couples danced around them.

"Good evening, Mr. Parker," Henry said, bowing. "Have you met my wife? Lady Amelia Banks?"

Mr. Parker, who was nearly as round as he was tall, bowed to her. "What a pleasure."

No, a pleasure would be when Elijah arrived and Henry could leave her side.

"Ho there, Elijah," Philip said, clapping Henry on the back.

"Philip," Henry clipped.

Philip was clad in solid black and wore a silver demi mask. He gave her a low bow. "Amelia. It's very nice to see the doting groom is treating you so well. May I have this dance?"

"Actually, I've claimed her first waltz," Henry cut in. "You wouldn't want to waltz with your sister anyway, would you?"

Philip's lips thinned. "Very well, but I'd like your next dance, then."

Henry nodded stiffly, then led Amelia to the dance floor.

"Why are you pretending to be Elijah?" she whispered.

"I had to introduce you somehow," he murmured, his eyes looking everywhere but at her.

She stepped on his foot to get his attention. "Not to my brother."

He ignored her and kept spinning her around the floor.

"Is there a reason there's enough space for another body between us?"

"I don't want to seem too eager. It wouldn't be good to make tongues wag."

"You're absurd. Tongues are more likely to wag *because* we're so far apart."

He frowned. "Do you think someone might think we have an unhappy marriage?"

She stared at him, unable to think of a suitable quip. Fortunately, this was a short waltz and the end was very near. Then she'd put as much distance between the two of them as possible. She'd promised Elijah she'd stay close to his mother, she'd never said anything about spending the evening with Henry.

"When we finish, perhaps you should make a visit to the little room Caroline set off for ladies of the family to retire in for a bit and read your note."

"Yes, I think I shall," she agreed. She'd been wanting to since he'd given it to her but hadn't found the right time, yet. From the corner of her eye she saw Henry shoot a wolfish grin at the young lady dancing next to them. She swatted him. "If you want to pretend to be Elijah, then you'd better have better manners than that."

Henry ignored her and quickly spun Amelia around so her back was to the lady and his eyes could focus on the side of the beautiful young lady's very generous curves.

A moment later, the music ended and Henry abruptly loosened his hold on Amelia in favor of making the acquaintance of the young lady who'd caught his attention.

Amelia scowled at him. If he didn't stop his wandering eyes and lustful looks while pretending to be Elijah, she'd brain him.

Putting it from her mind, she walked as slowly as she could to get into the little room. She'd been to a few balls in London held by some of the Banks ladies and always heard they set off a private room for family at balls. Amelia didn't know why. Perhaps there were better foods waiting or Caroline's personal lady's maid to mend a ripped flounce as opposed to hired help. She didn't really know, and would be slightly more interested if only she wasn't so intent on reading the slip of paper she'd tucked in her glove.

She closed the door to the dimly lit room behind her and sat down beside a candle, then removed the folded paper. It smelled of Elijah, spicy and of the fresh outdoors. Slowly, she unfolded it.

PLEASE, TRUST ME. I LOVE YOU.

Her heart pounded. He loved her? Why he hadn't just told her, she'd never know, but he loved her! She looked down at the note and read those three simple words again and again. He loved her. He loved her. Elijah loved *her*. She took a deep breath and refolded the note. She couldn't sit in here and reread it over and over again like a ninny. She needed to go back out there and find him and tell him that she loved him, too.

She tucked the note back into the top of her long white glove and stood.

Just then, a floorboard creaked. Her pulse raced. Was someone in the room with her?

Slowly she turned around to a pair of cold grey eyes in a demi mask. She opened her mouth to scream, but her cry was lost, buried against a firm, gloved hand.

***

Elijah stood motionless as Amelia scurried away from Henry. Elijah had wanted to be the one at her side, but Henry had convinced him that he was the better person to be down there with her because it'd be easier for Henry to drive her away to the room, nor would he appear besotted.

Which was true. Henry was better at keeping his feelings separated from his duty; not to mention he didn't love Amelia, and Elijah's love for her might have given himself away.

Still, he wished he'd been down there by her side and able to confirm she was locked safely in the drawing room, away from Philip and any danger he might present. Instead, he'd spent the last hour lurking behind a giant marble statue on the balcony which overlooked the top of the two-story ballroom, waiting and watching.

Just as they'd planned, when Philip approached them, Henry took Amelia off to dance and suggested she visit the blue saloon after the dance. Of course, Henry might have gotten a little too dramatic with his ogling of Lord Mobley's daughter, but it helped build credence for why Amelia was stalking off, he supposed.

Henry was supposed to have slid the lock once she was safely inside, keeping her secure. And if he didn't, so help him, Elijah was going to kill his own brother.

A boot scraped against the concrete and chills ran up Elijah's spine. Remaining stock-still, he shifted his eyes. It was Bertie, the footman he'd bribed to tell him who arrived with Philip.

Elijah stepped out from behind the statue and into its shadow. "Well?"

Bertie scanned the throngs of people. "I—I don't see him now, sir."

"How was he dressed?"

"Black. All black."

Elijah sighed. That could be half the gentlemen here. Costume balls, he'd learned, were generally attended only to appease one's wife. No gentleman enjoyed dressing up in anything different than he'd typically wear and most usually opted to wear black and a demi mask. "Anything else? Was he tall? Short? Did he keep his hat on?"

"Tall, sir. Taller than most, six foot, mayhap."

"Are you sure you're not describing Philip?"

"No, sir. This man was taller than Lord Kirkham, he was."

"All right," Elijah said with a sigh. He and Henry had agreed that Henry wouldn't collect Amelia from Caroline's sitting room until he'd seen Philip's coachmen park the carriage. Their best chance to catch either of them now would be to wait for them in the east lawn where the carriages were parked.

Elijah slipped out the side door to the exterior balcony and jumped. He bit off a vile curse when his feet collided with the hard ground, then dusted off his trousers. He was getting too old to be jumping off second story balconies. He slipped behind the tall bushes that lined the house and walked in the thin alley between the bushes and the house. Truly he didn't have to walk this way. In fact, it would have been faster to have gone the other way, but call it years of always being careful or perhaps love that he felt compelled to peek in on Amelia and make sure she was all right. A part of him wished he could have been hiding in that room and seen her reaction upon reading his missive. Did she smile? Did she cry? Or did she sigh with uncertainty? She'd seemed interested in their physical activities and spending time together, but did she love him, too? Or was her love only that of a friend? The uncertainty was enough to kill him.

Stepping carefully so not to alert anyone to his presence, he crouched down to stay hidden behind the bushes as they decreased in height from six feet tall down to three as he neared the window of the blue saloon.

He came to an abrupt halt.

The window was open.

Every ounce of blood in Elijah's veins pumped through his body, carrying with it, rage, fury, and nervous excitement.

"Calm down."

Elijah jerked his eyes to the right and in the moonlight locked eyes with his twin. "What are you doing?"

"The same thing you are," Henry whispered. "Waiting."

Elijah recognized the warning right away and it took every ounce of strength he possessed to stay still long enough to hear what Henry had to say.

"Someone's in there," Henry whispered again.

Elijah's heart slammed in his chest. "Why?" It was the only word he could form.

"I don't know. After I locked the door and asked Andrew and Benjamin to have a conversation right outside it and keep it guarded, I came out here to meet the constable. Just as I was walking past, I heard the sound of breaking glass and watched someone go in there."

"And you just let them?" Elijah hissed.

"Yes. I have Andrew and Benjamin guarding the door and I gave Hiram my best pistol and stationed him to wait in that room and if any foul play happened, he was to start shooting."

That would have made Elijah feel better if Hiram was a crack shot and not a chubby stableboy. "Do you realize he could shoot Amelia?"

"Not likely," Henry said, his voice calm as could be. "I told him to start shooting—and I specified not in the direction of a person."

A measure of relief washed over Elijah but was gone in less than a second when a shot rang out. Then a second. And a third. Followed by a fourth.

Elijah and Henry momentarily locked gazes, but not for more than a fraction of a second. Just long enough for Elijah to make sure Henry understood that if a hair was harmed on Amelia's head, Henry had better run into exile.

"Wait," Henry whispered, grabbing Elijah's shoulder to keep him from crawling into the window.

The force of Henry's grip held Elijah back just far enough that a booted foot coming out of the window missed his face as the intruder jumped out, taking a squirming and kicking, but silent Amelia with him.

"Now," Elijah and Henry whispered in unison, lunging for the duo who'd just come through the window.

The foursome tumbled into the grass; shrieks and grunts erupted as everyone struggled. The man at the bottom struggled to get up, Amelia struggled to get free and Elijah and Henry struggled to let Amelia get up while holding her captor down.

Elijah placed his hand firmly on the man's throat and rolled off to the side. "Go, Amelia."

Amelia scrambled to get up and ran to where a small audience had gathered a few feet away. Just then, a flash of silver caught Elijah's attention. He released his hold on the masked stranger and began chasing after who he was certain was Lord Kirkham. The crowd of onlookers was too large now for the other man to get away. Besides, Henry and his small army of constables were there. They could handle it. The only person Elijah cared about right now was Philip, Lord Kirkham. He still didn't understand what Amelia had to do with any of this, nor did he want her hurt ever again, and the only way to ensure that was to capture Philip who was running toward a little cusp of trees near the conservatory.

A twig snapped, followed by a whispered curse. Elijah froze. Philip was near. Very near. Elijah moved behind a thick tree and waited. Philip obviously knew to be careful while walking in the wooded area, but his mistake had been running into a grove of trees he was unfamiliar with, especially at night. Elijah crept closer to where he thought Philip was standing until he glimpsed what appeared to be the back of a human form through the shadows. At his side, Philip's left hand clenched and unclenched, while his right hand stayed hidden in the darkness.

Elijah lunged forward, taking them both to the ground and a shot rang out. Elijah reached for Philip's gun, but was stopped when an elbow collided with his right cheek. He grunted through the sharp pain and reached again, pressing down on the middle of Philip's back with the heel of his left hand.

Philip half-gasped, half-grunted and threw the gun. Not far, but far enough that Elijah couldn't reach it without allowing Philip a means of escape.

"Damn you," Elijah grunted.

"No, damn you," Philip countered. "She was supposed to marry Friar, then I'd be free of this mess."

Elijah placed his arm down on the back of Philip's neck, adding just the slightest amount of pressure as he continued to pin him to the ground. "Explain yourself."

"Amelia. She was supposed to marry Friar. Until you got involved, that is."

"Why?" When Philip didn't immediately answer, Elijah added more pressure to his neck with his arm.

"She was to be the madam," Philip shrieked, his body trying fruitlessly to move under Elijah's weight.

"Why?" he bit off again.

"People were starting to question Friar's activities."

"People? What people?"

"The ones he was selling the girls to."

Elijah pressed down a little harder. "What were they questioning?"

"Their willingness."

That's because they weren't willing! "And how does Amelia fit into all of this?"

"She was to act as the madam, say she'd recruited the girls and that they were willing."

Elijah's skin crawled at the very suggestion. "And Friar thinks he could have made Amelia bend to his will."

"Physical force is a powerful weapon, wouldn't you say, Mr. Banks?"

Elijah had the strongest urge to punch him in the side for that remark, but had long ago decided he'd only use as much force as was necessary to complete his tasks. That night in Brighton he'd only bloodied the man so badly because there were two against one and the only gun in sight was in the hands of the enemy. "All right, and was it by physical force that you took those other girls?"

"Of course. We couldn't very sell them as virgins."

A bitter taste filled Elijah's mouth and this time he did punch Philip in the side, eliciting a high-pitched shriek that echoed through the night. "That's for what you did to those girls. And this —" he punched him again, so hard this time he broke a rib— "is for enjoying it. And this—" he punched him again— "is for even thinking about involving Amelia in this filth."

"I didn't have a choice." His voice was a mere whisper. "I owe Friar money. A lot of money. I was working down my debts by helping gather girls and he said he'd forgive my debts entirely if I'd convince her to be the madam."

"But we both know that would never happen. So you thought to abduct her, is that it?"

Philip didn't answer.

Elijah punched him again. "Was that your plan? To abduct her? Or just to get her ruined at your cousin's party so she'd have to accept his suit?" When he didn't answer again, Elijah delivered another quick punch to his side.

Philip groaned. "The latter. But when you beat him and had him in the gaol, he couldn't attend the wedding."

"Then it became abduction," Elijah finished for him. "And now, it will be the gallows." Elijah propped himself up on the arm he had going across the back of Philip's neck and placed his knee in the man's spine so he could reach up and grab Philip's gun. Keeping his position, he cocked the gun and trained it at Philip's head. "Now, I'm going to release my hold on you and you're slowly going to get up and walk back to the house. You take one step in a direction more than five degrees away from the direction of the house, and you'll have a permanent limp. You try to run, and you'll never walk again."

"And if you don't explain *everything* to me right now, you'll never see Mr. Henry Hirsute again," came the sweet voice of his wife.

The hair on Elijah's neck stood on end. Not because of the threat Amelia had issued or what she might have heard, but that she was out here alone.

Henry placed a hand on Elijah's shoulder, instantly extinguishing any feelings of unease. "Go. You have much to explain to her. Friar has been unmasked and is in the care of the constable, as Philip will be. I'll speak to our inquisitive family. Just go to her, Elijah. You owe it to yourself as much as you do to her."

~Chapter Twenty-Seven~

Amelia clutched the tree next to her for support. So much had happened tonight, but she honestly couldn't explain what it all was.

One minute she was having an intimate moment with Elijah, then his brother intruded and she was dumped into a room with his female relations only to be told to wait there until he came back for her, but he sent Henry instead, who danced with her, then sent her off into a room where she was nearly abducted (and dare she forget shot at); stopped only by Elijah and Henry jumping out of the shrubs to take her and her captor—who apparently was Lord Friar, of all people—to the ground. And that was before she was helped to her feet and made to stand with a crowd while her husband ran into the forest, where she found him moments later holding a man to the ground who wheezed something about a madam, physical force and abduction.

Quite frankly, it was exhausting just to *think* about the night's events.

Nevertheless, there were several large holes of missing information and there wasn't a chance the sun was going to rise in the English sky again without her having each and every one of those holes filled in.

Still clinging to the tree for support, she strained her eyes to watch Elijah hand his brother the gun before taking to his feet and turning to face her. Henry, who now held the gun pointed at her brother barked for him to take to his feet and fired a warning shot scant inches above his head.

Wordlessly, Elijah walked over to her and scooped her up in his large arms.

Amelia would have protested had she the strength to walk

back to the house on her own. But she didn't. Nor did she mind being held this close to him.

Nearing the house, he took a shortcut; one that allowed them entry without having to pass by the crowd.

"Here we are," he said, lowering her onto the feather mattress in a way reminiscent of the way that stranger at Lord Nigel's house had done. Her eyes widened. Was he?

Elijah nodded once. "It was me in Lord Nigel's study."

"Wh-why?"

Elijah raked his hand through his hair. "I am—no I *was*—an agent of the Crown."

"Wh-what?" she gasped. His answer had created far more questions than she'd already planned to ask.

Elijah went over to the fire place and lit a small fire. "When we were eighteen, Henry and I became spies."

A memory of the other day when she'd accused him of being the worst spy in the world flashed in her mind and she blushed. "Why?"

He repositioned the logs in the hearth and poked them with the iron fire poker. "We were caught trying to escape the law—"

"You and *Henry* were caught doing something *illegal*?" The idea of it was laughable.

He nodded once. "It was a mistake, I assure you, but it happened all the same and when we were caught we were given the choice of the gaol or to become agents of the Crown."

She certainly understood why they chose to become spies. "So your travels, they weren't just the usual cavorting about the continent that most young lads do?"

"No. I was told to go to all of those places. What to do." Satisfied with the start of the fire, he set down the fire poker and closed the screen. "And even how to dress."

"Which explains your expertise with corsets," she murmured. In the low light of the room, she noticed a large bruise was forming on his cheek. So much made sense. His being a spy explained the scars she'd seen on his body. "But what does all of this have to do with my brother and Lord Friar?"

"And you," he added, pulling a chair over to sit next to her.

A shiver ran down her spine at his words. "Me?"

Elijah reached for her hands. "Yes, you. In March, Mr. Robinson, the fellow Henry and I took orders from while working for the Crown asked us to investigate and shut down a prostitution ring. He didn't have much to go on except the name of the boat—*Jezebel*."

Amelia gasped. "Philip always wanted to name his mare that and Mother wouldn't let him."

"And understandably so," Elijah said. "For weeks we chased the *Jezebel* all over the channel, unable to catch her. On a tip sent to us, we went to Dover. That's why I was at your cousin's party. Henry was there to act like an interested party, and I was to be unseen, lurking between the rooms that were supposed to be kept private in hopes of overhearing a private conversation or heaven forbid, an exchange. Instead, I happened upon you."

"Did you know who I was?"

"Not until you said my name. I should have known before then as all the signs of your presence were there: your perfume, your giggle, even the way my heart races in your presence, but my brain refused to believe it was you—just some young lady who'd been drugged and was in need of saving from whatever fate might hold for her if she were found in such a state in Lord Nigel's study. It wasn't until I got you upstairs to a hidden bedchamber and you kissed me and called my name that I realized my heart had been right."

"So you left when you realized it was me?" she asked, unsure of how to feel. In a way, it was a compliment that he'd been such a gentlemen as to excuse himself and not take advantage of her; at the same time, was it because he'd found her undesirable once he learned her identity that he had no desire to finish what she'd started.

"No. I stayed." He squeezed her hands. "When I realized it was you, I went down to the kitchens and asked one of the staff to make you a tonic that would help your head and stomach. But when I arrived back in the room, you were already asleep, so I set it down, loosened your gown as much as I dared so you could still breathe but also be decent enough to get home the next day, then I waited in your room. I should have been downstairs, lurking; but I couldn't leave you."

He swallowed. "But for as much as I would have liked to, I couldn't stay forever. Working for the Crown, I wasn't in a position to marry and if we were caught alone together, that's what would have happened and I didn't want that."

"But you said yesterday that you and Philip had a disagreement about your asking for my hand."

"We did. I went to see your father as soon as I learned of your engagement to Lord Friar, but he refused me." He didn't have to say why, they both knew: Father needed her to marry someone who wouldn't need a dowry and who might be generous enough to help his bride's family. Someone like Lord Friar, not an untitled, seemingly unemployed younger son of a baron.

"And what of your conversation with Philip," she prompted.

"He came in while I was speaking to your father and hinted that you were accepting Lord Friar's suit because you were without virtue."

Stung, she sucked in a harsh breath. "That explains your stoic expressions and candid discussions with Henry regarding bedding me as your duty. One you just needed to get done."

Elijah winced as if she'd slapped his freshly formed bruise. "It wasn't like that. I just wanted you to know that you weren't—" he sent a pointed look to her abdomen— "that was my hurry. Had Philip not hinted that you'd given your virtue to a man whose identity you didn't know, and I'd convinced you to ride off with me that day, I wouldn't have approached you about intimacies so soon because it wouldn't have mattered. I was the one in the room that night. I know what did and didn't occur. But since you didn't, I needed to find a way to tell you without actually telling you."

Now it was her turn to recoil as if she'd been slapped. "Well, I'm sorry you felt bedding me was a duty, but I do appreciate your willingness to suffer it in order to ease my mind that I hadn't given my innocence to a stranger whose bastard I might have been carrying." She pulled her numb hands from his and attempted to stand.

His hands encircled her waist and eased her back onto the edge of the bed. "That didn't come out right." He took a ragged breath. "What I meant was none of this happened how I wanted it to. Regardless of whether you thought your virtue was gone or not, I still would have been at that church to persuade you to marry me instead. But I didn't want you to fret over something that wasn't real, which is why I kept making attempts to bed you." His cheeks turned red. "There wasn't any other way. I'm sure you had no bursting desire to tell me of your nonexistent secret shame and if I were to tell you it was me that night, it'd only invite more questions." He reached up and scratched his left temple. "As I said, none of this happened the way I wanted it to."

"So then you did want to marry me?" She might be a little bold at times, but even she had enough modesty not to ask his true feelings about bedding her. But she needed to know the truth. Did he seek out her father because he was trying to right the wrong he'd inadvertently made or was he there because he genuinely wanted to marry her?

He nodded, his hands found hers again. "I have for some time now, but I knew you didn't see me that way any longer." He ran the pads of his thumbs back and forth across her knuckles. "I'd hoped when I was done working for the Crown that I could court you, but when I heard you were marrying Lord Friar, I went straight to your father and tried to persuade him differently. He wouldn't have it. Neither could I convince Philip." He twisted his lips in distaste. "And now I know why."

"Because I was supposed to be sold to Lord Friar," she guessed.

"That's it in its simplest form."

And simplest form was all she wanted on that score. "When will you be done working for the Crown?"

He flashed a boyish smile at her. "Tonight I made my last capture."

"Well, that's good to hear since I don't enjoy being used as live snake bait." She cringed at the shrillness of her own voice.

"Snake bait?"

"Your note."

"What about it?"

She stared at him. Did he really want her to embarrass herself and elaborate? "You and Henry conspired to get me in the blue saloon, did you not?" When he nodded once, she continued. "While I have no difficulty trusting you, I don't like being used as a pawn to catch the villain."

"That wasn't part of the plan," Elijah rushed to add. "I thought you'd be safer there than in the ballroom. I didn't know Friar was planning to break in and abduct you."

"So then your note it was..."

"Genuine," he said, coming to sit next to her. He pulled her trembling body onto his lap.

"Why are you telling me all of this now?"

"The simple truth is, I didn't want you to get hurt. I didn't know until tonight it was your brother who was involved—"

Amelia pressed her lips to his in a quick kiss. "Not that part."

"Then which part?"

"The part about you wanting to marry me and what you said in your missive."

"That I love you?" he asked, looking into her eyes.

She nodded. It was all she could do. Was this a romantic love or one of friendship like it seemed his marriage proposal might have been inspired by the latter, considering she was to marry Lord

Friar.

"Because I didn't want to hurt you—"

She lifted her finger to halt his nonsense, but he stayed her hand.

"—No, listen. I couldn't have anything to do with you before because I didn't want you to get hurt because of my job. If someone I was after found out how I felt about you, they might try to hurt you, and I could never live with myself if they did. I love you too much for that. And I'd hoped—" he swallowed convulsively— "I'd hoped once I was done I could convince you to love me, too."

"You had, had you?"

He nodded once, his jaw locked and a muscle in his cheek ticked.

"And just how much do you love me?"

A hooded expression came over his face. "I have a feeling I've just been asked to incriminate myself and I don't like it."

She lifted one eyebrow. "Incriminate yourself, sir."

~Chapter Twenty-Eight~

She wanted him to incriminate himself, did she?

That, he could do.

He shifted her in his arms until she was almost lying in his lap, then bent forward and brushed his lips over hers. Her response would have hardened him in an instant if he wasn't already. He licked the seam of her mouth, seeking entry. She granted it. As his tongue explored her mouth, his fingers reached for her hair, sliding out each pin one by one until the mass of her thick, silken tresses were down.

He pulled his mouth from hers and ran his fingers through her hair, an action he'd only dreamed of doing for far too long. He removed those hideous feathers and ran his hands through it again, then leaned her back against the pillows and stood to remove his clothes.

Her grey eyes roamed over his naked body. He'd stand in the firelight as long as she wanted to look. He walked toward her, her upturned face with the sensuous lips his target. He wanted her. Craved her. And now that everything was exposed, he could enjoy her and not wrestle with guilt afterwards.

Elijah climbed into bed and rolled onto his side. He propped his head up with his left hand and used his right to untie the bow at the top of her bodice. It wouldn't afford him much access, but it'd be a start.

She watched his face as he went about freeing her breasts from their confines. He'd never tire of seeing them. Never. Slowly, almost reverently, he cupped one, tamping down his own desire at the look of hunger and desire on her face. She wanted him just as much as he wanted her.

Her right hand closed around his erection, startling him in the best way. He knew she was bold, but had never imagined she'd touch him there by her own volition. He moved closer, hoping—nay praying—she'd continue her caresses.

"Do you like this?"

"You know that I do."

A siren's smile spread her lips as she pushed him over onto his back, then rolled onto her side, her bare breasts mere inches from his chest. That wouldn't do. Keeping his position because it'd be a shame if she stopped, he reached one hand behind her and started untying the row of knots that went down the back of her dress. "No corset," he remarked as each knot he undid loosened her gown that much more, allowing it to fall away from her body and giving him a beautiful sight to feast his eyes upon.

"No," she confirmed. "I was allowed to breathe tonight."

He would have chuckled if not for her nearly killing him with pleasure as she moved her hand up and down his shaft with a slowness that could rival that of waiting for a volcano to erupt.

She moved her dainty hand all the way to the tip of his erection, then stopped.

"You're torturing me," he commented.

"Perhaps." She gave him a quick squeeze. "Perhaps not."

"You minx," he said through gritted teeth. He fumbled with the remaining ties on the back of her gown, making it completely fall open in the front.

Her hand tightened a fraction on him, then she slid it back down to the base.

He groaned and she repeated the gesture while his hands worked to remove her gown, a task much easier done when not being both pleasured and tortured at the same time.

Inside him, excitement mounted. He shot his hand out to stay hers.

They locked eyes, but neither of them said anything. They didn't have to. It wasn't just twins who had the ability to know what the other was thinking without saying a word, the same could also be said for that other extension of oneself. The one that wasn't bound to you by blood or family history but by love.

With no other words, he rolled her onto her back. His lips and hands roamed aimlessly over her body and her lips and hands roamed just the same way over his. He squeezed and shaped, touched and caressed every inch of her skin that he could.

He loved the way her soft body molded so well around him and how her legs parted just the right amount for him to fit between—a better place on earth he had yet to discover. Scattering slow kisses over her chest, he reached for that apex between her legs, touching her most intimate flesh.

She arched her hips up toward his hand. "Please."

It was such a simple word, but one that almost pushed him to his limit. She was asking him for a pleasure he'd given her only once and was trusting him with her body that he'd do it again. And he had no intention of letting her down.

Shifting his weight onto his left elbow, he moved his fingers over his wife's silky folds. Her breathing grew labored, as did his. He had no idea which of them was more excited: her, as pleasure built within, or him, knowing it was him who could give her such pleasure.

He slid two fingers inside her warm, slick passage, eliciting the sweetest sigh he'd ever heard. "Is this what you wanted?" he whispered, moving in and out.

"Y-yes."

"Shh," he crooned as he increased his pace. "Don't speak. Just feel."

She gasped for air, her eyelids growing heavy and her face turning pinker. He dropped kisses on each of her partially closed eyelids, then her mouth, then down the column of her throat to her chest. Her breathing was shallow, more of a desperate pant than anything else, as he placed openmouthed kisses over her breasts. She was close. So very close.

He stopped his movements and withdrew.

She choked on a sound of distress as her eyes fluttered open.

"Just a second," he panted, sliding his erection into her.

She bit her lip and her hands gripped his shoulders. Hard. Their eyes locked and she matched his thrusts with equal intensity, creating a fierier passion in him than the first time they'd made love. Perhaps some might say it was this way because it wasn't both of their first times and they knew what to do. But he knew better. There was nothing between them to keep them apart. No lies. No secrets. Not even uncertainty.

Her fingers dug into his shoulders. It wouldn't be long for either of them now.

"I love you, Amelia," he said in a rough voice he barely recognized as his own.

Just then, her wide, grey eyes looked straight into his as inner muscles squeezed around him in a response more powerful than if she'd said the words with her lips instead of with her body, triggering his own release.

Gasping, he collapsed on top of her, then rolled them over where she was laying on his chest.

"I meant it," he said sometime later.

She looked up at him. "Meant what?"

"That I love you." He ran his fingers through her silky hair. "I wasn't just writing it so I could lock you in that room."

"I believe you." She inched her fingers toward his waist. "The part about you loving me, that is," she said, closing her hand around his thickening member. "I might still need some convincing about the other."

"You're mine now," he growled, rolling her back onto the pillows.

"I've always been yours."

~Epilogue~

Watson Estate
July 1819

"I daresay, you had more fun traveling through Italy on our wedding trip than I did," Amelia teased as their carriage rolled down the drive to Watson Estate.

Elijah shrugged. "I know I'd already been there a time or two, but never just to go and enjoy the city."

"What do you think has happened while we've been away?"

"Nothing too terribly interesting, I wouldn't think."

Amelia lifted a single eyebrow. "You wouldn't think? And what do you suggest *that* is?"

Elijah turned to see what had caught Amelia's attention outside the carriage. "Well, I never..."

"Never what? Thought your brother was capable of courting a girl or thought said girl would actually be smiling in his presence?"

"Either," Elijah admitted, dumbfounded. They were a good thirty feet away—and in a moving carriage—from where Henry was escorting a young lady down the lane from the dowagers cottage, but he'd swear she looked familiar. That was impossible, any young lady who already knew Henry wouldn't be interested in him that way. He was certain of it.

"They look happy together," Amelia commented, drawing his attention back to her.

Elijah lifted her hand and brought it to her lips. "Not as happy as we are, I'd wager."

"No. Most decidedly not." She peeked at the couple again. "At least not yet."

"Then you think there's hope?"

"Of course. I think there's hope for everyone and everything. It might have taken you almost two decades longer than it took me to fall in love, but you did, didn't you?"

"As usual, I concede." He dipped his head as if he were bowing to her. "Your boon, my lady."

"I think I shall finally collect on that slice of cake you still owe me."

He grinned. "I love you, did you know?"

"I did know." She leaned her head up and kissed his lips. "But I'll never tire of hearing you say it."

"Nor will I ever tire of saying it."

"And what of hearing it?" she asked before kissing him again.

"Never."

"Good, because I loved you when we first met, I love you now, I'll love you forever, and I'll never stop saying it. I love you. I love you. I love you."

If you enjoyed *His Jilted Bride*, I would appreciate it if you would help others enjoy this book, too.

Lend it. This e-book is lending-enabled, so please, share it with a friend.

Recommend it. Please help other readers find this book by recommending it to friends, readers' groups and discussion boards.

Review it. Please tell other readers why you liked this book by reviewing it at one of the following websites: Amazon, Barnes and Noble, or Goodreads.

Other Books by Rose Gordon

BANKS BROTHERS' BRIDES

His Contract Bride—Lord Watson has always known that one day he'd marry Regina Harris. Unfortunately nobody thought to inform her of this; and when she finds that her "love match" was actually arranged by her father long ago in an effort to further his social standing, it falls to a science-loving, blunt-speaking baron to win her trust.

His Yankee Bride—John Banks has no idea what—or who—waits for him on the other side of the ocean... Carolina Ellis has longed to meet a man whom she can love, so when she glimpses such a man, she's determined to do whatever it takes to have him—Southern aristocracy be damned.

His Jilted Bride—Elijah Banks *cannot* sit still a moment longer as the gossip continues to fly about one of his childhood playmates, who just so happens to still be in her bridal chamber, waiting for her groom to arrive. Thinking to save her the public humiliation of being jilted at the altar, Elijah convinces her to run away with him, replacing one scandal with one far more forgiving. But when a secret she keeps is threatened to be exposed, it falls to Elijah to save her again by revealing a few of his own...

His Brothers's Bride—Henry Banks had no idea his brother agreed to marry a fetching young lady until the day she shows up on his doorstep and presents the proof. To protect the Banks name and his new sister-in-law's feelings, Henry agrees to marry her only to discover this young lady's intentions were not so honorable and it wasn't really marriage she sought, but revenge on a member of the Banks family...

Coming 2014
Gentlemen of Honor Series (Regency)

Secrets of a Viscount—One summer night, Sebastian Gentry, Lord Belgrave hauled the wrong young lady to Gretna Green. When her identity is exposed, the only obvious solution is to get an annulment. Only, just like his elopement plans, things didn't go as planned and while she has reason to believe they are no longer married, he knows better. Wanting to make things right for her, he offers to help her find a husband —what neither counts on is it just might be the one she's still secretly married to.

Desires of a Baron—Giles Goddard, Lord Norcourt is odd. Odder still, he has suddenly taken a fancy to his brother's love interest, the fallen Lucy Whitaker. Lucy was once thrown over by a lord and she has little desire to let it happen again, but she's about to learn that his desires just might be enough for the both of them.

Passions of a Gentleman—Having been thrown over twice already, Simon Appleton has given up his pursuit for a wife—especially if his only choice is the elusive Miss Henrietta Hughes. But when he discovers a secret about her, he's not above helping to protect her...

Already Available:

SCANDALOUS SISTERS SERIES

Intentions of the Earl—A penniless earl makes a pact to ruin an American hoyden, never suspecting for a moment he'll lose his heart along the way.

Liberty for Paul—A vicar's daughter who loves propriety almost as much as she hates the man her father is mentoring will go to any length she sees fit to see that improper man out the door and out of her life. But when she's forced to marry him, she'll learn there's a lot more to life, love and this man than she originally thought.

To Win His Wayward Wife —A gentleman who's spent the last five years pining for the love of his life will get his second chance. The only problem? She has no interest in him.

GROOM SERIES

Four men are about to have their bachelor freedom snatched away as they become grooms...but finding the perfect woman may prove a bit more difficult than they originally thought.

Her Sudden Groom—The overly scientific, always respectable and socially awkward Alexander Banks has just been informed his name resides on a betrothal agreement right above the name of the worst chit in all of England. With a loophole that allows him to marry another without consequence before the thirtieth anniversary of his birth, he has only four weeks to find another woman and make her his wife.

Her Reluctant Groom—For the past thirteen years Marcus Sinclair, Earl Sinclair, has lived his life as a heavily scarred recluse, never dreaming the only woman he's ever wanted would love him back. But when it slips out that she does, he doubts her love for his scarred body and past can be real. For truly, how can a woman love a man whose injuries were caused when he once tried to declare himself to her sister?

Her Secondhand Groom—Widower Patrick Ramsey, Viscount Drakely, fell in love and married at eighteen only to be devastated by losing her as she bore his third daughter. Now, as his girls are getting older he realizes they need a mother—and a governess. Not able to decide between the two which they need more, he marries an ordinary young lady from the local village in hopes she can suit both roles. But this ordinary young lady isn't so ordinary after all, and he'll either have to take a chance and risk his heart once more or wind up alone forever.

Her Imperfect Groom —Sir Wallace Benedict has never been good with the fairer sex and in the bottom drawer of his bureau he has the scandal sheet clippings to prove it. But this thrice-jilted baronet has just discovered the right lady for him was well-worth waiting for. The only trouble is, with multiple former love interests plaguing him at every chance possible, he must find clever ways to avoid them and simultaneously steal the attention—and affections—of the the one lady he's sure is a perfect match for him and his imperfections.

FORT GIBSON OFFICERS SERIES
American Historicals based in Indian Territory mid-1800s)

The Officer and the Bostoner—A well-to-do lady traveling by stagecoach from her home in Boston to meet her fiance in Santa Fe finds herself stranded in a military fort when her stagecoach leaves without her. Given the choice to either temporarily marry an officer until her fiance can come rescue her or take her chances with the Indians, she marries the glib Captain Wes Tucker, who, unbeknownst to her, grew up in a wealthy Charleston family and despises everything she represents. But when it's time for her fiance to reclaim her and annul their marriage, will she still want to go with him, and more importantly, will Wes let her?

The Officer and the Southerner—Second Lt. Jack Walker doesn't always think ahead and when he decides to defy logic and send off for a mail-order bride, he might have left out only a few details about his life. When she arrives and realizes she's been fooled (again), this woman who's never really belonged, sees no other choice but to marry him anyway—however, she makes it perfectly clear: she'll be his lawfully wed, but she will *not* share his bed. Now Jack has to find a way to show his always skeptical bride that he is indeed trustworthy and that she does belong somewhere in the world: right here, with him.

The Officer and the Traveler—Captain Grayson Montgomery's mouth has landed him in trouble again! And this time it's not something a cleverly worded sentence and a handsome smile can fix. Having been informed he'll either have to marry or be demoted and sentenced to hard labor for the remainder of his tour, he proposes, only to discover those years of hard labor may have been the easier choice for his heart.

About the Author

USA Today Bestselling and Award Winning Author Rose Gordon has written eight unusually unusual historical romances that have been known to include scarred heroes, feisty heroines, marriage-producing scandals, far too much scheming, naughty literature and always a sweet happily-ever-after. When not escaping to another world via reading or writing a book, she spends her time chasing two young boys around the house, being hunted by wild animals, or sitting on the swing in the backyard where she has to use her arms as shields to deflect projectiles AKA: balls, water balloons, sticks, pinecones, and anything else one of her boys picks up to hurl at his brother who just happens to be hiding behind her.

She can be found on somewhere in cyberspace at:

http://www.rosegordon.net

or blogging about *something* inappropriate at:

http://rosesromanceramblings.wordpress.com

Rose would love to hear from her readers and you can e-mail her at rose.gordon@hotmail.com

You can also find her on Facebook, Goodreads, and Twitter.

If you never want to miss a new release, visit her website to sign up to be notified and you'll be sent an email each time a new book becomes available.

Made in the USA
San Bernardino, CA
14 May 2014